A TIMELESS LOVE

He moved like a panther. His gaze never strayed from her face as he eased between dancers and tables, closing the distance between them with a slow but steady pace. The roar of the cheering crowd in the bull pit, the crash of the dishes as the busser cleared the next table, the speaker throbbing with a heavy bass beat; none of it could drown out the sound of her heart singing with joy at the sight of him. Five years evaporated in a flash. It was as though they'd never been apart. Mackenzie could taste him on her mouth, smell him on her skin, and feel him on her, in her, hot, hard, and alive. She felt his whispers teasing her tender flesh and the old urge to yield to him without reservation.

TIME ROGUES

KAY AUSTIN

LOVE SPELL

NEW YORK CITY

To the Rogues in my life who taught me how to take risks and trust my heart, thank you.
To my hero, my Dad, who soars with angels, all my love.

LOVE SPELL®

February 2005

Published by

Dorchester Publishing Co., Inc.
200 Madison Avenue
New York, NY 10016

ISBN 0-505-52621-2

Printed in the United States of America.

AUTHOR'S NOTE

What if you could save the future by fixing the past? Would you?

Time Rogues exist. They live among us as everyday heroes capable of extraordinary acts. Watch for them and treasure the fire in their bellies and the truths they hold dear.

Core only exists in my imagination; however, I've mapped the boundaries and explored many of its hidden worlds. If you would like a copy of the map or want to share your own Rogue sightings, please write or email me at:

Kay Austin
PMB 125
1401 Marvin Road NE, Suite 307
Lacey, Washington 98516
kay@kayaustin.com
Or visit my website at www.kayaustin.com

TIME ROGUES

Prologue

Ancient Pompeii: August 24, A.D. 79 9:57 A.M.

"We made it." Maude's voice bounced between octaves. The first seconds post-transit were always iffy for her. She scanned the horizon for something familiar to hold her in place and time. Dirt here. Sky there. Charlie's landing coordinates had dumped Maude and her traveling companions on the outskirts of civilization; the transit was a full-body immersion guaranteed to upset a person's equilibrium—even a seasoned time-traveler's. And, Maude wasn't seasoned. With less than two-dozen transits notched on her identlog, her anatomy reacted within neo-class parameters, the worst of which was hives.

She didn't bother to complain, though. She'd volunteered for this crazy mission to save the world by rescuing Dak. She clawed at her legs and jiggled her raspberry-spotted flesh. The antidote wasn't working: the hives were worse than ever.

"Are you guys okay?" she asked her companions. One glance at them and Maude forgot all about herself.

"Oh, crap!" No, her transit buddies were far from okay. They were a mess.

Hair standing on end, Mackenzie Cates and the handsome-as-sin Professor Rick Mason were dazed and mute, though alive. This unscheduled mission was a rough scenario for a first transit. And, Maude had forgotten about the hair thing. A standard prep would have denuded their flesh, among other precautions.

Maude automatically touched her own head and righted the wig that concealed her baldness. Mackenzie and Rick's temporary static-stiff hairdos reminded her that nothing about this transit was standard—or legal, for that matter.

Pompeii was a surprise. Of course, that hub of ancient commerce was beyond her rural vantage point: a dirt road cutting through one of the Mount Vesuvius vineyards overlooking the city. Charlie's dead-on accurate transit coordinates had dumped them into a setting that offered temporary protection from any inquisitive inhabitants. Numerous tombs, bushes, and several nearby burial mounds were around to hide behind.

Ah, Charlie, you think of everything, Maude silently conceded. It was another comforting reminder that, although her boss lacked the demeanor of a super-brain or mastermind, he was one. He certainly was the only man who could pull off the necessary miracle or two for Core and the Continuum. Ensconced in a time and place in Earth's future, Charlie skillfully orchestrated the clandestine transits of all the Time Rogues. It was no small feat, even for an intellect such as his.

A cloud of worry filled Maude's thoughts. Charlie was human. Humans made mistakes. But her mind didn't need such excess baggage right now; it was filled to the brim with mission programming.

Maude noted a suitable thicket to conceal her companions, if necessary. She wrinkled her nose. Decay released unmistakable fumes, and she didn't relish discovering the source of the pungent aroma wafting from the shrubbery.

"You better cross your fingers, Maudie-girl, that you don't have to drag those two into that stuff," she warned herself.

The mid-morning sun felt hot, and her scanty toga garb exposed too much of her freckled and sunburn-prone flesh. The bugs were biting, or maybe it was just another wave of hives. Drutz! What she wouldn't give for a quick dip in Charlie's all-purpose protectorant, a lovely pink mist that was standard for almost every transit. But, it was too late to nitpick what this top-secret transit lacked.

Minus almost every tool, rule, skill, and protection mandated by Charlie's very own guide—a bible for safe time travel—this mission was handicapped by its rushed nature. As a novice time traveler, Maude could only guess at the personal peril involved in such a venture. But damn the risks, it was worth it. Nothing, absolutely nothing, compared with the shake-up in the cosmic Continuum if she and her companions failed to fix the future here in the past.

"Don't panic, Mackenzie," she said to her female companion. "No hurry. Try to blink or bend your knees. That usually gets the ball rolling." Thankfully Maude's American slang and jargon subroutine kept feeding her phrases that Mackenzie and Rick could understand.

She checked her chronometer. *Crapola!* She kept that comment to herself. Charlie said rushing acclimation for new transits only caused more problems. She'd have to squelch her anxiety even though these were precious moments she didn't think they could afford to lose.

Arrival and departure were always rough. Transit wasn't perfect, especially now with the expanding rift wreaking havoc in numerous timelines. She'd heard about the recent tragic reentries at Core. But accounts regarding transit errors on destination were nil. She shrugged. They'd arrived alive; she'd worry about the return trip later. Besides, if there was a problem, Charlie could fix it.

He'd invented the whole transit process, and had insisted on personally handling the controls for this mission.

"That's it, you're doing fine," Maude called to her companions while she scanned the pastoral landscape and deflected interest from a passing native. The child with the bleating lamb slung over his shoulders didn't pose a threat, but the hum and thud of blurry brown blobs coming into view farther down the road triggered more anxiety. Maude blinked and her ocular implants zeroed in. An oxen team with a driver cracking a whip approached at a sedate pace. She squinted and refined her focus to match the distance. A half dozen tethered slaves trailed the team.

Ha! *Doing fine?* Who was she kidding? The seconds were ticking away. Wasn't it enough of a handicap that she wasn't a historian or a linguist and was out of her element in ancient Pompeii without wasting crucial time mothering new transits? Their garb helped them pass for the moment, but unless Mackenzie and Rick could deliver on their promises, the rest of the mission would fail miserably—especially if the guy with the team of slaves assumed they were available to join him.

"Hey, you two. Shake it off. We're attracting attention," Maude hissed and jabbed Mackenzie in the shoulder. Pain sometimes helped. She squashed the urge to kick Rick in the shins; in open-toed sandals it would probably hurt her more than him.

Mackenzie was blinking and bending her knees. Good sign. Rick was flapping his arms and burping. Poor guy. Maude knew all too well what that meant. Charlie's transit food supplement had gone south and then north again, as it was wont to do on one in fifty applications.

With her two companions coming around, Maude felt her panic subside. They'd be off in another couple of seconds. But off where? Which way? Licking her finger and holding it up to catch a breeze was useless. She needed a damned map to shortcut the maze of Pompeii.

She wasn't totally prepped with the facts and tools of the era, either. She lacked the usual super-dose of proficiency with the regional dialects, a geo-conscious mapping overlay of surface and substrata landmarks, and marginal-to-adequate skills in several trades. There hadn't been enough free space in her short-term memory to carry the load; armament-and-destruction commands were space hogs. Besides, Rick and Mackenzie were the pros in all those areas. To sum up, if they didn't start contributing to the mission, Maude was worse than handicapped. She was lost.

Yes, she was a middling survivalist without total transit prep. On one of her previous missions, she had slogged her way through twentieth century Dallas and wasted a week before stumbling into Mackenzie and Rick at a drive-in burger stand. Charlie's skills at transport were dead-on, but what he didn't know about time-travel prep could fill a black hole.

And this was an illegal mission by Core standards—civilians were involved. It was another time-travel jaunt on the economy plan, fraught with risks and innumerable pitfalls not only for her but possibly the future harmony of the Continuum. Maude and her companions might alter the fabric of history.

Might? Hell, what was she saying? She and Charlie were thumbing their noses at Core dictums, the very preamble and bill of rights constructed to safeguard the future from meddlers in the past. On this mission, with Mackenzie and Rick along for the ride—none of them prepped, vaccinated, or sterilized for the duration—the odds of error and risk increased exponentially.

What were those tolerances again? Zero point zero two five seven percent? Percent of what? Would Charlie's last gift—a dab of ancient Latin pumped into Maude's brain while she, Mackenzie, and Rick re-garbed in airy togas and sandals at the transfer point on the Rogues' hijacked transit pad—change their odds of success?

What she wouldn't give for at least a hint of a landmark or access to some wheels. "Aha! What's that?" she asked herself.

A muffled shout from the opposite direction and a plume of dust announced trouble. Maude's telescoping implant found the threat. A chariot crested the rise and hurtled toward them.

"Drutz! Move, move, *move!*" Maude kicked Rick in the butt and sent him sprawling into the convenient hedge of noxious-smelling brush, locked arms with Mackenzie, and tumbled after him.

"Wow! That hurt," Mackenzie cried. She rubbed her rear, which had struck a nondescript tomb concealed behind the greenery.

"You two are in great shape," Maude encouraged them. "I can't believe this is only your second transit."

Mackenzie responded, but Maude wasn't really paying attention. She pointed off into the distance.

"Hey, Rick," she cried. "Transportation!" The clatter of the approaching chariot mounted in volume.

Rick nodded. "Showtime!" he replied, and pulled Mackenzie off her rump.

Showtime? Maude's slang subroutine cleared up her confusion. She nodded vigorously, then joined Mackenzie and Rick at the break in the hedge.

Ready or not, it was Showtime. The clock was ticking and everything hinged on locating that bum Dak and dragging him to safety before the volcano blew its top. Timing was everything, and Charlie was a stickler on that point if not on others. Dead or alive, in 180 minutes with zero point zero two five seven percent tolerances, the three of them would be zapped back to Bravo transit launch.

Chapter One

Dallas: 2005. Tuesday, one month earlier

It moved. Mackenzie gulped and held fast to the rail of the hoist. The damned statue had moved.

She glanced down at her museum intern, "Gil" Gillespe. The kid didn't appear to have noticed a thing. In the requisite white coat and white gloves, he was absorbed in the measured movements and exacting process of unpacking exhibit crates and checking the inventory against the manifest. Apart from the statue's movement, the world seemed normal.

Whump!

"Whoa, boss! What the heck was that?" Gillespe yowled and grabbed the edge of his crate of artifacts.

Mackenzie couldn't respond. Suspended above an irreplaceable piece of history with a death-grip on the hoist rail and her imagination a thousand leagues left of center, she didn't feel smart or bold. Gillespe was going to have to hang on a second. She couldn't talk to him about noises; she had her hands full juggling her own panic and shock.

Had the damned statue moved or not? Geez, she was starting to see things. Too many late hours and missed meals were catching up with her.

Museums weren't hospital emergency rooms. Crisis management and triage for the faint of heart weren't routine for Dr. Mackenzie Cates, museum curator and lead exhibit designer. And, Mackenzie didn't suffer fools gladly when priceless relics were at stake, especially when she was the fool in question.

Whump, whump, whir.

Mackenzie nearly fainted with relief. She offered Gillespe a reassuring smile. "That's the new ventilation system kicking in. Guess they're still anchoring the ductwork."

"Well, it nearly scared the bejeezus out of me," Gillespe replied.

Mackenzie didn't dare share the sentiment—aloud, that is. But her heart was beating like a jackhammer in her chest. A moving statue? Puh-leeze! That kind of stuff had happened to her Granny Moon all the time, but not to her. Not ever.

"Matter of fact, boss," Gillespe continued, "ever since the crew unpacked that guy, I've been getting weird vibes."

Mackenzie swallowed hard. Impressionable Gillespe was her intern, and male. Her persona as a rock solid role model and mentor was at stake. She wasn't going to slip up at this late date and start pulling a shrinking violet on the verge of a vapor attack routine.

"Is Mr. Pompeii getting to you?" she asked.

"Yeah, I'm spooked. Aren't you? Just look at him."

Spooked? Yeah. Weird vibes? Bingo. But the statue sparked in Mackenzie a host of other emotions, too—legitimate ones, linked to the care and study of artifacts.

"I've been looking off and on for the last two days and he looks great to me. A grade-A hunk." Mackenzie heaved a huge sigh. It had been love at first sight.

"A hunk! Gosh, boss, I know you're between boyfriends, but don't get desperate. I can set you up with someone who's alive and kicking. Mr. Pompeii is a two-thousand-year-old dead guy!"

"Ah, Gillespe, you don't have the heart of a museumologist—yet," Mackenzie said, and maneuvered the hoist until she was down to eye level with the subject of their discussion. "When you do, you'll be nuts about old stuff, body casts of dead guys included."

Gillespe snorted. "I suppose it could happen one day. Right now, I'm weirded out. I get some odd mojo every time we set up one of these exhibits, and this Pompeii stuff is the worst ever. It even has Harry jumpy."

"Harry? The guard? He's the rock of Gibraltar. Nothing shocks Harry."

"Well, this stuff does. I heard him telling Proctor that he didn't want the graveyard shift anymore."

Mackenzie laughed. "That doesn't mean Harry's spooked. He's romancing Bernadette from the Rib Joint, and she's off the clock at ten."

"Oh." Gillespe sounded disappointed.

Mackenzie pulled off her protective smock and gloves. Gillespe did the same and tried to look interested. Maybe the kid didn't have it in him after all. The museum business attracted a wacky breed of historians intent on discovering, preserving, and protecting relics from the past. It wasn't a sensational job with big bucks attached, but it could be passionate and rewarding. If Mr. Pompeii didn't inspire Gillespe, he needed to switch majors fast.

Mackenzie leaned on the hoist's rail and stared at the statue. Heart and soul, she was lovestruck.

In reality, Mr. Pompeii was a stone man, a plaster body cast of one of the countless victims of the Mt. Vesuvius eruption in A.D. 79 that rained fireballs and entombed a city and its inhabitants in ash. Like the other victims, he had been discovered during an excavation. His remains had long ago turned to dust, but had left a hollow within the rocklike ash: a clear impression of his physical body. Using an age-old method of casting, the team of excavators had flooded the hollow with a quick-dry ooze to preserve his features. And, once the ooze had solidified into a replica of his human form, they had chipped it free from the surrounding debris and plunged it into liquifix for a master mold and copies.

Mr. Pompeii, however, wasn't a copy. He was the original. He was both tragedy and mystery. A virile male cut down in his prime. A life of promise snuffed out. Yet here and now, as the focal point of Mackenzie's exhibit, he lived again and invited all to imagine those last hours before Pompeii ceased to exist.

It had been a major coup, all right. Winning the rights to the exclusive exhibit of these Pompeii relics was a career achievement for Mackenzie, and a financial boon for her budget-constricted Dallas museum. And, she owed it all to this dead guy—Mr. Pompeii, her inspiration and hero.

"But I know what you mean," she admitted at last, "and weird just about covers it for me." She looked at Gil. "Can you imagine what it was like for him when Mount Vesuvius erupted?"

"I sure can," the intern replied. "And if it'd been me, I would have freaked. I wouldn't have hung around like he did and get buried alive. Why didn't he get out of town in time? Lots of them did."

Mackenzie didn't answer. She couldn't. An all-consuming image of the horrific event flashed through her brain. A city aflame, the air thick with smoke, the metallic taste of fear, the sickly sweet smell of burning flesh, the pleading cries of lost children, and the frantic bleats from tethered sheep and goats. And, a man struggling in vain to free himself. Was Mr. Pompeii the guy, and was she suddenly clairvoyant?

For a split second, she felt like she was there—her body plunged deep into the scene of chaos when Vesuvius erupted. A moment later, she popped back into her own skin and time. Yikes! She was stunned and breathless. She grabbed the handrail again before she tipped head over heels down onto the exhibit.

"Hey, you okay, boss?" Gillespe cried.

Heck no! Her worst nightmare was becoming a reality, if this was a sample of Granny Moon's gift of second sight. Maybe it hadn't skipped Mackenzie's generation after all. Wait a sec, she didn't believe in all that bunk. She was a scientist, damn it! She shook off her dizziness and waved Gillespe to her side.

"Bring me that magnifying spot, will you?" she said. "I want to check this guy over again. These raised surfaces might be flaws in the casting or damage during shipment."

She accepted the blue light from Gillespe and moved around the standing statue with studied concentration. Were the marks on his wrists and ankles from jewelry or restraints?

And had he just moved again? Mackenzie blinked, counted to ten, and forgot to breathe. Hadn't Gillespe seen it too?

Evidently not. The kid looked right as rain, nonplussed, and almost bored.

Jeepers, am I going nuts? Snap out of it! Stand up straight and shake out the cobwebs.

She followed her own command and tried to blot out the fantastic idea blinking on and off in her brain like a rabid firefly. But, her brain wasn't cooperating. Her dogged adherence to probabilities wasn't holding up against the assault on her senses. She was dripping cold sweat, smelling brimstone, and was queasy—like someone had stomped around inside her mind and exposed her deepest, darkest fears.

"Didn't Dr. Mason make Mr. Pompeii's body cast?" Gillespe asked.

That sobered Mackenzie like a plunge in ice water. She hissed, an involuntary reflex whenever Rick Mason's name popped up in conversations. She quashed her venom and attempted to school her features into a less viperous expression.

"Yep, this is Rick's work, and he's good. He perfected the technique of casting the remains of the Pompeii victims that the original archaeologists developed with the very first excavations. Plus, he directed the excavations in Pompeii last year and catalogued the exhibit pieces. If anything's amiss with the shipment or installation, he'll catch it. He's got special radar for that stuff."

Gillespe groaned. "Okay, what's wrong with him? You've got that look."

"What look?" Mackenzie asked.

"The look all women get when they're dumped. Did he?"

"Dump me? No! We went to grad school together, that's all. End of story."

But that wasn't true. Mackenzie couldn't end the subject of Rick, their past, or what went wrong and why without a complete brain scan or a mind-meld with a slug. Rick Mason was the enemy. Their passionate grad school relationship hadn't ended with a cordial handshake, but a declaration of war. He'd betrayed her trust. Unforgivable. He'd accepted that damned dream job, traded in his horse and his cowboy boots, and moved to Pompeii without even consulting her.

Did he really think she'd drop everything, friends and family and her own career, and chase after him? Ha! Maybe that's what females did in Granny Moon's day and age, but not hers.

Sure, he'd sounded sincere when he bartered for a long-distance relationship, but she wasn't going to fall for that line of bull twice. She'd been burned by a cheating boyfriend early on, solid proof in her mind that males equated fidelity with proximity. Maybe that was wrong and unjust, but Rick's relocation to the land of *Amore* had demanded a leap of faith that she wouldn't—couldn't—make.

At the first hint—a mere smidgen of a rumor—that linked Rick with one of those dark Italian lovelies, Mackenzie had dumped him flat out. No questions, no argument. It broke her heart, but she'd had to do it. Poop on his peachy promises, and to hell with all that white-hot, sweaty sex and unquenchable passion they'd shared. She hadn't been about to waste her love and her life on a lying, faithless hunk.

When she'd married a steady-Eddie, button-down collar type of guy on the rebound, she'd figured she had closed the book on Rick and their tempestuous romance. Wrong again. Two wrongs hadn't made a right. For five years, her insatiable craving for bad-boy Rick had simmered like hot magma in a dormant volcano.

But, Gillespe didn't need to hear all of that story. Mackenzie flashed a smile that felt as fake as the new highlights she'd added to her hair.

"He's collaborating with us on the installation, of course, and for the remainder of the six-week exhibit he'll be doing guest lectures." Mackenzie's smile flagged. She might be forced to work with Rick again as a condition of the exhibit, but no way no how was she going to allow that overbearing authoritarian with his infamous attention to detail to compromise her stellar exhibit design or bulldoze her museum staff—or her heart.

"That explains everything," Gillespe said. "The new hairstyle and French manicure. You're a dead ringer for Ashley Judd—and she's one hot lady!"

Whump, whump!

"Gawd, that's awful," the intern added. "They better fix that before opening night."

Mackenzie silently agreed. Heads would roll if it wasn't

fixed. It was one more thing she didn't relish adding to her long list of tasks. Time to delegate!

She checked her watch and sighed. It was five minutes since the last blip on her internal scanner charting the "weird" and the "strange." She was either turning nutty like Granny or blind to the obvious. Which was it? She had an idea how to find out. But first she needed to ditch Gillespe.

"Time to get back to the office, Gil. The installation team will be checking in, and we need to stay out of their way."

Gillespe didn't require any more prompting. He grabbed their smocks and gloves and loped off. "See you there, boss," he called over his shoulder.

Mackenzie took her time rolling up the cord for the mobile spot, savoring the moments alone with Mr. Pompeii. The work crews were due and soon the place would be an orchestrated madhouse. If she was going to break a cardinal rule without witnesses, it was now or never.

She wasn't a saint, but she'd resisted the urge time and again, year in and year out, to commune in the most elemental way with artifacts. It was part of her training and discipline as a curator to never make physical contact. But the gloves were off, so to speak. Her sanity was on the line. And the temptation to sin was a powerful drug for a lovesick female with a crazy idea that maybe, just maybe, Mr. Pompeii had truly moved.

Readjusting the hoist, she climbed aboard for one last look—up close and personal. The displays were taking shape and tomorrow the invisible security grids would shroud many of these objects, Mr. Pompeii included. As always, Mackenzie's intellect warred with her instincts—inherited no doubt from Granny's side of the family. Fact: inanimate objects didn't move without help from another force. But, Mackenzie felt deep down that somehow this stone man had.

She stood nose to nose with the ancient male. With a quick glance to confirm she was alone, she reached out one finger and touched the cheek of the victim of Vesuvius and whispered in his ear. "Here I am, big guy. If you've got it in you, do it to me one more time."

Chapter Two

Dak's mission was a failure and he owed it all to love. If he hadn't fallen for the slave girl Falah and broken every time-travel commandment in order to steal her out of Pompeii before the volcano erupted, he wouldn't be caught in this trap.

His senses hissed like moisture scatting across a blazing iron griddle. Mackenzie's presence was a balm for his spirit. He savored the whispering chill and fed it kindling—memories of life, love, and happiness—and the icy flame grew.

As a veteran Time Rogue he'd suffered innumerable hardships, but this was the worst. Trapped in limbo, he was technically dead but not deceased. His human shell was gone, but everything that summed up his existence lingered within the body cast. Whether it was a curse or a blessing, he didn't know. But only Core's time-transit mastermind and Dak's best friend, Charlie, could have cheated death on his behalf.

Dak guessed that Charlie had activated the stasis-lock prototype—or something like it—which he'd been tinkering with for eons. Whatever it was, it had worked. Somehow Charlie had harnessed the power to intervene as the maelstrom of volcanic ash claimed Dak's life, and had stalled the decay of Dak's essence—all that made him unique, stubborn, friend, foe, lover, and time-traveler. It was another first for Charlie, time-transit guru and supra-genius.

Yes, Dak's body might be dust, but his intellect remained intact—and aware that limbo represented a tenuous safety net. He accepted that Charlie's power wasn't infinite. Limbo couldn't last forever. It was only a stopgap solution until the Time Rogues could launch a clandestine rescue—a rescue he didn't deserve. And if rescue wasn't possible? Termination. That seemed a cold, hard fact.

But, somehow, likely thanks to the archaeologist who'd excavated the site and made his cast body, Dak's limbo state now included mobility. He'd managed to move himself a few times. And Mackenzie's presence sparked hope by connecting him to a time and place and lifeforce that hummed and vibrated with passion.

Dak tentatively stretched his consciousness and sampled the world beyond his plaster shell, and the limits, if any, on Charlie's stasis lock. He could only manage a moment within Mackenzie's skin. His memories and intellect collided with her foreign and utterly female urges, fears, and curiosity. The sensory assault was too much to assimilate at once. He felt burned by her body heat, and all cohesive thought dissolved. Was the stasis lock failing? He snapped back into the safe, dark cocoon of his body cast, utterly drained of energy. Had he just jeopardized everything—his rescue, his stasis—with another of his infamous impetuous mistakes?

His mission to Pompeii had been one such mistake. He'd known it then and he knew it now. As one of the head honchos of the Time Rogue program, he was doubly cursed for making it. He'd handpicked and trained the first squad of Rogues to travel to the past to repair and prevent time rifts. He was their damned kingpin, mentor to a whole generation of warriors intent on saving the future by fixing the past. He'd helped Charlie test and set the standards, then broken every rule and safeguard established by Core for time travel. And he'd paid dearly for it.

Still, Charlie had saved him. And that could only mean that help was on the way.

Ah! He again felt Mackenzie near. Her fingers lightly hovered over his cheek and brow, and he ached to respond again. To reach out and connect with her mind. Should he?

This was virgin turf. Testing the limits of his formless state involved risk, and could jeopardize a rescue attempt. But he'd been in limbo a long time. And, for a man who thrived on action and commanded a garrison of like-minded Rogues, waiting was hellish torture. Yet, he didn't have a choice, did he?

Enduring stasis for almost two thousand years was a lesson of sorts, he guessed. Finally he had some small appreciation for the victims he'd been sent back through time to rescue, desperate people with nothing but a thread of hope to sustain them. Victims could do nothing but wait and trust. So Dak clung to the same belief and held fast. If it could be done, Charlie and the Time Rogues would save him.

Hope. As fragile as a spider's thread, it trembled and flashed in Dak every time Mackenzie neared his shell. Such closeness was new. It energized, teased, and taunted him. In the year since the excavation, after they'd poured the body cast and unearthed him from his tomb of ash, human contact had been restricted. No one had touched him without gloves, yet.

Mackenzie. That was her name, but he called her angel because she was his vision of mercy and hope. With her presence, she reached beyond the ages and touched his soul. He was more than a victim to her. In that brief moment within her skin, he'd shared the image of his last moments in Pompeii, racing through the streets choked with the dead and dying, struggling to reach Falah before it was too late, and failing.

Curses still bubbled within him. His last day of life was a mistake, a fatal blunder in a lifetime of missteps. He knew his weaknesses, but even in death the sin of pride consumed him. He wanted justice. He deserved a second chance to undo that last day, relive his final hour, and escape the fate at Pompeii. He might be a trapped victim, but he was also a Time Rogue—one of the best. And, Mackenzie's merciful touch renewed his belief that he could do more than wait.

Dak sighed with immeasurable pleasure as she touched him a third time. Women remained a constant. In death as in life, they stirred him, lured him, and fed his hope for freedom as this one did now.

Mackenzie! See me!

Dak eased into his demands, amassing sensations from his memories. She reminded him of his lover Falah. The same look and touch—yes, great heaven above, her touch—and Falah's kiss of promise. Cool fingers. Dared he hope that this slim, dark-eyed female possessed a heart that would lead her to help free his trapped soul?

Dak willed the spark of awareness to ignite between them. He fed the flame with the agony of his death, the fury of losing Falah, and his bitter regret for the fool's errand that had cut short his life and denied his love and his salvation.

He could see Mackenzie's face now—lovely, if not Falah's—soft curves and satin skin, with almond-shaped eyes that were nut brown and lit from within. Her sun-kissed hair was short and curling at her brow, and a little damp from the beads of sweat sprinkled across her forehead.

Falah would have sensed him, but could Mackenzie?

Could she see beyond the shell and feel him hidden within, or would she turn away like all the others since he'd been on display?

"Here I am, big guy. If you've got it in you, do it to me one more time." Mackenzie's sweet invitation and faint sad smile were irresistible.

Her teasing breath touched him like fire and seemingly transformed stone into man, at least for a heartbeat. Another image of his once vital life was all that Dak could manage, but it was enough; he filled her with it. He filled her with himself. Then, drained, he returned to the cast.

Mackenzie didn't jump back. Her eyes flashed, the tips of her breasts hardened and pressed taut against her silky pink blouse, and her heart pulsed in a rapid staccato at the base of her creamy throat.

Yes, she'd sensed him. And, her reaction pleased him. She was a woman indeed, and she hadn't fainted or snatched her flesh away. Dak felt smug and thick with pride—a damning trait he hadn't lost with conversion to rock. After all, he was still a man, inside.

Chapter Three

Earth's Core: A.D. 2151, Day 219

"Bingo! I found Dak in A.D. 79," Charlie's assistant said. Before he could say more, alarms sounded—a call for all Time Rogues to man their stations and await instruction. A time rift was pending.

"It's Dak's emergency SOS requesting auto transit," the assistant whispered. "From a no-transit zone!"

"Lock onto him," Charlie yelled, and rolled his stool over to the monitor.

The assistant feverishly punched buttons. Charlie leaned in and adjusted the static on the strobing viewscreen. "I've got him," the assistant cried.

Charlie stroked his jaw thoughtfully. "It's a faint signal and it's well inside the no-transit zone," he muttered.

The assistant looked up. "You mean we can't pull him out of there? We've got to. It's Dak! He never abandons a mission until he's run out of options."

Charlie's usually jolly features were sober. He shook his head. "I can't do it." He rocked back on his stool and pondered the puzzle. “You’ve really messed up this time, Dak old buddy.”

“You can save him. You’ve got to!” the assistant demanded.

“Turn off the alarm,” Charlie replied, and pushed him away from the transit controls. The assistant complied, then watched with wonder as Charlie’s fingers flew across the sequence buttons and safeguard links and fed an endless stream of commands into the system.

Rogues poured into the vast tunnel that served as Charlie’s headquarters, circling the mammoth transit hub and the genius who’d designed it. The walls here, deep within Core’s third ward, were riddled with fractures, and Charlie’s spartan base housed only the necessities. There were no viewscreens with simulated environments, no cushioned lounging alcoves, no creature comforts of any kind save the essential ones for life, though his laboratory and living spaces were one and the same. Only the rumble of magma and the pumping station beneath them intruded from time to time.

Rogues weren’t a secret but many of their missions were secret by necessity. They served as an elite rescue team for Core’s time-traveling population—few of whom knew of their dual role or clandestine missions, or understood their essential tasks to safeguard Core’s future. The tasks were often demanding, mostly thankless, and always dangerous. But Rogues—one and all—were committed to protect humanity. They were tough, decisive, and selfless. Egos were rare but pride was rampant among the commando-like teams, from the novice Rogues to the veterans. And, they were always on call.

Several Rogues nodded in Charlie’s direction. His assistant shook his head and shrugged his shoulders. Only a time rift of colossal proportions could unnerve an easygoing guy like Charlie. And Charlie looked pale and deadly serious, a sight none of the Rogues had ever seen.

“Done! I’ve got him locked in stasis,” Charlie crowed.

He laughed and spun around on his stool and faced a sea of worried faces. "It's one of our own, this time. It's Dak. And I don't give him better than a fifty-fifty chance of survival—or the Rogue who tries to rescue his damned hide. So, I'm asking for volunteers on this mission."

More than half of the Rogues tried to step forward. Charlie grinned and waved them back. "Not so fast. We've got our work cut out for us. We're also dealing with an especially tricky time rift."

He looked around the room and made eye contact with Maude. She squared her shoulders and tried to look serious. It was hard; she was ecstatic. Dak was in trouble, but a time rift was a jewel of a mission and she wanted a shot.

"As usual, Dak's broken one of my prime transit directives and finally he's in over his head," Charlie continued. "Let that be a lesson to you novice-class Rogues. Even the most experienced among you are vulnerable to the laws of time travel. I can't pull Dak out of a no-transit zone; it's impossible. And, a Rogue can't just go back and grab him either. A time rift of this magnitude can't be ignored or patched; we're going to have to stop it from happening. To protect Core and the Continuum, we have to change history."

If Charlie's pause was for dramatic effect, it worked. The dull thud from the pumping pistons and the deep rumblings of magma echoed through the cavernous space.

"Change history. Have we done that before?" one of the younger Rogues finally asked—a novice class hulk with a visible eager puppy wiggle when he walked. The Rogue's mentor, a senior-ranking female cut him off with a glare.

Maude stiffened her spine. She felt just as eager but hoped to Hades she didn't look it. It was a sure sign of a greenhorn.

Other Rogues were mumbling under their breath, but not about changing history. And while Maude didn't join in, she shared their concerns. Dak wasn't a typical Rogue.

His vast ego, stubborn streak, and notorious temper were sure to complicate the mission. It'd take a Rogue with special skills to convince one of the team's founding fathers that he was going to cause a major time rift and stop it from happening.

"I'm going to need mechanics, scouts, and planners," Charlie said. "We've got to establish a path around the no-transit zone. The stasis lock will buy us time to conduct reconnaissance and plan the mission."

Charlie explained the rest of the situation. The erupting volcano and other hazards might be standard, but the subject of the rescue—Dak—wasn't. When Charlie finished outlining the specifics, detail by detail, most Rogues wore a silent, stiff-jaw expression of determination.

Maude looked around at her peers. They all owed Dak something. It was payback time. She'd need something extraordinary in her favor to win the coveted slot. And just being a natural at time travel didn't quite do it. Ah, but something else did! She was a woman, and Dak's taste for females might be enough to tip the scales.

When Charlie asked for volunteers for the initial reconnaissance transits to pinpoint Dak's exact location, Maude stepped forward. "I'll do it," she said.

Charlie half-shook his head. Maude knew what he was thinking. Although a recent graduate from novice-class, she still hadn't logged more than scout hours on her ident-log. Still, she didn't need to point out her assets or restate her willingness to commit. Charlie knew her strengths and weaknesses. Either she was capable of the task or she wasn't. Still, she struggled with the urge to beg.

"All right. You've got it," Charlie decided. "Head on over to retrofit. I'll send a list of implants and subroutines you'll need."

He winked. Maude couldn't keep the smile off her face. She'd only won the reconnaissance assignment, not the rescue itself, but this was a vote of confidence from one of the guys at the top of Rogue command. All she needed was a chance to prove herself—and this might be it.

Woo hoo! Only time would tell.

Chapter Four

Dallas: 2005, Tuesday evening

"What's wrong, Mac? I thought you were over Ben." Bubba swirled the last inch of beer in his bottle before he chugged it.

"Hm?" Mackenzie replied. Tucked into a corner booth at the Rib Joint with a bird's-eye view of the reactivated mechanical bull, Mackenzie could indulge in one of her favorite pastimes—male-watching. Not just any males, of course, but the dark, dangerous, cowboy tough-types.

The speaker above the table she and Bubba shared was hooked into the main jukebox, and it occasionally complicated chitchat when selections strayed from soft country ballads to rough and rowdy drinking songs, but at the moment a sentimental Collin Raye tune was playing and Mackenzie was distracted by something else. The bucking and tossing action on Bessie the bull was getting interesting. So far the score was Bessie, seven; customers, zilch.

Bubba repeated his question with a dose of attitude. That

got her attention and triggered a few perimeter alarms. Sweet old Bubba was up to something.

"Hell, yes, I'm over Ben. Why the third degree?"

Conversations with her cousin weren't ever deep. They always focused on a get-rich-quick scheme or how to make up with his sassy bride. Mackenzie could usually get away with nods and grunts, but this last-minute dinner date was demanding better than average concentration. Bubba wasn't just letting off steam over brewskies and a super-sized rib platter. He was milking her for details on her love life.

When Bubba didn't answer right away, it tipped his hand. The guy was a hopeless matchmaker.

"Wait, don't tell me. You've got a friend and you want to set me up." Mackenzie put down her margarita and glared at him.

"Now, Mac. Don't get in a lather. I just want to you to be happy. And you don't look happy."

"Bubba! I don't have time for this right now. Trust me, I'm happy. I'm busy and don't need or want a good ol' boy to cheer me up."

Bubba held up his ham-sized hands in surrender. "Won't you just hear me out?"

The guy had a heart as big as Texas and was tough to resist. Mackenzie took a long drink from her margarita and then waved him on.

"Okay, start talking."

"Face facts, Mac. You've got a rusty picker when it comes to finding Mr. Right," Bubba started.

"Oh, Lordy. If you're going to rake me over the coals you better order me another margarita."

Her cousin whistled in the direction of the bar. "Another round for the lady, Marv." Marv hooted okay, and Bubba turned his attention back to her.

"I'm not gonna rake you over the coals, honey. I just

think you need some help from a pro to settle this once and for all."

She licked the salted edge of her second margarita. "And, you're the pro. Right?" It was a rhetorical question he didn't bother to answer. Bubba wasn't a pro at anything except generating ideas and punching cows, but everyone in Dallas knew he was an outrageous romantic. He wanted the whole world paired up and producing lovely little cowpokes. It was his life plan, and he was sticking to it like a tick on a hound.

"Guys like Ben aren't your type, Mac. Those Wall Street types haven't ever owned a pair of cowboy boots, ridden a horse, or eaten barbecue with their fingers." Bubba paused to gnaw on a hunk of meat from his platter of ribs and sucked the sauce off his fingers.

"And, that's my type?" Mackenzie wasn't challenging the assertion. Bubba was right on target, but two years too late. She'd figured it out the first time she'd dragged Ben to the charity rodeo and chili cook-off. A watershed moment. The marriage had been on a downhill slide anyway, but Ben's selective allergy to the Wild West and two-step dancing hadn't improved the situation.

"I'm not saying that, but I know what it ain't. And it ain't another guy like Ben!"

"Relax, Bubba. I realized that a long time ago. By the way"—Mackenzie grinned and raised her margarita in a solitary toast. "I hear Ben's going to be a daddy soon. Let's drink to that one."

Bubba whistled. "Sorry, that must sting a bit." Her cousin had never liked Ben, but even now, now that her marriage to the cheating jerk was finished, he was sensitive to Mac's feelings.

"It should but it doesn't. He's moved on with his life. And, frankly, I haven't looked back either." Mackenzie's smile flagged a bit under Bubba's intense scrutiny.

"Okay, so it's not Ben, but something's wrong."

Bubba didn't frown often; it scared babies and offensive linemen alike. Her cousin was frowning now, and Mackenzie was suddenly terrified that he'd put two and two together. Had sweet, loveable, cousin Bubba figured out she was still quaking deep in her bones from the encounter with Mr. Pompeii?

"Bubba, I can't explain it," she started.

Bubba shook his head and eased out a heavy sigh. "Don't even try. It's the motherhood thing, isn't it? Your female body clock starting to bug you again?"

"Well, no. Not exactly. I've still got time." Mackenzie fiddled with her bare ring finger, wondering if that were true. She was fresh out of husbands and options. Motherhood had been forced to the bottom of her list of life goals. Again.

Bubba groaned. "I know you've got time but why wait?" He snapped his fingers. "Easy as pie. This little old matchmaker has a few aces tucked away. In fact, tonight—"

"Hold on, Bubba," Mackenzie cut in. "Did you get me here under false pretenses?"

Bubba didn't have a poker face. "Just hear me out."

"You little poop!" Mackenzie reached for her bag and started to stand, but Bubba's large warm hand forestalled her.

"You don't need to spruce up for this guy. You *always* look great."

"Bubba! This isn't about clothes or makeup. This is about coercion. Read my lips: No blind dates. Not now, not tomorrow, and not until I say okay. Deal?"

"Okay, okay, I'll cut him off at the pass. Let me give him a call. Where's your cell phone?"

Mackenzie tossed him her car keys. "In the glove box. Make it quick or else . . ."

As a former tight end for the Texas Aggies, Bubba could move like the wind when he wanted. He disappeared into the Rib Joint's crowd of patrons before Mackenzie could finish her threat.

"Damn his hide!" she growled. "I don't need this right now!"

Between Bubba and her lovable but nosy next door senior neighbor, Mrs. Jay, Mac would never be short on companionship—if and when she decided she needed it. Bubba apparently had an endless supply of hunky ex-football-playing buds and rodeo pals to access. And, with Mrs. Jay's connections through her weekly poker, church, and garage-sale crowds, eligible widowers were just a phone call away. As Mrs. Jay regularly reminded her, a woman should never shut down the pumps at the service station if she still has gas left in her tanks.

Still, for all their good intentions, Mackenzie was tired of their proddings to get back in the saddle. She hadn't fallen off a horse. She didn't want to get "serviced." And, she didn't need to answer to, stumble over, or worry about another male—not just yet. Marrying Ben had been a *huge* mistake. It had amounted to a rebound effort to purge Rick Mason from her system.

Yes, she wanted to fall in love again and raise a family before the next ice age hit. But, Bubba was right. Her picker was rusty. She'd tried her best to avoid the lying, cheating males of the world, and she'd managed to hook up with three of them. Well, two and a half, really. Rick hadn't technically cheated on her before she dumped him.

Mackenzie fumed. Rick Mason. It always came back to Rick. A full-circle journey around heartbreak hill. When would her bruised and battered heart heal?

Now a Vince Gill ballad was playing. Somebody out there in that sea of smiling faces had romance on the brain. Mackenzie closed her eyes and let the music cut through her anger and slide right into her soul. Amazing how a little tequila and a sappy song could turn a frown upside-down.

Truth was, she needed sleep and lots of it. She didn't have the energy to jump into *the* relationship of her life until she recovered from the Pompeii exhibit, both physically and emotionally. But, aside from that, Bubba's offer was interesting. She needed a hiatus from seriousness. And all of Bubba's pals were fun-loving guys who knew how to laugh and had sense enough to own a decent pair of cowboy boots.

Bubba trotted back to the table and sat down looking mighty pleased with himself. "Done. Want another round? I do."

He waggled his fingers and Marv shouted assent. "By the way, cousin, I need to borrow your rig tonight. That okay?"

"Sure, sure," Mackenzie agreed. She grabbed his hand for a moment. "Bubba, I appreciate the effort. I really do." She waved off the waitress who'd brought another beer for Bubba. Two margaritas were her limit. Thank goodness Bubba was driving, otherwise she'd need at least an hour to process the booze before she dared to get behind the wheel.

"I'll tell you what I told Mrs. Jay. Hold on to your aces, Bubba. Let me get through the exhibit, deal with that backstabbing know-it-all Rick Mason, and then I might want to talk turkey."

Bubba's stool slammed down on all four legs and nearly slipped out from under his rump. "Your Rick Mason?"

"Rick was *never* mine."

"But I thought . . ." Bubba stammered and choked on his beer.

"I know what you and everyone else thought. But you were wrong."

She looked away. The band was setting up for the first set of the evening, and folks were inching toward the dance floor. The sight of them coupling up for the two-step triggered a wave of sadness. She'd fallen in love with Rick for many reasons, and following his lead in the Texas two-step was one of them. She'd felt sexy and primal every time he took her in his arms. It was a mating ritual that flushed her cheeks, slicked her skin with sweat, and stoked a raging desire into an unquenchable passion. Once she'd thought she could never get enough of the man. And now—now she knew better.

"We were all wrong about Rick. Especially me."

"What's all this about backstabbing?"

Mackenzie waved her cousin off. "Trust me. You don't want to know. Besides, it's all water under the bridge as far as I'm concerned. I'm damned lucky the guy showed his true colors before he broke my heart."

"Sure he didn't succeed?" Bubba asked.

Mackenzie snorted. "Ha!"

"That's probably why you married on the rebound," Bubba offered. "Ben's the complete opposite of Rick Mason. Rick's an old Azel Texas boy who knows his left from his right when it comes to horses, and who earned a shiny rodeo belt buckle before he turned seventeen. For the life of me I still can't figure out why he didn't go pro and work the circuit."

"Because as good as he was at calf-roping, he was even better at book-learning, Bubba. The guy got a full scholarship to North Texas and it wasn't because he played sports."

"That so?" Her cousin stroked his chin and looked a little too pleased with himself. "He's not what'd I call an egghead—like you."

"I'm not an egghead, Bub! I'm an academic."

"There's a difference?"

"Are you baiting me for a reason, Bubba Cates, or are you a couple of beers past your limit?"

"Honey, I don't want to rile you but it just seems like if you and Rick could kiss and make up—"

"Don't even go there! I dumped Rick a long time ago for damned good reasons." She held up a finger. "Unfaithful." Not quite accurate, but she wasn't about to split hairs at the moment; she was on a roll.

She held up a second finger. "Plus, he's stubborn. A hard-headed, Joe Friday, stick-to-the-facts kind of a guy." She held up a third finger. "He took a job halfway around the world and I *don't* do long distance relationships." She held up a fourth finger but Bubba interrupted her.

"I get the point!" He chugged the remains of another beer.

How many beers was that, Mackenzie wondered. Bubba's beer keg days were long over. He'd turned into a near tee-totaler since he'd become a papa. Something was driving him to drink, and she had a sneaking suspicion that something was her.

"Damn, Mac. This is all news to me. I was looking forward to hanging out with him again. We go way back. And when I heard he was coming home again, well, I just thought maybe you two might get back together."

"Not a chance! Rick Mason broke my heart," Mackenzie snapped.

"You said he didn't."

"I lied."

"I'll be damned. That changes everything."

"What are you talking about, Bubba?"

"Well, it's like this. He asked me to step in, sort of smooth the waters, offer the olive branch—"

"Oh, no!" Mackenzie lunged at her cousin, grabbed the neck of his shirt, and reeled him in. "Not Rick Mason! He wouldn't. You didn't."

Bubba's eyes pooled with concern. The big baby wouldn't hurt a flea. Maybe he'd thought he was just rekindling a romance between two old lovers. Instead, he'd ripped open a festering wound in her heart.

"Sorry, honey. Rick said he wanted to get you back, and I didn't see any harm in setting it up."

"For *tonight*?" Mackenzie cried. "Oh my!"

Her heart was in her throat. Rick? Not here and now—not with a band and a dance floor within spitting distance. She wasn't ready.

Although she was sure that her "rehab" had worked, that she was cured of Rick, she'd planned their first encounter and all the rest of the upcoming six-week exhibit. It was a complex scheme that kept their two schedules in conflict and limited all but the most basic interactions to group settings. She had backup plans and contingencies but nothing to circumvent a chance meeting like this. She pressed her fingers to her ears and tried to blot out the music and think.

"Wait," she cried. "You called and canceled, didn't you?"

"I left a message at his motel, but he might not get it in time," Bubba replied. Her cousin couldn't get more hangdog if he tried. He was taking it hard. "If he shows, I'll kick his butt back to Italy if you want me to."

Mackenzie released her hold on Bubba and settled back into her seat. After a deep cleansing breath, she tried on her best greet-the-public smile. "How do I look?"

"Just like you did when Barbie Gaston beat you out for first place in junior barrel racing. That's how!"

"Nooooo!" Mackenzie wailed. "Not my expression, you lunk-head! How do I *look*? Is my hair okay?" Mackenzie fished around in her bag for her compact and a tube of lipgloss. She groaned when she looked in the mirror. Her mascara was smudged. The "new" look of her hair needed some emergency help. And her pink silk blouse was dappled with barbecue sauce.

Bubba shrugged his shoulders and Mackenzie quickly rubbed, glossed, fluffed, and pinched herself until she gave up. "What am I doing? This is hopeless," she hissed, and tossed her emergency fix-it equipment back into her bag and snapped it shut.

Bubba was trying hard to smother his grin but his cheeks kept twitching. "Relax, cousin. You look beautiful."

"Thanks, Bubba." Several deep breaths and she'd regained as much composure as possible. "You're not off the hook, you know. If he shows, I'm going to kill you. Even if he doesn't, I might just have to kill you for trying to set me up with him."

"Gotcha." Bubba stood up and backed away from the table. From a safe distance he held up her car keys. His lips moved but Mackenzie couldn't make out the words; a roar from the pit with the mechanical bull drowned out the sound.

"What? I can't hear you," Mackenzie shouted above the din.

Bubba pointed to the nearest exit and waved, then disappeared into the throng of customers encircling the bull.

"*Bubba!*" Mackenzie started to run after him, but a sight stopped her in her tracks: Rick Mason was standing at the far end of the dance floor.

Chapter Five

Rick felt rooted to the spot. In the next few moments, everything would change. He'd waited five years, traveled halfway around the world, and stuffed all of his pride in his back pocket to get to this point of no-return—a face-off with the woman he loved and craved morning, noon, and night.

He squared his shoulders and nodded as Bubba passed him. They didn't speak. Mac's cousin's dour expression said volumes. Winning back Mackenzie was going to be a challenge.

Meeting her at the Rib Joint had been his idea. Once upon a heartbreak, this had been "their" place—their dance floor, their corner booth, and their crowd. The music was still loud and the aroma of mesquite-smoked barbecue still permeated the rough-planked space from the floor to the rafters. And, although he didn't see a familiar face, Rick felt like he was among friends. He was back in Texas. Mackenzie didn't stand a chance against his home court advantage.

He caught sight of her then, standing beside their booth

and staring at him. Her smoldering gaze was fair warning that she hadn't forgiven him. But it was proof she hadn't forgotten him either. Half wildcat, half Madonna; she was a beauty with a beast of a chip on her shoulder. And, where there was smoke, there was still a fire—one he was determined to fan into an inferno. With that first glance, Rick's love-starved libido unleashed a full-scale riot. Primal urges flooded his brain and extinguished all reason. Mackenzie was all woman. *His* woman!

Mackenzie couldn't budge a muscle. One look at Rick and all signals between her brain and her limbs jammed. The only time when she probably would have forgiven herself for cowardice, for having turned tail and run, and her body wouldn't accommodate her commands. Heavens above, she could barely concentrate on the simple task of remaining upright. Just watching him mesmerized her.

He moved like a panther. His gaze never strayed from her face as he eased between dancers and tables, closing the distance between them with a slow but steady pace. The roar of the cheering crowd in the bull pit, the crash of dishes as the busser cleared the next table, the speaker throbbing with a heavy bass beat; none of it could drown out the sound of her heart singing with joy at the sight of him. Five years evaporated in a flash. It was as though they'd never been apart. Mackenzie could taste him on her mouth, smell him on her skin, and feel him on her, in her, hot, hard, and alive. She felt his whisper teasing her tender flesh and the old urge to yield to him without reservation.

He was tanned, tall, lean, and lethal. He was the hunter and she was the prey.

The straps of her bag slid through her fingers. She couldn't move a muscle to stop it from falling to the floor. Her knees shook. Her gaze fixed on the pulse in his throat, the sheen of sweat on his brow, and his dark searching eyes. He wasn't a dream. He wasn't a mystery. He was a man with a past and a future. But for Mackenzie, all that mattered at that moment was that he was here and now.

He stopped. Two feet and a lot of history stood between them. Could she reach beyond the pain and anger and offer something more?

"Dr. Mason." Just like that, she'd drawn a line in the sand: *This far, Rick Mason, and not an inch closer to me or my heart.*

"Can we work together?" she asked.

Whoa! Work together? What the hell was she talking about? And, what was all this Dr. Mason crap? They weren't strangers.

This was the woman who'd seen him down and out and higher than a kite. Skinny-dipping in the campus fountain after he'd passed his oral exams. Wasted on Jim Beam after putting down his aged quarterhorse. She knew his secrets, his weaknesses, his passions and faults. And, he knew hers. They might not be lovers anymore, but they sure as hell weren't strangers. Good or bad, close or distant, they'd always be more than coworkers because he'd never forget those countless steamy nights in her big brass bed. He'd pleasured her until she wept with joy, fed her icy strawberries until she shivered with delight, and traced every curve and hollow of her satin flesh with his tongue and committed it all to memory.

Rick clenched and unclenched his fists. The raw edge of his passion was out there, visible to the whole world. Up close, Mackenzie was more than simply lovely. She was an intoxicating blend of earth, wind, and fire that called him home. His loins throbbed with heat as her special scent of ripe peaches and wild cherries swamped him. The husky edge to her sweet voice nearly felled him like a ten-ton velvet hammer and whetted his appetite for more. How long had he craved the taste of her red-wine mouth? And, how long had he waited to hear his name on her lips to ransom his heart? It seemed like forever.

"Well, can we work together or not?" Mackenzie snapped again. She wasn't offering him the warmest of welcomes. A scalded cat looked friendlier.

Rick sighed and muscled his desires behind a steely reserve. It was going to be tough to keep them in check. Friendly or not, Mackenzie bewitched him. Her eyes were dark chocolate pools of mystery that still seduced him with a glance.

"I can if you can. This is business," he said.

"That's all it is!" she quickly added.

"I see," he returned, managing to sound cool and collected—part tough guy and part old friend.

Mackenzie inwardly groaned. Damnation, this wasn't going well at all. Not only did Rick still look better than George Clooney, his Randy Travis drawl was liquefying her muscles and sending alerts to every sweat gland to increase production two hundred percent.

"Do you? Do you really?" she asked, and tried to ignore her clammy palms, soaked armpits, and soppy brow.

"Mackenzie, I'm sorry. I owe you an apology and a whole lot more. I was a fool. I caused all this." He paused, chopping the air between them with the edge of one hand. "We had something really great together and I want it back. Don't you?"

"I don't want *this,*" Mackenzie snapped. "This is making something personal out of a purely business situation. I learned my lesson. I never mix the two."

The music shifted tempo. And, from where Rick leaned against the railing, she realized—and half hoped—he could snag her arm, pull her out on the dance floor, and melt all her resistance with a few sexy moves.

She needed to pinch herself and wake up. This wasn't

another fantasy where she indulged every whim without recourse. This was real. Obliging her libido even for a single gratifying act with Rick would wreak havoc on her emotions. She'd done the broken-heart routine complete with tears on the pillowcase and a rebound romance five years ago because of Rick Mason. Once around heartbreak hill was enough.

She pressed her trembling lips into a thin smile. "Since you're here"—she waved her hand in the direction of Bubba's vacated stool, "we may as well clear the air. And, I can give you my ground rules. Have a seat."

Rick sat. He was smooth, cool, and too damned close for comfort. Had the table shrunk? Sitting across from Rick she could feel the blast of heat from his body. She was stiff, nearly afraid to move for fear of accidentally brushing against his skin or knocking knees under the table. And, she didn't dare make eye contact for more than a second or two at a time. Rick Mason, friend or foe, unnerved her. Strike a match and she might just go up in flames.

"Your ground rules?" Rick prompted.

"Thanks, I'll take it from here." Mackenzie shoved aside the remnants of Bubba's dinner and tapped the top of the planked table with her fingernail.

"First, the exhibit is my number-one priority. Second, our professional collaboration is necessary on the signage, lecture series, and promotion. But third, this is my museum, my staff, and my exhibit. What I say goes. It's not open to debate or challenge. Are you following me so far?"

"There's more?"

The band finished the first set. At least one thing was working in her favor. Now she could hear her heartbeat—oh dear! It was loud and strong and thumping faster than an Olympic-class runner sprinting for the finish line.

"Of course," she replied. Did her voice really sound like fingernails on the chalkboard, or was it her imagination?

She downed the rest of her margarita but it didn't calm her nerves. On the contrary, her insides felt like she'd just tossed gasoline on a campfire. She coughed until her eyes watered and her nose dripped.

Rick pushed a fresh glass of water into her fist. "I guess this is bad timing, Mackenzie. Want me to leave?" He handed her a wad of napkins.

She shook her head as she dabbed at her eyes and nose. Great! If she looked a mess before, she hadn't improved the situation one bit. She'd better wrap it up pronto before she embarrassed herself further.

"No. This won't take long. There's just one more thing I'd like to add," she said. But before she could finish, the band launched its next set with a boot-stomping sing-along that threatened to rattle the rafters and shake the foundation.

"You want to get out of here?" Rick yelled above the noise.

Yes, yes, a thousand times yes—out of here and away from Rick as fast as her little pitter-pattering heart and heavy-as-lead tootsies could carry her. Mackenzie bit her lips and nodded.

Chapter Six

It was crisp and cold outside. It felt delicious for a few minutes, till the shivering kicked in and reminded her that she was coatless and without a car.

"Damn it, Bubba! Damn, damn, damn!"

"I take it there's a problem," Rick said. He looked great in his leather flight jacket, of course. He wasn't a clotheshorse, but that didn't change the fact he looked hunky and handsome in just about everything.

Stop drooling! Remember you dumped him! she silently chastised herself.

Mackenzie glared at him. "Nothing I can't handle."

"You're shivering."

"I know, but like I said, this won't take long," she snapped.

"All right." He snorted. "You were going to add one more condition?"

Yeah, and just what had that last condition been? The cold was zapping her anger and her focus. All Mackenzie really wanted was to pull Rick back inside, find a nice warm corner, and nuzzle up against his body. But that wouldn't help keep her chin up and her pride intact.

"Professionalism," she finally said. She'd earned it, she demanded it, and she couldn't afford to let it slip for a blessed second whenever this dark and dangerous cowboy was nearby.

"Professionalism? What about it?"

"Mutual respect. You stay on your turf and I'll stay on mine."

Rick laughed out loud. "That last bit sounds like a truce to me. Let's shake on it." He held out his hand.

Mackenzie couldn't refuse, could she? It was a quick one-pump affair, but the instant replay in her brain stretched it out like a slow-motion scene in a movie. The swooping approach, followed by contact—pressing the flesh, Rick's warm fingers curling around her cold ones and transferring a goodly amount of heat—and finally the breakaway. She had to give Rick credit. He didn't take advantage of the situation. He didn't pull her close or tuck her inside his warm coat or attempt a modified version of CPR to breathe his heat into her mouth and restore their lost passion for each other. No, Rick was all gentleman, damn his leather-coated hide!

"That's all of it?" he asked.

Mackenzie nodded while her teeth chattered. "Yep."

"Where's your truck?" He looked around the large dirt lot that hosted a sea of vehicles. "You still have the Jeep Willy, don't you?"

"Not tonight. Bubba borrowed it."

Rick nodded. "Want a lift home? It's no trouble."

She could do that. It wasn't breaking any of her conditions. Besides, she didn't have another option at the moment. Cabs weren't impossible to get, but it would be a damned long wait for one.

"I'd appreciate it. Thanks."

Rick's rental car was silver and sleek and looked like it could run on jet fuel. He opened the door and Mackenzie slid into a seat that fit like a glove. Umm, nice.

And when he got behind the wheel and shut the door, he cut off the rest of the world. It was just the two of them nesting in cushy leather seats with only six inches to spare between their bodies. The engine sounded like a jungle cat purring beneath the hood. It took only seconds for the space to warm and Mackenzie's teeth to stop clattering—and a split second more for her to realize that the soft melody coming from the speakers was a re-mix of *their* song, "This Kiss." The mood was perfect, the guy was available, and it would be oh-so-nice to feel his arms around her one more time.

And let him break her heart again? No way!

"This was a mistake!" She grabbed the door latch and started to get out.

"If we're going to work together as a team again, I've got a few ground rules too," Rick said.

Mackenzie knew that take-charge tone all too well. It had suckered her many times in the past. Team? What a bunch of bull. She sat up straight and folded her arms across her chest. "Okay. Let's hear them."

"Accept my apology for my part in our breakup. And say my name."

"Your name?"

"Yep. Say it."

"Rick," she snapped. Short and sweet, nothing to it!

Rick closed his eyes. "Sounds like you're popping bubblegum. Could you slow it down a bit and try again?"

Jeez, Louise, she silently groaned, and a niggling germ of a warning surfaced. *It's a trap. Don't do it.* She swallowed once and tried to relax. She closed her eyes and was suddenly swamped with the thrilling image of Rick standing across the room in the Rib Joint and her heart calling out to his.

"Rick." She couldn't stop herself. Joy was spontaneous, rounding out the sharp edges of the consonants. His name sounded like a lover's whispered prayer.

He nodded. "Better. Thanks. I've waited a long time to hear that." He groaned and scrubbed his face with his hands.

Mackenzie's reserve was crumbling. Quicksand surrounded her thoughts. She needed a branch, a helping hand to pull herself out of the mire of emotion threatening to drag her deep into Rick's enticing snare.

He cleared his throat. "And, the apology. I'm sorry. I was wrong, you were right. Does that about cover it?"

It felt like he'd slapped her. "You think *that* covers it? That's the sorriest excuse for an apology I've ever heard, Rick Mason—*not* that I want to talk about it."

She fumed in silence for about half a second before she changed her mind. Sure, she wanted to talk about it. She wanted to dissect it and tweak it until she'd turned it into a happy ending instead of what it was—a sad story of jealousy, fear, and infidelity.

"You took the Pompeii museum job without consulting me, Rick," she cried. "We were a fine team, weren't we? Didn't you think I'd care that you were going to move to the opposite side of the planet? It was selfish, mean-spirited, and flat-out rotten. After what you did to me and to us, I'd think you could do better than a mere 'I'm sorry.' "

"If that'll fix it between us, Mackie, I can and I will—but I'll need a rain check for the full-blown version." He leaned back against the headrest and rubbed his eyes with the back of his hand. "God, I'm tired. Jet lag is catching up with me, I guess."

"We can't work together for six weeks! We're barely able to stay cordial," Mackenzie cried.

Rick chuckled. "We'll manage, Mackenzie, because you're a lady and I'm one motivated cowboy."

A lady? Well, Mackenzie wasn't exactly making her

Mama proud tonight. Exhaustion, out-of-the-ordinary events, and stress had won the day. She was certifiably snippy and snotty and more than a little in-lust with an old flame. If that wasn't a volatile combination, then neither was a case of nitro strapped to a bucking bronc.

"Why don't you just drop me by the museum," Mackenzie said. "It's closer to the motel you said you are staying at, and besides I've got some more work to do tonight. I can grab a cab when I'm done."

"Is that a good idea? It's not safe." He revved his car engine and put it in gear. The big cat had power. Rocks spun under the wheels, and before Mackenzie could muster an indignant response they were cruising toward Big D's skyline.

"If treasures from Pompeii are safe, I'm safe," Mackenzie replied. "Guards, alarms, locks, and vaults seal me off from the big bad world."

Rick folded too easily. "Agreed." His lips pressed into a thin line. "So, I'll see you to the door and hand you over for night deposit."

Mackenzie admired his restraint. They'd been over this turf many times. A verbal misstep and they'd cycle through the old argument and not solve a thing. She had worn out the soapbox on the subject of her ability to take care of herself and fight her own battles.

"Thanks, I appreciate the escort service," Mackenzie said.

The sudden quiet was awkward. It was instinctive for Mackenzie to want to smooth out the tension between them: an urge born of five generations of southern females to *always* be polite to friends, strangers, and sworn enemies alike. She quashed the urge and dismissed the looming image of her mom shaking a finger of warning.

But Rick, still a West Texas boy and a gentleman at heart, didn't shirk his duty. "Is there something else that's got your back up? I mean something other than having my sorry ass hanging around your exhibit and dredging up old memories?"

"No. We're on schedule for the opening."

She stared straight ahead and avoided even the most casual glance in his direction. Once they'd been close enough to nearly read each other's minds. If he picked up on her issues with Mr. Pompeii and the idea that the body cast might have moved, it'd be a disaster. Wouldn't it?

Or, would he understand? Rick, enemy or not, was probably the only one she could tell and not be laughed right out of a job. He knew all about weird Granny Moon, and once she could have talked to him about anything.

"If we're going to work together, we'll need to exchange more than grunts," he said.

"You're right." She nodded and sighed heavily. "I'm tired too. Pete Proctor owes me for all the overtime I'm putting in on this project."

"Teamwork a little one-sided with my old mentor?" he asked.

"I don't have any complaints," she returned.

And, she really didn't. Working with the museum director was on par with her collaborations with other professionals; it was the garden-variety give and take. Not up to her ideals, but very few associations were. After all, she'd started out with Rick, and nothing since could match that level of challenge and intellectual stimulation or equal the sheer poetry of how their minds melded around issues. Rick had once called it brain sex. For Mackenzie, that summed it up perfectly.

"It's going to be a great exhibit," she said. She glanced down at her hands. The one that had touched Mr. Pompeii felt burnt. She shook herself and smiled. "The body cast is remarkable. It gets to me every time I see it."

"I know the feeling," he said.

"Yeah, you do, don't you." Her smile felt linked to her heart. It wasn't the first time that day, week, month, year, or decade that Mackenzie acknowledged the kinship they had once shared, born of common interests and trials by fire. When one of them breathed it had felt like the other exhaled. For five years now, Mackenzie felt like she had been breathing with one lung.

He didn't prod. That was the Rick she remembered. It was so easy to be with him, listen to him, talk to him.

"I think it moved," she said. *Holy poop, did I just say that?*

Rick gripped the wheel. "Repeat that."

"Mr. Pompeii, the victim. I think he moved."

"The body cast. The one I made, moved." It wasn't a question but a statement.

Mackenzie finally looked at him. Rick's own features could have been etched in stone. Noncommittal for the moment, he was clearly listening, waiting, knowing there had to be more. He didn't even blink.

"Yep. Moved." There, she'd said it.

Rick exhaled audibly and leaned back against the seat and stretched. The silence between them felt thick with tension.

Mackenzie held her breath. Damn, damn, and double-triple damn. Getting in the car with Rick was mistake number one. Mistake number two had been telling him about the statue.

He flipped on the blinker and turned into an oasis of neon in the moonless night, a Dunkin Donuts, and cut the engine. "I need coffee and sugar. Lots of it."

"You don't believe me," Mackenzie said, crushed even though she'd expected it.

"Hell, no. But I'm certainly not going to get any sleep until I hear the whole story."

Chapter Seven

"I really don't know what to think," Mackenzie said and shrugged. She kept her focus on the action behind the glass partition in the nearly vacant doughnut shop.

Rick groaned. It was his turn. Time to step up to the plate and support her delusions or call her a kook.

The doughnut-making machinery was operational, and Rick was thankful for the distraction. It allowed him a moment to formulate a response. He swallowed another chunk of cinnamon roll and washed it down with hot coffee. Damn, who was he kidding? He needed more than a moment to sort through the glut of information she'd just dished out.

He knew there was a fine line between wanting and having that even some of the roughest, toughest folks couldn't cross. He wanted Mackenzie back. And he'd prepared for a long siege, if necessary, to get her. He was ready to run the gauntlet and defeat any obstacle she could throw at him—or so he'd thought until he heard about the moving statue.

Believing Mackenzie had inherited any of Granny

Moon's physic gifts was a wrinkle in his nearly foolproof strategy. It didn't jibe with the scientific precepts that he embraced. Still, it unveiled fascinating and complex aspects about the woman he adored, and it suspended the hostilities between them, for the moment, while she summarized her encounter with Mr. Pompeii.

After wolfing down sugary pastries and tanking his system with pure black java, he felt his jet-lag fog lift. He was puzzled and curious about Mackenzie's paranormal experience, though truthfully he'd feign interest in anything if it would prolong the truce with her. It was bogus and underhanded to take advantage of the situation and feed into her delusion when he couldn't muster a valid micron of support . . . but he was going to do it.

She wasn't watching the machinery now. She was staring right through him, her eyes seeing all, knowing all—or so it seemed. He flexed his jaw and tried on one of his practiced smiles.

"I don't know what to think either, Mackie. But I . . ." He stopped before he could dig a deep, deep hole he couldn't get out of. Lying to Mackenzie didn't come easy. Thanks to the body cast, she'd lowered her guard. They were talking again. That was all that mattered to him. If he had to fake an interest in astrology, UFOs, and pots of gold at the end of rainbows to ultimately win her back, he'd fake it!

He reached across the table and brushed a crumb of doughnut away from the corner of her mouth. She grinned and his brain instantly turned to mush again.

"Want to go check on Mr. Pompeii and tuck him into bed for the night?" he asked. "I'm game if you are."

"Sure!"

Her relief was obvious, and Rick instantly felt like a jerk. Was he crazy too? Why didn't he just spit it out and tell her the truth instead of stringing her along? An upright guy would tell her straight out, No dice, it's all in you're head. But, when she'd dumped him five years ago, he had changed. Upright guys didn't always win. And, honorable or not, he'd stop at nothing to win her back.

"You're breaking the rules," Rick whispered. He leaned over Mackenzie's shoulder as she punched in the code.

"We both know it. Stop reminding me." Mackenzie held her breath while the keyless lock processed. It wasn't always instantaneous. Sometimes she flubbed the number sequence, like now when she was nervous or excited. *Not about the rules.* No, that wasn't the reason her heart thumped like a piston in the *Titanic* trying to reverse engines and avoid the collision with the iceberg. This was something else. This was fate. Her life shifting on its axis and something cracking—changing forever the way she sounded, acted, thought. The split in the Liberty Bell wasn't as profound as this breach in Mackenzie's character. It was a wide rift that allowed possibilities to ebb and flow at will. New stuff. Not prohibited acts, like touching relics with her bare hands or slipping Rick past security before he'd been officially cleared for access, but the rash of inexplicable and profound twists to a single breath that caused a quiver in her voice and trembling along her spine.

Damned if she knew just how this was happening. But she had a pretty good idea that the focal point of the Pompeii exhibit triggered the urge. The stone man was a mystery that begged solving. It flipped the switch on her amateur sleuth persona, a compelling and obsessive Sherlock Holmes nature she struggled to keep under wraps because it lacked caution and reserve. But here she was again, intent on ferreting out truth even if it meant bending a few rules to do it.

The lock finally clicked; the door popped open. They were in.

Mackenzie led. Rick, close on her heels, hummed the *James Bond* theme music, adding a clandestine feel to the trudge through the main offices and labyrinth of storage rooms.

Well, I've done it now, Mackenzie admitted to herself. *Too late to back out.*

She flipped on lights as they passed into the netherlands of the museum; a small factory at the heart of the showpiece, accessible by staff and service personnel. This was home. Quiet pervaded the space. Odors too. Elemental smells of metal and mortar blended with the plastics and stirred her appetite for enigmas and conundrums and mimicked a craving for illegal drugs. She knew Rick felt it too—another bond between them.

She led him deeper into the stockroom for artifacts, past the caged areas with oversized booty and orphaned tapestries, and between florescent-lit gray-green holding pens with study cribs for undergrad researchers. They'd shared a desk here early in their careers. Rick touched her shoulder and held fast for a moment as they passed Gillespe's littered desk in number six, a minor disaster area compared with their tenure in the same space. Mackenzie smiled, glad that he still remembered those days.

The staircase accessing B-4 level was cooler than the rest of the museum. They were getting close to the Pompeii staging area. Mackenzie pushed open the thermosealed door to the maze of temperature-controlled areas, vented spaces, and labs that held the priceless artifacts and readied them for display. Pausing at the portal, the last lock and final checkpoint before entering the exhibits, Mackenzie tapped on the glass of the security booth.

Harry the night guard grinned when he saw Rick. The three of them had bonded years earlier when all-night efforts were essential for those post-grad museum research projects. Harry was a sentimental old Scot with a passion for doughnuts and a good story, both of which Rick had provided in excess. Harry mopped his jolly face with his trademark tartan hankie and checked his watch.

"Thought you were done with this kind of work, Dr. Mason," he said, and wrung Rick's hand twice before letting go. "Good to have you back again, even if it is only for a little while."

Rick nodded in Mackenzie's direction. "I'll check in tomorrow and get my official clearance. Okay if I tag along tonight to make sure this workaholic gets to bed before dawn?"

"Good idea. She still works too hard. You might want to haul her out of here before Joseph checks in for the midnight-to-seven shift. He's a hard-nosed cuss about staff and guests bending the rules."

Good old Harry, he'd keep Rick's visit off-the-record. But Mackenzie would still bring him a half-dozen Krispy Kremes and a thermos of coffee on his next shift to ease her conscience.

"Thanks, Harry, I'll keep it short," she said. She thrust a lab coat and gloves into Rick's hands and ushered him through the door.

Adjusting the lights, she stood for a moment. Rick flanked her, silent and alert. It was hushed, almost sacred, as though they had just stepped into a tomb. The display provoked the sensation. The installation team and display construction folks had made significant progress since Mac's early morning visit to Mr. Pompeii.

Mackenzie flipped one switch on and off several times before waving at the security cam. "Harry, will you note that the spots on the alpha grid are out?" It wasn't a two-way transmission, but she knew Harry would pass on the data to maintenance.

Rick donned his coat and pocketed the gloves. Mackenzie followed suit.

"Let me lead," Mackenzie said. She didn't add the rest of the warnings. Rick knew them all. Minimize contact with the exhibits, stay clear of the equipment, watch your head, watch where you step, and generally stifle all urges to fondle the artifacts. So what if she'd torn up the rulebook six hours ago when she touched the body cast with her bare hands. She still couldn't believe she'd really done it. And now this, sneaking Rick into the exhibit. Yep, the crack in her principles was getting bigger by the minute.

The exhibit still lacked crowd-control devices and info placards. And it looked like a workshop. Scaffolding, sawhorses, crates, and mechanized lifts nested around most of the artifacts. But the presence of something else permeated the scene. Age. Centuries encapsulated by the stark white walls and boxlike space. Yes, like a tomb. It was a bonus point for Mackenzie's exhibit design.

In the half-lit cavernous exhibit space thick with shadowy artifacts, if someone played a few bars from the *Phantom of the Opera,* Mackenzie would have jumped right out of her clothes. Hell, a squeaky shoe would have set her off.

She offered Rick a weak grin, but he didn't seem to notice. His talent for visualizing an exhibit minus construction paraphernalia was activated. And his mumbled commentary was a by-product.

"It's a great design, Mackenzie," he said. "You have a knack for capturing the essence of the moment."

Mackenzie agreed. Her goal had been to invite visitors to experience a pivotal event in history and the layout worked. She'd tested it in flat, 3-D, and virtual formats, but only now could the true impact of the design be realized.

"This is cutting-edge exhibition design. The pseudo immersion in the era with the artifacts I excavated last summer will truly bring it to life. It's a testament to Boca Frendal, the grand master of exhibit design himself. You're proving his adage that less is more."

"Interesting," she mumbled and led him deeper into the exhibit that replicated a streetscape in ancient Pompeii.

"Interesting? That's an understatement," he replied.

Mackenzie was viewing everything with a critical eye, but she had to admit her design was taking shape nicely. It wasn't finished yet. Frendal's requisite light and sound enhancements would be added next. But, even without them, she could easily assume the role of a time-traveler and witness the prelude to disaster and the aftermath of devastation when Mount Vesuvius erupted on August 24, A.D. 79. More than a mere snapshot of life frozen in time, the exhibit promised to treat avid museum-goers to a lingering you-were-there-too hangover.

"Once it's fully lit and open to the public," Rick said, "I guarantee a few new gray hairs for more sensitive visitors."

Mackenzie detached from her assessment long enough to chuckle. "Maybe more than gray hairs. Are you current on your CPR?"

"We sure might need it," he added.

Mackenzie reached over and tugged on his sleeve. "Come on. I want to show you where I planted Mr. Pompeii before they throw us out of here."

She pointed to the bakery as they passed. "Frendal's atmospherics include piping in the scent of bread left burning in the ovens."

Rick murmured his approval as they rounded the corner and confronted carts loaded with loot, abandoned in the middle of the street, casks and urns of wine stacked at the tavern door, and, at last, the man. The stone man—Mr. Pompeii. A victim caught in motion, upright, apparently attempting to flee disaster.

"Wow." Rick stopped in his tracks. "He looks sensational."

Rick circled the man. The lighting glanced off both of them and Mackenzie marveled at the sight. Nearly two millennia separated the men. That and the small matter of Mr. Pompeii being stone—or plaster, rather. Otherwise, they were very similar. No great leaps in evolution separated one version from the other. Both shared physiques that tempted virgins to sin. Both had strong limbs, broad shoulders, chiseled chins, and eyes that seemed to see beyond the world.

Rick was the animated, *GQ,* colorized version. His tanned body pulsed with life. His lean muscled mass reflected his obsession with horses, sports, and the great outdoors. His dark hair contrasted with his golden skin.

Mackenzie shifted her gaze between the two men. Rick was fact and life in motion; Mr. Pompeii was an ancient version, stilled and silent. Both would qualify for the title of Mr. Heartbreak. Both looked dangerous with a capital D.

Chapter Eight

Mackenzie kept her distance and lingered just beyond the edge of the pool of light created by the spots. She studied the body cast's profile again. The guy wasn't a local from Pompeii; she'd bet her granny's hope chest on that, even though she lacked hard facts to prove it. He had the brawn and bulk of a gladiator and could be Greek or Roman—yet none of it mattered now. His final destination labeled him for all time. Victim of Pompeii. Or, rather, of Vesuvius. Fate had called his number, and life had ceased for this man in his prime one sweltering day in A.D. 79.

Mackenzie cleared her throat. "What do you think?"

Rick mumbled. He was lost in the same mists of time that fogged her brain when she worked with artifacts. He was struggling with the shift.

It had been a bond between them since grad school. They shared the obsession and the power of age embodied in tools, toys, and ornaments from the distant past, objects fingered and discarded by hands long turned to dust.

To be honest, her fascination with Mr. Pompeii surprised her. He wasn't really an artifact. Not a mummy or a skeleton, he was only a cast of the man entombed by smothering ash. The form represented the imprint of his body, not his remains. Still, the addition of the statue to the exhibit was a plus.

"Nice job on the body cast," she said. Rick nodded in thanks but continued to study the placement and positioning of the object. She added, "You've mastered the casting of victims and my guess is you've probably advanced the craft to a science."

"I don't know about that. But I am the authority on the techniques used by the early excavators of Pompeii and their dedication to casting the remains of victims. Of course, I've switched to synthetic materials for the molds and copies."

He tugged her over onto the hoist, raised it level with Mr. Pompeii's shoulder and pointed. "That's my site entry into the cavity. I made six copies off this guy. After this exhibit, we're going to stabilize him in long-term storage and use only those copies for display. He's too fragile to showcase for extended periods.

"Still, whether they're originals or copies, victims such as this are crucial to a Pompeii exhibit. They represent the human equation of the historic disaster." Rick looked at her. "That's why I always try to include one in the manifest. Although, I don't mind telling you"—he mimicked wiping sweat off his brow—"getting permission to ship this original off-site took some fancy finagling!"

"I'm glad you did. I'm not so sure I'd feel the same way about a copy."

Rick laughed. "I make a swell copy. I don't think too many curators can tell my duplicates from the originals."

"I can." Mackenzie wasn't bragging. The burned feeling on her fingertips had something to do with the original body cast; she was sure of it. It was another gut instinct, but she'd stake her soon-to-be-shaky reputation as a curator on it if necessary.

Rick didn't challenge her. They were skirting the fantastic idea that the body cast had moved. She was enjoying the banter between them. It was foreplay to brain sex. And after a five-year drought, Mackenzie was loath to shift gears.

Then Rick broke the silence. "Where were you standing when it moved?" he asked.

Mackenzie adjusted the hoist to the point where she'd first experienced the phenomenon. "Here."

"And what about the racket from the ventilation system you described? I don't see any ductwork."

"It's hidden in the ceiling panels. But they must have finished stabilizing the monster now. I haven't heard it cycle on and off once tonight, and we have a regular schedule on air exchange."

Rick nodded, then continued his silent survey of the statue and surroundings. It really was too quiet, Mac admitted to herself. She shifted her weight, drummed her fingers, and finally filled the void with nervous chatter.

"Why do you think he's standing when all of the other victims you've excavated are prone?"

"I'm still researching it, but I've got a few theories," Rick said. "None hold water."

"Try me. I won't quote you," Mackenzie said.

"Eruption characteristics for Vesuivus and the Pompeii victims don't jibe with this guy," Rick explained. "My best guess is that he was in motion when an avalanche of ash somehow stopped him in his tracks. What held him upright defies explanation and challenges the accepted theory that poisonous gasses killed most victims before the ash buried them."

Mackenzie gulped back a rush of emotion. "But death was instantaneous, wasn't it?"

Rick's brows knitted. "Yes, probably so."

She stepped into the pool of light and circled the figure, stopping beside Rick and looking up into that face again. A little sigh eased out before she could stop it.

"I don't think he's from Pompeii," Mackenzie said.

"Relevance?" Rick adopted the same tone he probably used with his archaeology dig crews. It was his brand of Morse code that warned off conversationalists from wasting his time discussing extraneous data.

"None," she returned. "A theory." Mackenzie glanced over at him. "Do you see or feel anything?"

Rick shook himself but didn't answer. His strong features could shift at will and shield emotion behind an impassive countenance. Mackenzie scowled.

"Yes or no?" she demanded.

"Where did you touch him?" Rick replied. He gave no hint of what brewed in his brain.

Oh, he was good, damn him. His noncommittal tone kept Mackenzie on edge. She couldn't guess what he was thinking. She accepted that it was too much to ask a rational mind to believe her story without evidence, too great a leap of faith. Still, if anyone could make the leap, Rick was her man.

"I touched his cheek."

Rick nodded. "I'll check that next. There's something I want to see first." He squatted down on his haunches, bending low over the ankle of the back leg.

Mackenzie smiled. Sure enough, Rick's radar for flaws still worked. She hadn't told him about the defect yet. There hadn't been time.

"Got a mobile spot?" he asked.

Mackenzie collected one from the neighboring scaffold and donned her gloves. She leaned in close and flicked on the lamp. "Is it damaged from the shipment?" she asked.

"Use your famous gut instinct and imagination, Mackenzie. What's your first impression?" Rick extended his finger and pointed to the ankle. Mackenzie stared for a moment and then her eyes grew wide.

"Jewelry?" she whispered.

"Or manacles. He has another one on his left arm. He

could have been tethered or chained." Rick stepped back and looked him over again. "But I didn't find evidence to support it at the dig site."

Rick's voice thickened with the progressive deliberation. It wasn't a vote of confidence by any means, but she was grateful for the studied effort. Applying his own exacting methods of historical detection, Rick could uncover clues and extract elusive facts most specialists might miss. She trusted his ceaseless research would eventually solve the mystery about the nameless victim.

"Wonder who he was," Rick mused.

This was often how it had started between them—their minds knitting together over a problem. Tit for tat. One sparking, the other providing kindling and vice versa.

Mackenzie frowned. "Process of elimination, I guess. He wasn't a Roman senator."

"Okay? Why not?"

"Well, his clothes for one, and the jewelry—if it is jewelry. It might be a trade guild ornament." Mackenzie tilted her head back and frowned. "Also, you discovered him in a brothel. The wealthy indulged themselves at home, services delivered so-to-speak in the privacy and luxury of their villas. This guy was a victim of his vice, caught in a pleasure palace on the last day of his life."

Rick shook his head. Quick jerks left and right. "Was that the ventilation system?" he asked.

"What?" Mackenzie glanced over at him. "Did you hear something? I didn't."

Rick turned away, his face pale and drained of energy. His fingers fumbled with the buttons on his lab coat as though they were alien objects.

"You okay?"

"Yeah, fine," Rick murmured. "Damned jet lag and sugar rush. I can barely keep upright." His voice sounded deeper, husky.

To Mackenzie, he didn't look fine and he didn't look jet

lagged. He looked like he was on the verge of something serious enough to dial 911. Rick looked at her, through her, beyond her. Mackenzie waved her hand in front of his face. He didn't even blink.

"Rick? Maybe this wasn't a good idea." Mackenzie edged toward him while running through a laundry list of emergency procedures that popped into her brain. *What was that again? Pump, pump, pump, and breathe? Or breathe, breathe, breathe, pump?*

"I'm *fine*—I just need some air." He swung around on her. "Don't you hear it? The dull roar? It's like a 747 is making a low-level pass over the museum."

Mackenzie gulped. No, not at the moment. But if it was anything like the sound she'd heard earlier, just before she'd touched the body cast, Rick was about to get zapped.

"Harry?" She waved at one of the security cameras. "Sixty-six on over here, will you? ASAP."

"Sixty-six?" Rick growled. "I don't need medical aid! I need a firm mattress and twelve hours of shut-eye." His movements had slowed to a crawl. He pulled off his gloves and dropped them on the floor as he staggered toward the nearest solid object of support. Mr. Pompeii.

"Rick!" Mackenzie cried. She rushed forward but was too late.

Rick's full-body contact with the plaster cast didn't appear to damage either party at first, until Rick's eyes rolled back in his head and he crumpled like a rag doll.

"Sixty-six, Harry!" Mac screamed. She slid to the floor beside Rick, scared to touch him but more scared not to.

Chapter Nine

Rick bobbed around in a numbing black void. It felt like he'd been sucker punched, minus the pain. And then, the darkness shifted. He wasn't alone.

Images of panic and death snapped on and off like a crude slide show complete with sense, sound, and aroma. *Wow! That's Vesuvius erupting,* he thought. The blast of heat and stench of sulfur hit him full force.

The next shot: a screaming child clinging to its dead mother's hand. The next: the roof of the Stabian baths catching fire.

Others: people fleeing the burning city, Vesuvius belching fireballs, ash choking the skies. And, another: himself racing to find Falah. Falah?

They came at him faster and faster until the images melded into one continuous stream of flashing light that resembled a scratchy home movie of a visit to Hell. Was he dying?

The raging inferno felt real enough to boil his blood. The fetid odor of fear seeped from his flesh. The distant screams for help were his own.

The last image was a freeze-frame. It was an ash-coated

hand grasping the armband and pressing the red flashing stone encaged in the metal. The images stopped and the sudden darkness severed all sensation.

Good God! Was he dead?

"Damn, woman," Rick growled. "Stop screaming."

He said more, but Mackenzie tuned out the stream of muffled curses and concentrated on assessing his other symptoms. "You're clammy." Mackenzie jerked off one of her gloves, slipped her fingers around his neck and took his pulse.

"My heart beating?" Rick snapped.

"You're alive, so I don't think you need shock therapy," she replied. She kept her fingers pressed against his flesh, absorbing the heat and confirming his pulse was strong and sure.

"Do you know where you are? Are your ears ringing? Do the tips of your fingers feel burned?"

"Hey, one question at a time," Rick barked as he rubbed his hands against his pant legs and flexed his knuckles.

"Okay, how about: What the *heck* happened?" Mackenzie returned.

Rick sucked air into his lungs and let it out. "I don't know, but something, probably the faulty ventilation system, knocked me on my ass. Gotta be fumes from the preservatives. I'm okay now."

"Damn it, Rick," Mackenzie cried. Her eyes were leaking tears, but she didn't wipe them away.

He cocked his head to one side as he looked up at her. "So you still care a little," he guessed.

Hell, yeah, she cared. And, jeepers, it felt great to touch the man again. Crisis or not, this moment of bonding was magic.

He grinned. "Thanks, but you can stop with the pulse thing. I think I'll survive."

Mackenzie jerked her hand away as if she were scalded. "Sorry." Hot. Africa hot. The heat of passion and embarrassment tumbled together as though a fireball had broken loose in her being.

She wrestled the seductive feelings back into their corner and mentally kept them at bay with a whip and a chair. She hadn't brought him here to jump-start a dead romance. This was supposed to be all about solving the mystery of the moving statue.

And they'd solved it—or rather, Rick had. He'd offered a rational and reasonable explanation. It was an air quality issue. Simple as that.

"Sorry," she said, "I should have guessed it was the ventilation system acting up." She sniffed. It did smell a lot like brimstone all of a sudden.

"Hey, don't be," Rick returned. "You're number one on my list of preferred CPR providers. I'd trust you to hotwire my heart anytime."

In spite of her protests, he pulled himself upright and flexed his knees. He did look better. His color was good. He'd lost that alien, guttural tone and uncharacteristically cranky attitude.

Mackenzie nodded back in the direction of Mr. Pompeii. Her breath was ragged, but Rick seemed recovered, which helped tweak her pulse down a few notches. Nothing like a dose of reality to jerk a gal back on course.

"What happened back there? Tell me exactly. Did you feel something or just faint?" She snapped at him. It was a sham. The urge to cuddle, pamper, and pounce on Rick hadn't diminished. She added one of her best frigid scowls to mask her emotions.

"I didn't faint," Rick snapped. "Men don't faint." And, standing there, mouthing off like a great macho solo artist, he was as convincing as General George S. Patton.

"They do and you did—or nearly did. Sit back down. You don't look good."

"Don't get bossy, Mackenzie. I'm fine." Rick sucked in air and pounded on his chest as if to prove his point.

"Knock it off," Mackenzie said. "Hand over the keys, I'm taking you to the hospital."

"Over my dead body," Rick returned. He relinquished his lab coat, but not the keys to his car.

"If necessary, I'll have Harry stun you senseless and we'll wait for an ambulance to haul you in for a stem-to-stern check-up."

"I called 911," Harry shouted. He appeared and loped forward from the access hallway, his badge and accessory belt jingling as he moved. His radio squawked and sputtered with static. "They'll be here in a jiffy."

Rick stifled another curse. "Call them off, Harry. I'm *fine*." He fixed his gaze on Mac's throat. Yep, he wanted to strangle her.

"Thanks, Harry. I'm taking Rick to the emergency room myself. It's faster." She snagged the keys from Rick's pocket and crooked one finger for him to follow.

"Bully!" Rick yowled. "All I need is a blast of fresh air."

"Let's go, buster—or do I need to get rough?"

Rick rolled his eyes. Macho needs never far beneath any male's smooth exterior, he managed a chuckle, clearly for Harry's benefit. It was one of those guy-to-guy messages that he was humoring a panicky female and capable of taking care of himself. Evidently, she silently groused, Harry bought it.

"Just like old times," the guard said and chortled. "Glad to see you two lovebirds squabbling again."

And then Rick and Mackenzie were off to the hospital.

A few hours later, Rick snarled as they left the medical building and started through the half-lit parking lot. "I got a clean bill of health. I can drive!"

Three hours of worrying while the interns checked and rechecked Rick's vitals had stolen the last drop of fortitude Mac had socked away. She was giddy with relief, but sick to death of Rick's full-scale "*I'm okay, so get off my back*" routine. Rick might be perfect at most things life tossed in his direction, but he failed miserably at being a cooperative patient.

"Go right ahead," Mackenzie yelled. Tossing him the keys, she added, "But I'm not going to risk my life to appease your bloody macho ego. I'll walk." She started across the pavement. The direction didn't matter at the moment. All she needed was distance from the man before she assaulted him with her handbag.

"Playing Florence Nightingale to an ungrateful cuss is not my idea of a dream date, you know," she hollered over her shoulder.

Rick threw back his head and bayed at the moon. It got her attention. Mac swung around and shook a finger at him.

"Knock it off, Tarzan, this is a hospital zone."

"Sorry. You're right. I'm wrong—again. Please, will you drive me to my motel so I can end this nightmare?" He bowed and gestured toward his car.

Mackenzie stretched her lips into a big fake smile. "Gladly," she said through clenched teeth, and she climbed behind the wheel. She ground the starter, not on purpose, but it felt good anyway.

"Let the engine warm up, will you?" Rick asked. He folded his arms and stared straight ahead. "Thanks for driving, by the way."

Mackenzie sighed and shook her head. "You're welcome."

The car warmed. The uneasy silence between them softened after a few moments. Mackenzie reached over to pop in a CD—not their song, but the next one in the collection in his console—but he stayed her hand from the knob. He slipped his hand over hers. Gentle warmth enveloped her fingers as he tugged them to his lips.

Oh my gosh. Oh my gosh. Mackenzie barely breathed while her mind chanted the fantastical phrase over and over again. Her mouth dropped open as Rick kissed her palm. Time stood still. Heat dripped into her veins as if she were hooked to an IV of molten lava. Her bones were liquid. She lacked the will or power to move a muscle. Jelly had more substance than she possessed in her hand at that moment.

Rick lifted his mouth from her palm and winked at her. His eyes gleamed dark and dangerous even in the dim light from the parking lot mercuries. Mackenzie gasped. She was staring into the eyes of a stranger.

"Rick?"

"*Angelus*," he whispered in deep and husky tones. It wasn't Rick's voice. Not Rick's touch. Not even Rick's language. Someone else was behind those eyes, breathing life into the *GQ* shell and possessing the palm that was still held to his lips.

Then Rick passed out.

Chapter Ten

Rick needed a stiff drink, or maybe several. Nothing much ever spooked him, not even as a kid. He'd never been afraid of the dark, and the only monster lurking around his bed had been the garter snake his kid brother Race had once planted beneath his pillow. Rick had survived, and so had Race—barely.

But he was spooked now. Blackouts were hell. He'd taken two plunges into the void now and didn't want a third. Was it a case of amnesia? Or, heaven help him, something worse? He was in Mac's living room, on the couch.

He didn't have any answers, and from the look on her face, Granny Moon's granddaughter didn't either. And for once in his life, he wasn't sure he wanted them. For the moment, he needed to maintain a white-knuckled grip on his sanity and keep watch for another sucker punch.

"Take off, will you?" Rick growled. His hand shook. He didn't seem to care that the water in it sloshed the front of his crisp shirt or damaged his silk tie. "High probability for puking."

"Take a deep breath," Mackenzie said, and applied another cold compress to his forehead. "I'll take my chances with the puking. It's my house, by the way, and I've seen worse if that's important."

Rick lifted an eyebrow and glared at her. "Total debasement? Yeah, pride is important to most males."

"Not to me. So, cut loose if you've got the urge. You'll probably feel better." Mackenzie replaced the cloth behind his neck and eased him back against the sofa.

Rick groaned. A wave of agony rippled through his body for half a second. When the torment passed, he mopped his face with the cloth and waved off the replacement Mackenzie offered.

"Mind telling me what I'm doing here, Mackenzie?"

"I'm supposed to keep an eye on you for the next six to twelve hours. That's the deal I made with the doc who cut you loose."

"I can take care of myself."

Mackenzie hissed. "Spare me from running through the whole routine again, will you? I know what you are. Macho; check. Independent; check. Proud; check. That's the lot, isn't it? I haven't left anyting out, have I?" She leaned in close and tweaked his nose. "Oh, wait. Ungrateful; check."

Rick growled when he suffered. It often frightened student interns and vapid blondes, but Mackenzie shrugged it off.

"Let me get you out of this straightjacket." She unfastened his tie and unbuttoned his shirt, ignoring the restraining hand he put up. "Forget the proprieties, Rick. Loosen up."

He gripped her wrist and eased her fingers away from his shirt. "Just what exactly are you watching for—werewolf tendencies?"

"Something like that, but don't worry. I've got it handled."

"Mackenzie, stop playing nursemaid for a minute and square up, will you? What's going on?"

He still held her hand. She looked down and flexed her fingers but didn't pull out of his grasp. "Do you remember the ride home? Any of it, I mean?"

He was looking down at their hands too. He turned hers palm up and frowned. "What happened?"

"You made a pass."

"Yeah, sure. What really happened?"

Mackenzie didn't answer. Rick stared at her for what seemed like an eternity—or at least a millennium.

"You're serious?"

"Uh-huh," she said, and tucked her fingers into her armpits. She looked a little nervous, like she'd wanted to touch him.

"No, I didn't," Rick decided. He kept his voice flat. He refused to accommodate the possibility that he'd hit on her, undoing their deal and their truce. Plus, he didn't remember it. He would have wanted to remember it.

Mackenzie looked annoyed. "It's your word against mine. There were only two of us in the car. I say one of us made a pass at the other. You figure out who."

A wave of darkness washed over Rick, but he sensed it coming and was ready this time. It was an invisible force tripping the perimeter wire on his psyche, pressing in for control, and Rick countered with all the resistance he could muster. He closed his mind to the images, ignored the sounds and smells, and concentrated on the one person who anchored him to reality. Mackenzie.

Aha! It worked!

The darkness receded to the far corners of his consciousness, and Rick shook off the clinging malaise. He'd won the battle, but had he won the war? He didn't think so. He was beginning to believe, and to understand. The blackouts and the invisible force had a name and a mission.

Rick blinked. The adjustment of his eyes to the light took time. But when they did adjust, Mackenzie's face was the first thing he saw. She was staring down at him in concern.

God, she was beautiful. Flawed and unique, and everything he craved in a partner for life. Loving, loyal, funny, and bright, she was heaven on earth. An angel.

Angel? *Angelus?* A snippet of recovered memory popped into his brain. Only, it wasn't his memory he recalled but that of a guy called Dak.

"Actually, I didn't make a pass. He did," Rick said.

Mackenzie felt confused. "He? He, who?"

"Who do you think?"

Uh-oh. Staring at him, she was pretty sure she knew. But she didn't want to believe.

She shook her head. Was this the *Twilight Zone?* She searched the depths of Rick's eyes for some hint of the stranger, the one who'd dominated and possessed him in those moments when nothing else seemed to matter except tumbling into a sea of lust. Rick stared back. Just Rick.

"Knock it off. You're scaring me, Rick."

"I'm scaring me too."

He shook his head. No, more than that, Rick stopped the forward progress of this irrational hypothesizing. Back and forth. Negative. Unacceptable. His brain rejected the information, as hers wanted to do. Rick was wrestling for control, beating back demons with his fierce gaze and firm hold on the present. Mackenzie reached for him, but he jerked back from her touch.

He said, "You're right. This isn't happening. I'm jet-lagged. There are a half-dozen rational and reasonable explanations for this delusion."

Then he looked up at her. His eyes were searching for answers that Mackenzie couldn't provide. Or wouldn't.

Rick believed in facts. He didn't go in for sci-fi, tolerate studies on crop circles, appreciate psychic abilities, or respect gut instincts. The explanation that Mackenzie withheld, the one that emanated from her belly and expanded as she applied her imagination, fell into the paranormal arena. To even suggest the possibility that "other worlds" had a bearing on the events of the evening would require a leap of faith that Rick lacked. And, she wasn't so sure she could make the leap herself.

"What exactly did he do?" he finally asked.

"Stop saying *he,*" Mackenzie snapped. She'd wanted him to not give in to this irrational happening. Her instinct was to run and hide her head under the covers until the nightmare ended. Fumes could have triggered hallucinations for both of them. So far, no harm done. They weren't operating heavy machinery—unless their bodies qualified. She'd wanted Rick to save her from this insanity, not be part of it.

He said, "Humor me, will you? It's been a long day, and it'll be an even longer night if we keep circling our wagons around nouns and pronouns. Answer the question."

"You didn't do anything egregious," she hedged.

That wasn't the truth. Hell, her heart pounded just remembering. In a solitary moment, the stranger's touch had propelled Mackenzie into bliss. Unfathomable. Excruciating. And addicting. But, if Rick wasn't in on the deal, Mackenzie needed to back up and regroup. Rick solo was enough to set fire to her brain. Someone inside Rick's body? That was a new brand of dark and dangerous!

"Well, *something* must have happened. I can see it in your eyes, Mackenzie. Spit it out. I want details!"

"No big deal. You just kissed my hand. Kind of sweet, really."

"If I did, you should have decked me," he said. He tugged off his tie, then seemed to rethink the action.

Rick was again honoring that damned promise for mutual respect she'd demanded a few hours ago. But that had been before the planets in her personal hemisphere collided and proved all bets were off. He was sure as heck succeeding at the don't-step-outta-line part. He deserved a gold star for maintaining the proprieties of a strictly business relationship. But whatever his motive, Rick's current no-touch, strait-laced routine was starting to bug the heck out of her.

"That's just great!" She muttered under her breath. "Serves me right for asking. I got my stupid wish."

Rick saw her annoyance. "I'm not a saint, Mackie. I want to jump your bones, but you were right about a lot of things—both five years ago and tonight. If I'm going to have a future with you, and I *am,* I'm going to play by your rules. And when I make the moves on you, and I *will,* I want it to be my idea. And I want to remember it."

"And you don't."

"No. Not all of it. Just bits. My memory is flashing on and off like a yield light at a crosswalk."

"What do you remember right now?" Mackenzie was grasping at straws. She didn't want to imagine this for a second longer than necessary. She wanted to believe her alarm would ring at any moment and this would all be a nightmare.

They stared at one another, united in fear that the truth wasn't rational. It was tough for two scientists. The answer wasn't fumes or jet lag or overwork, but *him*: Mr. Pompeii.

Rick gave in completely. Finally. Mackenzie could see his resignation penetrate and ping around in his brain. He said, "His name is Dak."

Mackenzie winced. "We're making a leap, Rick. A huge one."

"Don't I know it." He paused and groaned. He sounded like a wounded grizzly bear and looked just as dangerous. "Crap. What am I saying? No. It didn't happen. It couldn't. You seeing that body cast move, and then me . . ."

"A case of shared hysteria? It's surreal whatever is going on." Mackenzie looked down at her nails. Their smooth shapes polished with clear lacquer reflected the white ceiling. Nothing anchored her to the here and now. *Surreal* almost captured the mood of the moment. Almost but not quite. Everything felt timeless—the whiteness of her reality devoid of sound except for the thundering inside her chest. Her lungs sucked in air. Her heart pumped hot blood throughout her human form. And whooshing and whizzing thoughts bumped around in her frontal lobe.

Rick closed his eyes and nodded. Mackenzie left him like that. She wasn't abandoning ship. It wasn't in her to do that to a friend or enemy. But she needed to back off—and fast—until she dispatched her errant urges and marshaled her reason. She didn't know how Granny Moon had handled similar situations, but a bubble bath and some comfort food couldn't hurt.

Rick stood, eyes closed. It was an odd thing to know he wasn't alone in his skin. It bugged him. But it wasn't a permanent condition. He'd kicked some invisible butt already, and with some practice, a few resources, and a double dose of effort he knew he would finish the job and eject Dak once and for all.

Possession. It galled him to slap such a label on it. He didn't believe in possession, yet what else could it be? "Blacking out" didn't explain anything. He wasn't comatose during the episodes. He was functioning on a high level of awareness but without knowledge or control over his actions. To sum up, he'd been temporarily hijacked by a guy named Dak. How? It didn't matter. It was a done deal. All Rick could do was concentrate on limiting the visit to a one-night stand.

* * *

Mackenzie decided against a soak in the tub. She needed the force of the shower spray to pummel her body and the clean scent of soap to wash away the smells of artifacts, hospitals, and brimstone.

After washing, her fluffy yellow sweats were the only guaranteed non-sexy duds she could find in her closet. They felt like a well-loved blanket against her skin. She didn't need to send Rick any more mixed messages—or herself either. One last look in the mirror proved she wouldn't. Not a smidgen of makeup remained on her scrubbed face, and her freshly washed hair still dripped water. She felt like "ho-hum" personified, a "before" candidate in a glamour makeover contest.

She padded down the stairs and grabbed a frosty grape Nehi from the fridge. She'd done it. Refreshed and regrouped, her reason had returned and slowed her pulse to near normal levels. She'd have no problem keeping her emotions in check now.

She peeked in on Rick from the kitchen. He was up and in motion. And Mac's fuzzy orange tomcat Sam was keeping vigil from his perch on the mantel.

Rick was pacing. As he moved, his smooth, sleek muscles sliced through space with the heady beauty of an ancient warrior wielding a broadsword and mastering a warhorse. The steady creak of floorboards and the flick of Sam's tail measured Rick's paces to and fro.

In years past, Mac had watched and appreciated those movements, admiring them in the abstract. They weren't abstract now. The man wore out the carpet within five feet of her. And he was going nowhere fast. She could break the rhythm as she once did with a single embrace. But she refused to yield to the temptation and open her heart to the man again. It was easier to rewind the tape, erase all images of his vital energy in motion, and concentrate on mental snapshots of Rick that anchored him far away in Italy, cruising around in a sleek car. That vision of Rick wasn't touchable any more than the glossy images in the *GQ* magazines.

"Want a soda pop?" she asked from the doorway.

He shook his head. "Tequila, straight, if you still keep it on hand. A couple of shots will put me out of my misery."

Mackenzie smiled. "How's your puke meter? Think your gut can handle cactus juice?"

Rick laughed. "If you're worried, I'll haul my sorry ass out of here. Excuse me, I mean to say my sorry asses. Rick Mason and company."

Mackenzie shrugged her shoulders and got a tray with tequila, limes, and salt. She settled it on the coffee table between them and poured two shots. "Have at it, cowboy. I'll make up the couch in the spare room in case one of you decides to pass out."

"Crap, Mac, I'm not a total creep." He licked the back of his hand and doused it with salt.

"Prove it," she whispered. It was a dare—a double dare—that surfaced from deep within her cloistered reserve.

Good golly, what had happened to her steely reason, to her promise to herself to keep all these feel-good emotions in check? She couldn't stop herself and didn't want to even if she could.

She leaned close, aware of the scent of him and the sound of his breath catching as she neared. "Kiss me, Rick."

His gaze collided with hers. He dropped the lime and nearly the shot too.

"You're playing with fire, kid."

Lovely. She liked fire. She liked hot. She liked this lazy slide into the molten web that made her prey to this male, good or bad. Just inches from tasting, feeling, possessing his mouth, her bubble of bliss exploded into a flash of orange with claws attached.

"Yeow!" she howled, and fell back, juggling the furry mass of feline that just leapt into her arms.

Rick fell back too, and although he was sporting a few

flesh wounds from the cat, he was laughing. "Told you," he said. "You're playing with fire."

She'd been saved by the cat. It had been a lame idea anyway. There wasn't going to be any more of that. No fire and, damn it all, no kisses.

Chapter Eleven

Dallas: Wednesday morning

"So, the new ventilation system checks out," Mackenzie said, and switched the phone to her other ear. It was only ten in the morning, but she was already running late. Pete Proctor was notoriously long-winded for a museum director with a busy schedule. It'd taken half an hour for him to chastise her for the security breach last night, accept her explanation of events, and absolve Harry of any wrongdoing. At last, he'd gotten to the subject of the museum's air quality. She pushed aside the half-finished crossword puzzle in front of her and her stone cold cup of coffee.

"You're sure?"

She didn't have any reason to doubt the report. Both the mechanics had tested, cycled, and re-certified the new system. If Rick had fainted, it wasn't because of bad air. Damn, she wanted this whole woo-woo business about the Pompeii body cast to be over and done with.

"Guys like Rick don't faint without cause," she said. Oops,

she probably shouldn't have put it that way—especially to another guy. Rick would kill her if he found out.

So what! Let him get pissed. She was pissed too. In less than one day, he'd disrupted her life, jeopardized her job, and complicated her emotions.

"Yes, he's fine now," she replied. "The doctor said his vitals are good and nothing should prevent him from resuming all activities. We won't need to reschedule any of his lectures."

Proctor was finally out of questions and statements, and not a moment too soon. Mackenzie hung up the phone and unlatched the kitchen door to allow her neighbor, Mrs. Jay, and her pug Petunia in for their daily visit.

"How does scrambled eggs with extra-crisp bacon sound this morning?" Mrs. Jay asked before she'd cleared the threshold.

"Perfect," Mackenzie returned. She stepped out of the path of the pink-haired senior, who was being dragged across the linoleum by her pint-sized canine.

Her neighbor's temporary difficulties due to minor foot surgery had provided Mackenzie with a chance to help the woman out, this woman who was her mother's best friend and Mac's pseudo aunt. The first chance in two years, since Mrs. Jay moved in next door, to repay her countless kindnesses. It came at a price, however. Very little escaped Mrs. Jay's eagle eye or well-meaning critique. Like Bubba, Mrs. Jay was a diehard romantic intent on replacing Mackenzie's good riddance ex-husband with a more suitable mate.

"How's the bunion today?" Mackenzie asked, after collecting the leash and placating the pug with a doggie treat.

"Much better, thank you," Mrs. Jay replied. "I'll be able to walk the dog and squeeze my foot into some decent shoes in a few days. Hopefully, in time for your museum opening. I don't want to miss that." She paused. "Land's sake, I don't know how I would have managed all of this without you living next door."

Mackenzie waved her off. "Taking Petunia on her morning walk in exchange for breakfast? I'm getting the best end of this deal. You're spoiling me!"

Mrs. Jay's eyes twinkled with delight. "I'll whip up some buttermilk biscuits too."

"Thanks." Mac planted a kiss on Mrs. Jay's rouged cheek. "See you in a bit."

"Yes, you run along, dear. I'll take care of things here and leave your meal in the oven."

"Let's go, Pet. Walkie, walkie," Mackenzie said, and jangled Petunia's leash. She soon had the dog collared and ready.

Halfway down the block, Petunia—a doggie obedience school dropout—paused for her first delivery of the day. It was then that Mackenzie realized she hadn't told Mrs. Jay about the houseguest sleeping it off on her fold-out couch. She swore under her breath. She couldn't go back now and warn the woman. Petunia wasn't a cooperative pup. She didn't accept commands, and she didn't deviate from her daily rounds.

Mackenzie crossed her fingers and muttered a quick prayer. She'd lied to Proctor when she'd told him Rick was okay. She didn't know, or trust, anything about Rick Mason after last night. For a gal who valued gut instincts, she wished she had some cold hard facts.

The Lindstroms' Siamese was loose again and thankfully Petunia spied the feline and launched into a full-scale pursuit. Maybe luck was with Mac. At this rate, she and Petunia might make it home before the bacon was cold and Rick was roused.

When she returned to the house, Rick was lounging on the back porch stoop with a sheet wrapped around his lower half. Petunia challenged the strange male for about a half a second—until Rick held out a piece of bacon and won her over.

"I hope you didn't startle Mrs. Jay," Mackenzie said. She released the dog into Mrs. Jay's fenced yard and rolled up the leash.

"I don't think much in this world surprises Mrs. Jay," Rick replied. "When did she move into the neighborhood? Is she an ex-cop or former CIA? She's particularly observant—as she pointed out to me—and heads up the block watch. She saw us come in last night, noticed the car this morning, probably ran the tags past the DMV and figured out my flight arrival from the rental car company. She knows my name, birth date, and I think she even knows whether I still have my wisdom teeth.

"I'm the one suffering from shock," he added. "She brought me breakfast in bed and kept talking about 'burning daylight.' I take it Mrs. Jay is a lot like you used to be. She doesn't believe in sleeping past dawn."

"You're entitled to some extra snooze time. It was quite a night."

"Was it?" Rick wasn't smiling. His confident look—the one that always hung around like a golden glow—was missing too. And worst of all was the singularly haunting glint in his dark eyes.

"Don't tell me. You're still possessed." Mackenzie sighed. Her lucky streak was over, and the nightmare that had started with a moving statue was only just beginning. The cat was a stubborn cuss—a male, of course. And her usual bribe to dose him with vitamins wasn't working today. She led Rick inside.

"Come on, Sammy Baby. Come to Mama," Mackenzie called. Down on all fours, head half under Rick's fold-out bed; she shook a can of kitty treats. Rick chose that moment to step out of the steamy guest bath, and Mackenzie yelped.

"What now?" Rick backed against the wall and held up both hands. "I'm almost afraid to ask."

Mackenzie sat back on her haunches and tried not to stare. He looked just great. Freshly scrubbed with one of her fluffy terry towels loosely wrapped around his hips, he was all she remembered and more. She gave herself a little mental shake to break the spell.

"The cat's been hiding under your bed all night. And I almost had him," she said. She screwed the liquid eyedropper back into the medicine bottle she was holding, and tucked it into her pocket. "You won the battle, Sammy, but I'll win the war. You're getting your vitamin drops today and that's that."

"Sam?" Rick bent down and called to the longhaired golden brute. "Hey, buddy, long time no see. Come to Daddy."

Sam obliged and then accepted the affection from Rick as if it were his due, totally ignoring the fuming Mackenzie. "If you two fellas will excuse me, I need to get going," she grunted.

She started out the door but Rick called her back. "Aside from a minor spell of memory loss, what's my status?"

The answer didn't come easy. She wanted to rake him over the coals for his past offenses and she needed to boot him out of her house before she got too comfortable with him taking up space. She applied a frown to her face and tried to recall the exact smell of swamp gas.

The effect on her features must have been dramatic. Rick's reaction certainly was. "That bad?" he asked.

"Noooo," she replied, and rolled her eyes for comic effect. "Just the opposite. And it's way past the witching hour, so if there aren't any delayed symptoms to report back to the emergency room doc, you're free to go."

She grabbed the glass of juice from Mrs. Jay's breakfast tray, spilling half the contents before handing it over. "Drink your OJ."

Rick took the tumbler without a word. His gaze followed her progress as she prowled the room collecting clothing. She piled it all on the bed. She wrinkled her nose at the smell of tequila.

"Jeepers, Rick. You must have rolled around in these all night before you kicked them off."

"You didn't take them off me?" That flat tone was back. Rick obviously didn't remember.

Mackenzie glanced at him. Relief and disappointment warred within her. She couldn't have it both ways. It was a surefire way to make herself crazy if she didn't pick a side and stick to it. She could either love him or leave him the heck alone.

"No. You said you could handle it yourself." She held up a wrinkled shirt missing half its buttons. "You did, I'm sorry to say. What'd you do? Rip it off?"

"I don't remember." Rick leaned one arm against the door frame and furrowed his brow in thought. "How much did I drink?"

"You polished off the fifth before you hit the mattress. But there was only an inch or two in the bottle to begin with."

"What about later, did we . . . ?" He didn't manage the whole question.

"You didn't make another pass. You didn't revert to ancient Latin, and you eventually passed the good guy cat test—my ex-husband never did. So you're safe to get behind the wheel and make rowdy as you please."

"Not so fast," Rick said, then yowled when Sam circled through his legs and bit one of his ankles. "Hey, Sammers, that hurts."

Mackenzie raised one brow. "Maybe I spoke too soon about the cat test. Five years is an eternity for a cat. Maybe he can't forgive you either."

"Naw, we're old buds. Ouch. Sam? What's the matter? Hasn't she fed you breakfast yet?"

"If he wants seconds, you can take care of it—you know where I keep the cat food. I've got to run. Bubba's going to pick me up in a few minutes." She scooted past him and the cat to retrieve the breakfast tray, but Rick stalled her again.

"Bubba can wait," he said, "until you tell me what happened last night. I don't remember everything and I've got a right to know if . . ."

Mackenzie coughed. She tried to keep her features neutral, but her words came out a bit too fast. "You're intact, Rick. So am I."

She bit her lip. She was sorry about a lot of things regarding last night, and not kissing Rick was at the top of the list. She could have kissed him, except that her tomcat *and* her damned conscience had horned in. That was the rub. She'd wanted to—and still did. But, who did she want to kiss her back, Rick or that other guy?

"Honest. Nothing happened," she added.

He seemed to breathe again and his color returned. Damn his hide! Rick the male, the macho ego, needed to know that he had not lost control. Drunk or possessed, no excuse would appease him if he'd flagged where and when it mattered most. And obviously the kiss had been her idea, not his.

Rick looked at her, his smile breathtaking. His damp hair and bare chest were a turn-on at any hour of the day, but even more so now, when only a few inches of space and toweling separated their bodies.

"I'm sorry, Mackenzie," he whispered.

She shrugged. "No damage. We're back to mutual respect and strictly business, again. All's well in the real world." Maybe the ghost was gone. Life was back on track. Along with all the rules of propriety.

"No, babe," Rick said. "You don't understand."

She shook her head, puzzled. “Guess I don’t. What is it?”

When Rick didn’t answer immediately, the hairs on the back of her neck stood up. *Danger, danger, danger,* her brain silently screamed.

“I wanted to kiss you last night,” he admitted. A thrill shot through her.

But then his mouth thinned, and he looked at her with different eyes. They were the eyes of a rogue, a male, a man on the prowl.

“And Dak did too,” he added.

“Dak too, huh? Thanks for clearing that up,” she replied.

Her voice was shaking as much as her knees. Maybe the ghost wasn’t gone. She didn’t trust herself to not melt into those arms if he moved a muscle in her direction. He didn’t. But, her growling tomcat crouching next to Rick’s feet seemed to be considering it.

She backed slowly away from both of them until she bumped into the doorway to the hall. Even with the obstacles, the cat, and ten feet of space between them, she didn’t trust herself.

Honk!

Outside in the driveway, her truck idled with her cousin behind the wheel. Bubba had arrived, thank goodness. Mackenzie had her reprieve. She spun around and fled the scene without a backward glance.

Chapter Twelve

She ran out onto the front porch. Rick followed, sporting a devilish grin, his towel still loosely wrapped around his hips. "Have a good day," he called, and waved at Bubba.

Bubba revved the engine in the old Willy and returned Rick's wave as Mackenzie climbed into the front seat. "Don't ask. Just drive," she said.

"Whoa, cousin. He spent the night? Tell me everything. Start from the top," Bubba demanded as he backed out of the driveway.

Mackenzie buckled the seat belt, punched the door lock, and folded her arms over her serious, dark and elegant, double-breasted power suit. "I don't want to talk about it." But when tears threatened to well up and spill out of her eyes, Mackenzie realized that she did.

Her cousin seemed oblivious. "This is great! I knew if you two got together again, the sparks would start flying. Just talk through your problems, and you'll patch things up permanently."

"Bubba," Mackenzie snarled, "This isn't about chemistry. Of course we've got chemistry. It's all the other stuff

I can't reconcile. He's still at the top of my bad-guy list. Rick Mason's the enemy, and he's not going to get a chance to break my heart again." She didn't even want to get into all the weirdness regarding Dak.

"Hm." Bubba drove in silence for a half-a-minute. "You always invite the enemy for a sleepover, do you?"

"I can explain that," she started, then stopped herself and groaned. "No. I guess I can't. But trust me, it's *not* what it looks like."

Bubba nodded and didn't make another peep, not even after he made the sharp right off Mockingbird Lane and stopped in front of his house. He took the Willy out of gear and pulled on the parking brake, but he didn't cut the engine or get out.

"Thanks for loaning me your truck, by the way," he said. He jerked his thumb to the rear of the Willy, which was crammed with boxes of salsa, chips, jalapenos, and Girl Scout cookies. "I can't deliver this stuff till tomorrow. All right if I leave it in here till then?"

Mackenzie nodded. "Sure, come over for breakfast tomorrow and you can get them."

Bubba smiled evilly. "Shall I expect Rick too?"

"Run along, Bubba," she cried, and shooed him out with her hands. "I've got to get to work."

Her cousin leaned over and chucked her under the chin. "Chemistry isn't something I'd take for granted if I were you, Mackenzie. But, I don't need to tell you that."

No, he didn't. Mackenzie knew all too well about chemistry and the lack of it. She'd rebounded into Ben's arms, exchanged rings with him, and shared a toothbrush holder and nearly five years of days and nights together. But they'd never shared chemistry—not the volatile polarizing reactions that merged elements into compatible compounds. They'd remained oil and water to the end; no amount of shaking could bond them. Not so with Rick. He didn't even have to touch her and she felt linked to the man—shot through by Cupid's arrow, no doubt.

"No, but thanks for reminding me," she finally said. Realizing her eyes were filling with tears, she damned Rick Mason again. The man was still under her skin. And it wasn't just the physical attraction she felt for him and that ghost inside him.

Bubba dabbed at her damp cheeks with his shirttail. "Chin up, honey. It could be worse."

Bubba didn't know how wrong he was!

Rick stretched out on Mackenzie's big brass bed. He needed a couple more hours of shut-eye before he dared face the world. Trying to control two personalities and two libidos was hard work—not that he'd resigned himself to Dak's presence.

He'd excavated a monster. And Mackenzie's cat knew it.

"Ouch, Sam!" He rubbed his ankle. The feline had a pretty fierce love bite.

The cat rubbed up against him again and sneezed. Rick could smell it now, the lingering aroma of brimstone.

Damn. He checked the clock on Mackenzie's nightstand and swore again. Two hours were missing from his life and, by the look of his muddy bare feet, he hadn't spent them all in bed.

Mackenzie watched from the security booth. The female object of her attention could carry off the retro look; she was just about as tall and knockout gorgeous as Ingrid Bergman, so the enveloping trench coat and broad-brimmed hat from the last scene in *Casablanca* didn't look bad. The only problem was, it wasn't raining inside the museum.

"Who's this suspicious-looking character?" she asked, tapping the screen of camera one. The female made another circuit of the Women in History section of the main gallery, her image hopping from screen to screen as the cameras tracked her.

Harry bit into another Krispy Kreme and adjusted his bifocals. "Oh, her? She's a regular. Been here every day for a week trying to take a peek at the Pompeii stuff. Always wears that getup, rain or shine. Bet that wig is as hot as Hades."

Mackenzie leaned in for a closer look. "That's a wig?"

"You wouldn't ask if you saw her face-to-face. It's one of those synthetic ones like Bernadette wore to the Halloween dance last year. Watch." He pointed as the woman walked past the entry to the exhibits. "It picks up static every time she gets near the metal detector."

"Is she a problem?" Mackenzie asked.

"We're keeping our eye on her but, no, I think she's just curious. Everyone is."

Mackenzie sighed. "You're right. Our opening is forty-eight hours away. Maybe she's just an eccentric who's as anxious as the rest of Dallas to check out the exhibit."

"How are ticket sales?" Harry asked.

"We're nearly sold out, but there are tours during week five and six that still have openings. I have an extra for opening night if you need it for Bernadette."

"How 'bout giving it to *her?*" He jerked his thumb in the direction of the security monitors. "I hear she's on a waiting list for the opening—she's only in town for another few days. Bernadette can see it later."

"I guess so. . . ." Mackenzie chewed her bottom lip. "You really think she's okay?"

Harry winked. "The ones who dress like kooks usually aren't the ones to worry about."

"Thanks, I'll remember that." She laid a hand on Harry's shoulder. "Sorry again about last night. Hope it didn't get you in Dutch with Proctor."

Harry waved her off. "Proctor's a bigshot museum director. He doesn't have time to worry about stuff like that right now. But I owe Joseph half of these doughnuts. He backed me up."

Mackenzie laughed. "Don't bother. I'll bring him his own box."

"Good!"

Mackenzie started out the door, then called back to him, "It proves one thing, though. Every time I break a rule, I get caught."

Harry laughed. He hollered after her. "Then my advice to you is to stick to the rules. Don't rob banks and keep it under the speed limit!"

"Hi, I'm Gillespe. You must be Dr. Mason."

"Call me Rick," Rick said, and leaned against one of wire cage dividers that separated Gil's workspace from the museum storage areas. "A century ago this used to be my desk."

He tapped the torn Jimmy Hendrix poster hanging above a dartboard. "I like what you've done to the place."

"Want to grab a seat?" Gil asked. He started to shove boxes together.

"Nah. I know what it's like to have an old fart invade your space and start reminiscing about the good old days."

"Were they?" Gil asked.

"Good old days? Yeah, they were."

Gillespe nodded, but his grim expression contradicted it. He plopped down in his desk chair and shuffled a few file folders from one pile to the next.

"Having a hard time imagining that these will be *your* good old days?" Rick asked.

Gillespe sighed. "I'm not so sure I'm in the right field. I could've had my pick of half-a-dozen other intern positions. Maybe I should have taken one of them instead."

"I hate to admit it," he continued. "But I'm a lazy trust-fund kid who'd rather be out teeing up on the back nine of the country club links."

"Instead, you're here," Rick added. "Scratching up the face of your Rolex, hauling boxes, and cataloging artifacts."

"Yeah. Of course, I am finding out all this amazing stuff, like Pompeii and body casts. That would make just golfing kind of boring."

"I think it's too late, Gillespe."

"What do you mean?"

"Sounds like it's under your skin. When I got hooked on relics and research, I trashed my shot at one of the Fortune 500 companies and a six-digit salary."

"You did?" Gil looked stunned.

"Yeah."

"You liked this that much?"

"I was lucky. Early on I figured out what I was good at and loved to do, and I went for it. For me, there's not a better job on the planet—unless there's an opening for a superhero. You know, helping people? Archaeologist or superhero—if I was starting over again, I'd take either one in a heartbeat."

The trench-coated patron had disappeared; Mackenzie failed to locate her in a swift survey of the public areas. She left a message with the membership and ticket sales staff to contact her if the woman materialized. It was the best she could do at the moment. Other priorities were pressing, and she crossed the attempted good deed off her list.

She checked her watch. There it was, the pulsing reminder that they were almost upon the opening of the Pompeii exhibit and there was still a page and a half of tasks on her list of undelegated projects. But she was keeping a promise to herself to remember to eat. Just a quick stop at her desk to grab five bucks, and she'd join the rest of the staff in the museum café for a green salad and a fistful of carrots.

"Hi," Rick said as she dashed into her cubicle. He'd commandeered her high-backed office chair, rolled it over to the window, and propped his booted feet up on the sill.

Good gracious, his long limbs and muscled body filled out his jeans and cotton shirt better than any cowboy Mackenzie had ever seen. The mere sight of him turned her to putty. If she didn't sit down quick, she might fall down. But there wasn't a free surface to plant her rear end, and Rick wasn't budging. Mackenzie grabbed hold of the partition separating her pod from those of her peers, and tried to assume a casual and controlled pose.

Rick's grin lit up the deepest and darkest parts of her heart. She grinned back, a knee-jerk reaction.

"Can you idle your engines for a minute?" he asked. "We need to talk."

Her watch buzzed. It was the lunch alarm she'd set as a backup reminder to eat. Mackenzie silenced it and shook her head. "I'm at T minus forty-eight hours and counting till the opening, Rick. Can't it wait?"

"You can spare a minute," he said. "I'm scheduled to do a lecture myself in twenty-four."

Mackenzie sighed. She pushed aside a pile of folders on her desk and sat on the corner. Um, better. Her limbs were still shaking, but at least she'd averted the immediate danger of melting into a pool of hormones at Rick's feet. "Your lecture. That's right, for the museum board and some of our key benefactors. You know the agenda don't you? First is your talk, then an exclusive tour of the exhibit, followed by a special reception. It's a small group, so we're using the Hargrove auditorium."

"Hold on, you didn't!" Rick yowled and slapped his leg. "You didn't name an auditorium after him?" He rocked with laughter. "Great balls of fire, I hope to hell the museum board made the family cough up a fortune for the honor."

Mackenzie tried and failed to suppress a laugh. "Shh," she said, and placed a finger to her lips. She stretched to see above the partition. "We're not alone," she mouthed, and in *sotto voce* added: "His portrait is mounted in the hall between the two auditoriums. It always scares the primary school kids, especially troops of Brownies."

Rick's howls increased. Mackenzie had to take control of the situation fast. Not everyone within earshot would appreciate or understand making sport of the Hargrove name or bankroll.

"What will you need for your presentation besides the lectern and a slide projector?" she asked.

Rick shook his head and wiped his eyes with the back of his shirtsleeve. His amusement was cooling down a bit. "Neither. I can't do it. I have a conflict."

"What? I don't understand. We sent you the final itinerary weeks ago and you signed off on it. You can't do this to me, Rick. It's too late to back out now."

"I can and I am."

When the old Rick Mason made statements like that, Mackenzie never could budge him off the mark. But that was then and this was now.

"You'll do it," she snapped. "You'll be on time, make nice with the board and benefactors *and* Hargrove, and hold them spellbound for about forty-five minutes with the details of your archy dig. After that, you can split for all I care. We can handle the tour and reception without you." Mackenzie finished with a particularly satisfying "Hmph," and an I-mean-business-Buster glare.

Rick glanced over at the partition and crooked his finger. "Time to conference, Mackie," he said.

"I'm not a pushover, Dr. Mason, so this better be good," Mac hissed. She hopped off her perch and strolled over to his chair.

Rick snagged her hand and pulled her close them pointed to something out the window. Mackenzie saw it, surprised that she hadn't remembered in the last ten days its proximity to her office space. A Sonic drive-in—in her mind, home of the world's best foot-long, chili-cheese coneys, cherry lemonade, and roller-skating carhops. It was one of Mackenzie's weaknesses, and only a guy like Rick would play dirty and use it to his benefit. She folded her arms and tried to offer a token resistance to the suggestion, but her growling stomach delivered a complete and unconditional surrender.

Kiss that healthy green salad goodbye, she told herself. This was just what the doctor ordered. And, gosh darn it all, Rick knew he'd won.

"You're buying," she crabbed and led the way.

Chapter Thirteen

Mackenzie devoured her chili dog and Texas-sized onion rings with abandon. Food! Wonderful, colorful, fragrant, and salty complex carbs. Her system was going to have to put in some overtime just to process the stuff. She groaned aloud in satisfaction and choked back a burp before it managed to escape.

Since they'd walked over from the museum, they'd taken one of the booths inside. It wasn't quite the same as parking outside in a convertible while old Beach Boys and Jan and Dean songs blared from the post-mounted speakers, but this wasn't a date. It was lunch on the run. It wasn't about atmospherics or resurrecting memories. It was really all about the food. Lots of it.

"Pardon," she mumbled between bites. She had to forgo napkins, the messy meal required both hands and she dreaded the probable damage to her power suit. Chili stains were particularly troublesome.

"Want a slurp?" Rick offered. He held up a thick chocolate shake.

Mackenzie leaned over, sucked down a half inch of the

icy goo and crossed her eyes. "Brain freeze," she cried, and rubbed her forehead with the heel of her hand.

"Did you forget how to fix that?" Rick asked. "Hang on." He put down his burger and pinched her earlobe between his thumb and forefinger.

Mackenzie's eyes flew open. "Er, thanks. That's got it," she said, and swallowed with difficulty.

"You sure? I think I can hold on awhile longer without tanking on my promise and kissing your socks off."

They were nose to nose. She couldn't fit a basket of curly fries between them. Now, this was dangerous territory. Her belly was full, her brain was working hard processing orders for her digestive system, and, well, Rick looked delicious, himself.

"We're in public," she hissed. Then added, "I smell like onions."

"So do I, and I'm pretty sure I'll taste almost as good as that pound of deep-fried Vidalias you just inhaled."

He didn't have far to go to make contact. And if he spanned the distance, Mackenzie wasn't going to have much will to do more than simply shut up and kiss him back.

"Dr. Mason? It is you, isn't it?" The trench-coated museum patron had sneaked up on them without either noticing. Mackenzie and Rick jumped apart like two adolescents caught necking.

"Hey, aren't you . . . ?" Rick snapped his fingers, his voice fumbling around the sounds of the alphabet until he discovered a handful that labeled the stranger: "Maude?"

"That's right, Maude Kincaid. I was on your Pompeii dig last summer."

And, Mackenzie silently added, *fell into lust with you too, no doubt.*

Rick roared with genuine pleasure. "I almost didn't recognize you in that getup."

He turned to Mackenzie. "This is Maude Kincaid, Mackenzie. Say howdy."

"Howdy," Mackenzie obliged, albeit begrudgingly.

Rick didn't seem to notice her cool acknowledgment. He was too wrapped up in one of those fast and furious dialogues that happen when two long-lost friends try to catch up on all the details of their lives with barely a break to breathe.

On the first of these essential pauses, Mackenzie jumped in. "Rick, we need to talk about your lecture."

Rick didn't seem to follow. He was lost in the business he loved best: talking about archaeological digs. "Mackenzie, don't you know who this is?" he cried. "Maude's the one who found Mr. Pompeii. And, she's here for the opening. Isn't it fantastic?"

Mackenzie knew competition when she saw it. Ms. Kincaid didn't appear to be the accidental drop-in type.

She did, however, look like a female with a mission. And Mackenzie didn't doubt for a second that she'd found her Holy Grail: Rick.

"Great," Mackenzie replied in icy tones that would freeze most conversations on the spot. But neither Rick nor Maude seemed to notice.

It turned out Mackenzie didn't need to part with the opening night ticket after all. Rick went over her head and cleared it with Proctor and security to allow Ms. Kincaid a look at the exhibit later on that afternoon, when the installation crews took their last break of the day.

She rolled around in her desk chair, moving from project to project and trying to stay focused and forget about the woman. But, she couldn't. Ms. Kincaid and Rick were off somewhere getting cozy, catching up on old times.

She stubbed her toe on the row of labeled archive boxes lined up along the freestanding wall of her pod. She kicked off her Ferragamos. Why had she bothered with these sexy strappy things and one of her best designer outfits today of all days? They weren't part of her typical no-nonsense working wardrobe. Most of her behind-the-scenes museum duties were nonglamorous, dirty chores. This pulled-together look was something she saved for public presentations—or to impress old boyfriends.

Damn you, Rick Mason, she silently screamed for the umpteenth time that day. She opened the lid on the box of paraphernalia for Rick's first lecture. Gillespe had done a fine job. Everything she needed for the event was inside: programs, nametags, a short bio for her use when introducing Rick, and a list of attendees. Yep, everything was there, but would the speaker show? She didn't think he'd try to back out again. Conflict or not, this was his reputation on the line, not just hers.

She spun around in her chair and chewed on the end of her favorite pen—a cheap stubby-barreled device with three colors of ink. Right now she was using red, the color of highest priority on Mackenzie's hierarchy of effort. Could she safely mark this project finished? Or, did she need to draft some notes and prep Proctor as a possible stand-in?

"Rick!" she growled. "You're making me crazy!"

She rocked forward, marked a huge red check on the box lid and moved on. No sense involving Proctor. The poor guy had his own list of tasks. This was the biggest event of his career and his final hurrah as museum director. After the Pompeii exhibit, he was retiring. And Mackenzie just might be the right candidate to fill his shoes—if the board and Proctor himself approved.

Her promotion pretty much hinged on the successful management of this special exhibit. If she didn't get the advancement and—Heaven help her—Jeremy Hargrove did, her world wouldn't end. But she would need a long vacation to rethink the direction of her career.

Nope. If Rick bailed, she would do the honors herself.

She swore under her breath and wished to high heaven that she could kick his fine-looking butt across the room to let off some steam.

She suddenly had a better idea. She flipped through her Rolodex and dialed a number she'd called only once in her life. Just like before, the lady on the other end of the line agreed to a no-notice appointment.

Mackenzie laughed as she hung up. She was hedging her bets. Rick needed her help, and she was going to be ready. She hadn't earned the label Always Prepared just because she kept a first-aid kit in her truck. No, she still didn't exactly believe in possession—not absolutely, positively. But it was funny; once she'd entertained the implausible idea that she might have inherited some of Granny Moon's psychic abilities, the more her thinking leaned in that direction. Was it a case of mind over matter, or a last ditch effort to debunk the impossible? She shook with silent giggles. Whatever it was, she was ready. When Rick asked for help, he was in for a real treat. And it would be better than kicking him across the room.

Rick chose that moment to stick his head around the corner of her partition. Ms. Kincaid was shadowing him.

"We're heading down. Want to come along?"

Mac had better things to do than trail along behind Rick and his adoring protégé, but she couldn't seem to help herself. "Fine," she managed through clenched teeth, and nodded in Ms. Kincaid's direction.

But, she silently screamed at the other female, *if you so much as makes one false swoon in Rick's direction, I'm going to personally toss you out of my museum with or without Proctor's blessing.*

A short time later, Mackenzie was sure Maude Kincaid was a fraud. She'd watched the woman like a hawk, and Maude didn't appear to know the first thing about conservation, artifacts, or ancient Pompeii. How she'd snookered

Rick into allowing her to join his crew on the summer dig was more a testament to her skill in flattery than intellect. Her statuesque physique probably hadn't hurt, either.

Plus, Maude was jumpy and trying to keep clear of her. As they entered the exhibit area and started through the maze, Maude somehow managed to keep Rick's body between them.

"Ms. Kincaid," Mackenzie asked, with her best disarming smile as bait. "What are you working on now?"

"I'm between semesters at school," Maude replied. She started to scratch her head but stopped herself.

Mackenzie took note of the blotchy flesh at the neckline of the girl's trench coat, and where her makeup had rubbed off on her cheek. A bit of sympathy softened Mac's assessment. The girl had lovely features, but allergies, hives, or something worse plagued her. Still, that didn't account for her odd choice in clothing or her horning in on Rick.

"So, you'll be going back to . . ." Mackenzie's leading question didn't get her anywhere.

"That's him," Maude gasped as they rounded the corner and caught sight of Mr. Pompeii.

He was perfectly lit. The scaffolds and hoists were gone now, and Mr. Pompeii looked nearly alive and running. They all stopped as one. Mackenzie had known what to expect; she'd designed the scene and fussed till the lights were perfect. The surrounding display of artifacts set the stage for a life in crisis—a man trying to flee death. If she never did another exhibit again, she would be happy and fulfilled. This had been her great white whale, and she doubted that life would ever offer another.

"Charlie was right. It's him," Maude whispered, then clapped a hand over her mouth as if she'd just let the mystery of the universe slip out.

Suddenly Mackenzie was scared that maybe Ms. Kincaid was not less than she appeared, but a whole lot more.

Chapter Fourteen

More to humor herself than the curious Ms. Kincaid, Mackenzie retrieved a hoist and handheld spot from the stockpiled equipment awaiting removal by the service elevator. The security system was on, and Harry and his crew were beefing up on every aspect of crowd control. One of the uniformed team trailed them not only as an exercise in monitoring but also as a very real and serious reminder. The heat was on. Everyone's job was on the line. No one, not even staff, would be allowed to violate the strict rules of confinement for this priceless exhibit.

"Sorry I can't allow you on the hoist, Maude. Safety issues for one, and security for another." She nodded in the direction of the guard.

"That's okay," Maude replied. But her wistful glance in Rick's direction prompted him to devise a compromise.

He hopped on the hoist and grabbed the spot. With careful maneuvering, he used the spotlight to point out the detailing on Mr. Pompeii. It seemed to satisfy Maude's fixation on three irregularities in the body cast: a spot on his ankle, the mark where a band of jewelry had adorned his arm, and the scar on his brow.

"We know where he died," Maude said, "but what was he doing there? Surely you have some idea, Dr. Mason."

Maude might be fluttering her eyelashes at Rick, but the effect was lost on the man, Mackenzie was pleased to note—because for some strange reason the poor girl lacked them.

In fact, Maude lacked hair anywhere, Mackenzie realized. Harry was right; the glamour-gal wig was more comical than stunning up close, especially since it was slightly askew now that Maude had finally removed her hat. And she'd rolled up the sleeves of the trench coat, too, revealing hairless forearms freckled with hives.

Maude caught her staring and bit her bottom lip. The kid wasn't competing for Rick, Mackenzie finally decided, but whatever she was doing here, she was earnest if not obsessive in her desire to extract information about Mr. Pompeii. If flattery and cajoling didn't work on Rick, Mackenzie accepted the possibility that more desperate measures would be taken.

"I don't want to speculate without further research, Maude," Rick finally answered. "The fact that he's upright and all other victims are prone creates a mystery that begs to be solved."

"Surely you've furthered the hypothesis since our discovery last summer," Maude persisted. "Who was he? What was he?"

"His name is Dak," Rick said without thinking. Surprised, Mackenzie punched him in the shoulder to keep him from saying more.

Maude blanched, and ill concealed a gasp with a polite cough. Her big cornflower blue eyes didn't blink for what seemed like a full minute as she stared at Rick.

Mackenzie forcibly broke the trance. "We're calling

him Dak. We thought he needed a name," she hurried to explain. She glanced over at security and made a cutting motion at throat level. Time to evict their guest and haul Rick off to some deep dark corner and kick his butt.

"Dr. Cates," the security guard said, and gestured with his baton. "We'll need you to remove the hoist and clear the area now. We are running a full-system security sweep before we lock down for the night."

"Thanks for letting us stay this long, Bill. I hope we didn't put you off schedule." Mackenzie pushed a near stiff-legged Rick in the direction of the nearest exit. Before Maude could go with him, Mackenzie caught her by the arm and enlisted her services. "Help me with this hoist, will you?"

Then, "What's up?" she asked point-blank when she finally got Maude alone. After moving the hoist, she took the girl to the museum café, which offered a plethora of beverages to help soften her planned third degree. She ordered two thick and frothy hot chocolates with sprinkles and waited until Maude had sampled hers before launching the attack.

"If you're trolling for a thesis for your doctorate, you're going about it the wrong way."

"Thesis?" Maude genuinely looked baffled for a split second. Then the confusion seemed to clear. She licked her lips and sipped the hot chocolate like she'd never tasted the concoction before. "How should I go about it?" she asked brightly.

"What do you really want—Rick's research, or facts on Mr. Pompeii? One is theft, but the other could be a sound base for your *own* project."

It felt like she was reliving an old nightmare, though on the other side. Maybe that was why she was questioning Maude's real motives. In grad school she'd been on the receiving end of an inquisition conducted by her then-thesis advisor, Jeremy Hargrove. At the time, there had been a rash of plagiarized and stolen research, and all the doctoral candidates' work had been scrutinized. But Hargrove had conducted a witch hunt. Mac had survived the challenge of own her dissertation, but she was still sensitive to a cloud of suspicion that, no thanks to Hargrove, had never been fully dispelled.

"This is really good," Maude said and ran her tongue around the wide rim of her mug of hot chocolate to collect the whipped cream.

Mackenzie felt like she was talking to a child or an idiot savant. Maude was a mix of innocence and brilliance that defied standard labeling. She tried another approach, which finally connected like a home run to the left field bleachers.

"You said something curious while we were in the exhibit."

Maude's eyes went big as saucers. "Did I? I don't remember."

"Who is Charlie? And what is he right about?"

Maude dropped her mug and scooted her chair back. She managed furtive glances left and right, almost as though gloom and doom might descend and swallow her whole. She grabbed her arm and squeezed.

"I'v.e gotta go," she said. "Thanks for the hot chocolate."

Were Maude's teeth chattering? And, what was that muffled beeping sound—a watch alarm or a cell phone? Whatever it was, it obviously precipitated her hasty departure.

Mackenzie didn't try to detain the girl. She wanted information, but more she wanted to shake up Maude and deflect her curiosity about Rick's slip of the tongue regarding Dak. And she hoped she had. As it was, it was another task checked off her list and that was good enough for now.

* * *

Scaring off Maude hadn't taken long, but by the time she returned, her office area was a production line. Administrative staff and Rick and Gillespe were finishing up the packets for opening night and storing them in boxes. Gil was prodding Rick about carbon dating artifacts. Rick was obliging. And given Gil's rapt expression, one would have thought it was a firsthand account about a walk on the moon.

One of them had tuned the radio to jazz, and everything looked normal; but it wasn't. The brimstone smell, the husky voice, the dark eyes—Mackenzie's gut instinct told her that there was another presence in the cubicle that belonged in a grave; or at least back in the exhibit area in its body cast. But there was little she could do about it.

"You've got it all wrapped up as usual, Gil," Mackenzie said, and collapsed in her chair as the last box was packed and labeled. "You're making me look real good!"

"Thanks," Gillespe replied. "With Rick's organization and my sweat, we got it done in half the time."

Mackenzie checked her watch and suggested Gillespe take off. The kid lingered.

"I thought I'd sit in on the membership committee meeting tonight," he said. "That okay with you, boss?"

"Ha!" Mackenzie rolled her eyes and groaned. "Be my guest. I'm officially off the clock as of twenty minutes ago."

"Good," Gil said, and looked relieved.

Mackenzie rolled over to Gil's end of the workspace and cornered him. "Something afoot? Something I need to know?"

"Only that I'm supposed to pitch you out if you don't leave at a decent hour."

Mackenzie laughed. "Oh, you poor kid. I forgot about the trials and tribulations of being an intern. Who put you up to it? Cousin Bubba?"

"Proctor. Bubba just wants you to eat."

"Well, I'll take care of that," Rick said. He tugged her out of her seat. "Say good night."

He dragged her outside, and they got into her truck. He turned to her, looking obviously shaken. "I'm losing my grip, Mackie. Help me out, will you? Quick! Give me something to think about, to focus on. Something normal, mundane," he demanded. "I've been doing okay today, keeping him out, but . . ." He sat beside her in the Willy. A half-eaten box of Girl Scout cookies was on his lap, his eyes were forward, staring but not seeing anything from this world or the present.

"Just tell me what's going on inside of you," Mackenzie said in the calmest tone she could muster.

He turned to her. A look of utter helplessness was visible in his eyes. He was lost somewhere, and Mackenzie's gut compelled her to anchor him to the here and now.

"Hang on, Rick," she whispered. "I need you."

It made him smile, if sadly. "I've finally got you right where I want you and I can't do anything about it."

"Explain that, will you?"

"I've been trying. I'm not alone in here, Mackenzie." Rick tapped his head with his forefinger. He shook his head and groaned. "I'm carting around a freeloader."

"You still think you're possessed by Mr. Pompeii?"

He nodded. "Call him Dak. I do."

"I guess you are possessed then," Mackenzie said. She made a face like she'd tasted unsweetened lemonade.

Rick shrugged. "I guess so. I don't have much experience in these matters, but I prefer possession to the alternative."

"Which is?" More sugarless lemonade. Mackenzie wanted something with a kick to help wash down the taste of panic collecting in her mouth.

"Madness. There's a rumor of it in my family. It goes back to my great, great grandfather's brother, the one who survived Gettysburg."

"Your namesake?" she asked.

"You remember that?" he returned.

"Of course I remember. And, stop with the melodrama. You've got situational trauma and you're coping. You're not mad. Stress is your enemy, Rick, and it doesn't discriminate."

Rick ran his fingers through his dark hair and looped one arm around the back of Mackenzie's seat. "Okay, okay. Forget the madness theory—for now."

"Okay." Mackenzie scowled until Rick managed a half-hearted chuckle.

"Don't worry, Mackie. I'm a rock." He laughed again. More volume. More heat. He was settling in with some effort, but it helped shift the mood. "Okay," he continued. "Maybe I'm not granite anymore, but I'm also not about to flake out over this, whatever it is."

"Good!"

"But, now you know why I said there's a conflict. I can't do that lecture. Can you picture me standing in front of the board and benefactors and Dak starts kicking in his two cents?"

"You seem perfectly fine right now," Mackenzie said.

"I am. He comes and goes. But, I don't seem to have any control over the coming or the going."

"What about now? You all alone in there?" she asked.

"For the moment," Rick replied. "Why? What's going on, Mackie? Am I blacking out? Twitching? Foaming at the mouth?"

She wished it were a simple as that. She'd sensed Dak herself, when she'd touched his cast in the museum. But he hadn't possessed her. At least, she didn't think he had. And the difference between Rick with and Rick without company wasn't an obvious Jekyll and Hyde swap. It was more like Rick electrified—that shift signalled by the smell of brimstone, him looking like a solar flare was occurring within and radiating a cold wave that made her shiver with trepidation.

"No, it's not that noticeable. Have you blacked out again recently?" she asked.

"No." Rick groaned. He closed his eyes for a moment and shook himself. "I don't think. But it could happen again any minute. Where are we? What time is it?"

"Don't sweat about that, Rick, just tell me how you feel."

"Like I'm losing it." He groaned again, but his command of the present seemed intact.

His turmoil brewed inside him and threatened to flood him with panic. His shallow breathing marked his struggle, and it was a strange sight for Mac, who was used to Rick as the brawny male mold for macho men.

"We're in this together," she said, and reached over to grab his hand. There, she'd done it. She'd offered to tie her kite to the tail of Rick Mason and not even blinked an eye.

"No." Rick moved slowly. "This is my problem and I'll handle it."

His expression shifted, and his body followed suit. Gone was the scared friend. Back was the polished Dr. Rick Mason.

How much did it cost him to look, be, and stay so strong? Almost a feat for a superhero, she realized.

She fastened her seatbelt and started the Willy. "It's not your choice, Rick Mason, it's mine and I've made it. I've fallen for your story—hook, line, and sinker. I've lined up some help for you."

"No," he said again.

No? Rick's monosyllabic responses were an irritating habit that she'd tolerated long enough. Bullheaded recognizes stubborn all too well. She opened her mouth to enlighten Rick on the matter, and to tell him she'd already set up the appointment.

"You don't have to do this," he cut in. It was a crack in Rick's tough-guy facade. A gift.

"Always the independent cuss," she crabbed. "So, you'll

owe me." Though she'd be surprised if he thanked her for where they were headed.

He didn't seem to have an inkling of what was to come. A ghost of a smile played across his lips. "Thanks," he said.

Chapter Fifteen

"Where are we going?" he asked after Mackenzie caught I-35 and drove several miles in the opposite direction from her house and his motel.

"I know someone who can help you. Do you trust me?" she asked, then shook her head. "Never mind, forget I asked. We stopped trusting each other when you took the Pompeii job without consulting me."

He gave an exasperated sigh. "No, I didn't stop trusting you then—that happened later. But I'm glad you brought it up. That's part of our unfinished business. Since you're taking me on this road trip, I've got time to offer up the expanded version of my apology. You'll recall you rejected my short and sweet one."

Mackenzie squirmed in her seat and stole a glance at him. Keeping him talking seemed better than allowing him to brood. And he definitely wasn't possessed at the moment. He looked comfortable and better than any male should who was supposedly carting around the soul of a dead guy. Besides, he was right. This was unfinished business between them. It was stuff she'd tried to purge solo with zero success. And since the scab had been ripped off her wounded heart, here was a chance to complete the cure and give him a piece of her mind.

"It's a bit of a drive, you've got time," she agreed. "You left off at 'I was right and you were wrong.' "

Rick coughed and looked a bit sheepish. "Well, you were. The Pompeii job was a mistake. I shouldn't have taken it. Not when I did."

"It was a great opportunity. You made a career decision. People do it all the time," Mackenzie replied. She adjusted her seat and tapped the rearview mirror up a notch to see over Bubba's load of boxes.

Rick waved off her words and continued. "What I should have done was get you drunk, haul you to Vegas, and married you before you could think of another damned reason to put me off."

"Put you off!" Mackenzie yowled. "I never—"

Rick cut in, "And then, you married Ben." He stopped and scrubbed his face with his hands. "That cut me to the quick, babe."

Mackenzie was stunned speechless. She thought about their past. Rick was right. She had put him off and dumped him for all the "right" reasons. And when she'd made the colossal mistake of marrying Ben, she'd done it for spite—another not-so-proud moment in her life. She'd wanted to hurt Rick. She'd ended up hurting everyone—herself included—in the process.

"Maybe we should have gotten married back then," she finally said.

"It would have saved me five years in solitary confinement," Rick complained.

"Oh, no. I won't believe it for a second if you're telling me you didn't live it up in Italy. The whole damned country reeks of *amore* and passion. I bet you've got a fat little black book and a bevy of beauties at your beck and call."

Rick chuckled. His slow sexy smile, his casual shrug,

and his no-nonsense gaze pierced her armor and cut her deep. "I tried everything to get over you, Mackie. And nothing worked."

Rick Mason had turned the tables on her again. She'd been all set to roast him, but his down-home honesty had ripped the rug out from under her. Snits were hard to sustain when love was on the line. She'd have to yield something—but she still wasn't going to let down her guard completely.

"All right, all right," she snorted. "Apology accepted."

"Too easy," Rick replied. "I want the rack, or at least a bed of nails."

Mackenzie laughed. "You want torture? Well, I can deliver. This help I'm planning—I'm taking you to a psychic."

Rick cleared his throat and glared at her. He didn't say anything for a long time.

Mackenzie flipped on the radio and punched the pretuned buttons till she found a station playing something soothing. She wanted to keep Rick happy and off the subject of exhibits and possession, but his apology was playing through her mind. It had stirred up a few demons in her soul.

Their problems had started with Hargrove's witch-hunt about stolen research. Rick hadn't abandoned her, and when she landed on her feet and was awarded her doctorate, she was relieved. But the whole affair had shaken her to the core. Yes, she had put Rick off again and again. How could she think of love and marriage when her career was compromised? She'd become obsessed with proving she was above reproach. It was the tear in their relationship that ultimately sent them off in opposite directions for their careers, and to opposite continents for their lives.

"If you keep squirming around in that short skirt," Rick growled, "you're not going to be safe and I'm not going to be responsible for my actions."

Mackenzie wasn't sure she wanted to be safe or responsible. She had an idea that pulling off the road, kicking out a few of Bubba's supplies, and stretching out on the carpeting with a possessed cowboy wasn't either one.

She took the Waxahatchie exit and slowed to a crawl when she entered gingerbread row, a line of luscious ornamental Victorian homes that seemed frozen in a bygone era. Tea roses perfumed the air, kids played hide-and-go-seek around a vine-covered gazebo, a young mother on a porch swing rocked a little one, and a paint box sunset pinked the sky and cast a rosy glow on everyone and everything.

"Keep an eye out for a sign. It's a small one. I've only been here once and I don't quite remember where the place is."

"The psychic." Rick coughed again.

"Tarot cards are her specialty, but when I called her today she said she'd try to help."

"You called her before I even asked you for help? Oh, that's rich." He started to chuckle, and soon his whole body was shaking with laughter. "Mackenzie, love, you are one piece of work. If I live a thousand years, I'll never understand you completely, but I sure as hell won't ever doubt you again."

Mackenzie's face scrunched into a mask of confusion. "What are you talking about, Rick?"

"Don't you get the irony?" he replied, and pointed to the left side of the street. A line of parked cars nearly obscured the modest curbside placard sporting: *Psychic Services: Inquire Within.*

Mackenzie found a spot further down the block, pulled over, and cut the engine. "No, I don't get it. You're in trouble and I'm exhausting my Rolodex of resources to try and get you some help. That's all. Any friend would do the same thing."

"Not everybody would. That's my point. Without a

shred of solid evidence you're on my team. Don't you find this improbable, unlikely, and over-the-top kind of crazy?"

"You mean, like you did when I told you I thought Mr. Pompeii moved?"

"Well, yeah. Like that."

She pressed her palms together as if in prayer and rested her chin on her fingertips for a moment. "It happened to me too."

"Possession?"

Mackenzie shrugged. "Sort of. It was like I was there when it happened. Pompeii. Seeing it through his eyes." She shook herself and sighed. "Of course, because of the exhibit, I've been living that moment in history for nearly a year. And I haven't had a lot of sleep lately. It's not surprising that my imagination could supply a few extra details and for a split second make me think I was there. Hell, I designed a whole exhibit to do that very thing."

"But this isn't your imagination we're talking about now. It's mine," Rick replied. "And you don't doubt me one bit. I can see it in your eyes."

She shook her head. "No, you're right. I don't. But I really really want us to both be wrong."

Chapter Sixteen

Earth's Core: Day 227

"It's Dak all right," Maude said. "He's got the imprint of an identlog on his arm and a scar on his forehead."

Charlie sighed. "That's great. That's the confirmation we've been waiting for."

Maude smiled. She had rushed through post-transit to deliver her reconnaissance report. The Rogue contingent sitting in on the planning session in the elevated lounge overlooking Charlie's austere lab cheered and hooted their approval.

Charlie pulled out several holographic charts developed by the planners and laid them across the light boards in the center of the oval room. All idle chatter ceased, and everyone conferring on the project faced forward and waited.

"There's more," Maude said. "The people at the museum know Dak's name."

Charlie looked mildly surprised and nodded. "Dak has made contact. It could jeopardize the stasis lock, but I'm not too surprised. He's just the fool to risk it." He paused. "I can't guarantee it will hold. The lock is an untested prototype."

"But if they know his name, they could know other things about him too," one of the transit specialists interjected. "Can we establish a link and extract data? Details on Dak's movements an hour or two prior to the stasis lock could be helpful to the mission."

Charlie's eyes widened and he slapped the specialist on the back. "Great question and great idea, Frank. Get the retrieval folks to help you find answers." He looked a little less pleased. "But remember, Dak's not communicating with Rogues. People from that era don't have memory chip implants; our technology can't interface with their brains. You'll have to design something that can."

The specialist nodded. Several Rogues leaned over and offered to help. The "All for one and one for all" motto suited this tenacious lot crowded into the unadorned meeting space.

It suited Maude, too. The Rogues were fast becoming the family she'd always wanted but never had. She fit in. Most Rogues were junkies for danger and gluttons for challenge—she sure was.

Yes, Charlie's realm of scientific inquiry worked hand in hand with the special breed of risk-taking commandos she'd joined. It fostered imagination and inspired creativity. There wasn't ever a bad concept or a kooky notion as far as Charlie and his crew of inventors and technicians were concerned. So when the wild idea popped into Maude's brain to transit back to the museum herself to try and communicate directly with Dak, she knew Charlie would hear her out. And every transit she logged moved her closer to her goal: snagging the rescue mission assignment. But she'd have to wait to propose that. There were more weighty issues for Charlie and the planning team to discuss first.

Charlie illuminated the charts and tapped one of the images. The hologram lifted, rotated ninety degrees, and slowly spun in a counter-clockwise direction. To Maude, it looked like a spiderweb with a blister.

"Is that the time rift?" she asked.

Charlie looked pleased. "Yes, it is, as well as the affected area of the Continuum. We're mapping it as it continues to expand." He pointed at the pink-edged bulge in the upper quadrant of the rotating image. "This is our primary focus. Along the front, transit links have been terminated with Core time-travelers. And it's an example of what will happen to other time lines as the rift continues to expand."

"It's not progressing sequentially, is it?" one Rogue asked.

"No. The rift originated in a no-transit zone. The rule of random catastrophe applies, as well as other mitigating factors. By the way, it's a class-ten time rift."

Dead silence. No one spoke and Maude's thrill meter went off the scale. This was big. She didn't know exactly what a class-ten rift meant to the Continuum, and maybe she didn't need to know. Predictions of apocalyptic events went with the job, but they were a distraction too. Rogues needed to concentrate on specifics. Every time-travel mission was a controlled nosedive into the past with the potential to fix or screw things up.

The Scio-society, Charlie's branch of Core's governing arm, addressed the bigger picture. Maude didn't envy their task of determining how best to protect Core and the future of humanity. Every choice and every decision was critical. She preferred the Rogues' job description—glorified body-and-fender guys, they were the mechanics who kept the great Continuum on course.

"Class-tens are not reversible," Charlie explained. "However, their erratic nature is predictable to a degree, and we know the outcome if unchecked."

A Rogue supplied the information: "Yeah, yeah. Total annihilation of life as we know it."

Everyone in the lounge snickered or laughed, even though it was completely true and they were all serious about their roles in preserving life. For Rogues, the stakes were always high. Class-one rifts or class-ten, it didn't matter; a Rogue's commitment and dedication never wavered. All any of them ever needed to know about a mission was where and when to show up.

Maude stretched and yawned. Her post-transit treatment wasn't finished. Stage two was necessary to keep her Rogue status current. Transits were rough on everyone, including youthful natural talents like her. She still needed to complete reacclimation, debrief, and subject her body to a systemwide saline flush and prolonged infusion of nutrients. Drutz, what a waste of precious time! She could probably shortcut the flush, but the infusion? Not a chance. Charlie's nutrient sludge was key to getting transit recertification. And with the rescue mission assignment still up for grabs, she wanted recertification fast!

"Thanks to Maude's reconnaissance data, we can refine our mission parameters," Charlie continued. "We've confirmed Dak's physical location at the moment of stasis lock. Using the reference, we can extrapolate when and where he triggered the time rift with plus or minus five-point-two-five percent tolerances. I want to narrow that margin before launching the mission. The no-transit zone complicates precise calculations—we might be over or under—but I'm shooting for absolutes. Let's try to get them!"

"Frank"—he pointed at the transit specialist—"more data on Dak is critical. Keep me posted on your progress establishing a link with the locals at the museum." He stopped and grinned. In spite of the dire threat and impossible odds, Charlie was irrepressibly optimistic. The guy didn't harbor fatalistic thoughts for long, if he ever did. The effect on everyone who worked with him was extraordinary. Charlie's glowing enthusiasm was infectious. One by one, everyone gathered in the lounge grinned.

"The mission is on," he announced. "Let's go over the scenarios step by step. We'll need to pick one and start the prep work."

The planning session extended beyond two meal cycles. Maude's interest flagged but she forced herself to listen to all the options. She was learning that changing history wasn't a frivolous undertaking. And that *how* Rogues changed history figured as prominently in planning as *why*. For each scenario, Charlie's Scio-society considered and weighed merits against deficiencies until the safest and most expedient course emerged.

Ah, we finally picked one! Maude silently cheered. But it wasn't over. Reports followed.

Data Collections established the framework of the Vesuvius event from the first eruption to Charlie's stasis lock. Armament demonstrated a range of devices to disarm, disable, and dispatch the contrary Dak—if necessary. Mapping produced primary and alternate landing sites within free-transit zones, and Logistics countered with mobility and hazard constraints. And Wardrobe presented preferences for garbs and societal roles the selected Rogue would adopt for the duration of the mission.

Maude sighed in relief when the session concluded and everyone scattered. She'd contributed very little beyond her report and a few questions, but now was her chance to corner Charlie and introduce her idea.

"Let me transit back to Dallas," she said after trailing him to his lab. "I can try to contact Dak directly, and we won't have to link with locals. You could send me now; I'm ready to go again."

It was true. She felt great. Stage one of Charlie's post-transit treatment had left her tingly from the top of her bald head to the toes of her bare feet. No more hives, and nothing but a soft green toga encumbered her body.

Charlie scowled. "It's a good idea as a backup plan if Frank can't deliver. But you're wrong about being ready. You're not fully reacclimated. I'm suggesting stasis for seven rotations—not that you'll comply, of course."

Charlie couldn't act stern or gruff at all well. He was naturally good-humored and sweet. Although he was one of Core's elite super-brains, he didn't look the part. In terms of her recent transit to Dallas, she could put a finger on his strange wild-eyed, red-haired, and toothy-grinned looks—a cross between Carrot Top and Lyle Lovett.

"I will comply if you promise to let me go back to Dallas," Maude returned. "Or, if you assign me to Dak's rescue mission."

"I'll think about it," Charlie replied, stowing the holo charts in one of the tubes on the honeycomb wall file. "But no compromises. Do the full seven rotations with auto-nutrient supplements and a complete memory download, and maybe I'll put you on standby."

"That's rough, Charlie," Maude countered.

"Weren't you listening during the planning session? These aren't pleasure transits, Maude. We're collecting data to isolate Dak and install safeguards before we attempt the rescue and thwart his SOS. Things are serious now. The scope and dimension of the rift is expanding. I need reliable scouts who accept every safety precaution I deem necessary. If not, they're off the team."

Maude laughed. "I don't mind the rotations or even your foul-tasting supplements. But a complete memory download? That erases my emotions, right?"

"Just the superficial ones that accumulate during repeat transits to a time window. Affection, longing, and remorse can overburden a Rogue. It's for the best," Charlie swore.

"You'll retain your knowledge of the mission, which you'll need if I send you back."

"You let me keep my emotions after my first recon to the Pompeii dig," she argued. "Why do I have to give them up now?"

Charlie groaned. "Don't tell me. You've got a crush on someone."

Maude nodded and shrugged. "Rick Mason, the archaeologist who unearthed Dak and made his body cast. He's in Dallas. He's also the local who said Dak's name."

"You've got a crush on Dak's contact?" Charlie sighed. A moment later he winked. "Okay, I'll save them to file for you. Anything else?"

"Just one more thing. When you download my data about hot chocolate, try to stir up a replica, will you?"

Chapter Seventeen

Waxahatchie: Wednesday evening

Introductions took some time, since they weren't Madame Beefcake's only guests. The others were a group gathered for the Second Wednesday Séance & Supper Club.

Rick wasn't the only male in the collection, but he was the tallest. Mackenzie could keep tabs on him as they all mingled in the front parlor and waited for Madame to appear. Mac had last been in the house three years ago but nothing had changed. The renovation of the Victorian was still under way, with very little to show in the way of progress. Aluminum-backed insulation still lined every bare-to-the-studs wall in the double parlors, and metal folding chairs offered the only seating options. Still, the group didn't seem concerned with the less-than-hospitable setting.

"Will you be sharing this evening?" a keen-looking bird of a woman asked Mackenzie. "We have a regular agenda, of course. Everyone waits their turn, and I'm sharing first."

"Oh, don't listen to Hazel," a rotund male in orange

plaid walking shorts whispered. He held out a tray with lime Kool-Aid and Rice Krispy treats. "No one wants to hear her chew out poor Dudley again for dying on her birthday."

Mackenzie passed on the hors d'oeuvres. "We don't want to intrude," she started to explain, but the man moved away and offered his treats to her neighbors.

Rick waved her over. "I saved you a seat," he said a little too loudly, and pulled her down beside him. "What have you got us into, Mackenzie? I'm getting grilled on things like pendulums and whether my moon is rising. This is beginning to feel like a PTA meeting on LSD."

"Sorry about the crowd. I didn't expect this, but Madame Beefcake insisted on seeing you immediately."

"I can see why. I'm going to be the main attraction," he growled.

He looked mutinous, and she didn't blame him. Odds were slim that this would help him one bit. Fortunately, it wasn't the only idea she'd generated. After her call to Madame earlier she'd made a list. Granny Moon would have been proud.

"I'm counting to ten and then I'm out of here," Rick hissed.

"Count slowly, because she's worth the wait. If nothing else, you need to meet her."

"I need a lobotomy more," he returned.

Mackenzie clamped one hand on his knee. "Sit still and count slowly."

Rick mumbled under his breath, but it sure didn't sound like numbers. Mac decided holding on to his knee was a good idea, though she eased up on the pressure.

"I met her three years ago when Sam was having some adjustment problems," she said.

Rick raised an eyebrow. "Sam the cat?"

Mackenzie laughed. "Yep. She's also a pet psychic."

"And she helped?"

"More or less. I had to choose between Sam and the husband. Sam won."

Rick howled. "That's my buddy."

The bare-bulb chandelier winked on and off. Mr. Orange Shorts was doing the honors.

"Attention, everyone. Madame Beefcake will be joining us shortly. Please take your seats and try to clear your minds."

The birdlike woman, Hazel, switched CDs in the boom box and the sound of ocean surf and seagulls gradually mounted in intensity. Mr. Orange Shorts dimmed the chandelier to a medium glow. The curious collection of folks settled into the hard metal seats without a whimper.

Even though she was prepared for it, Mackenzie jumped a little when Madame seemed to materialize in the center of the floor, shrouded in a froth of sea-foam green. Like her dwelling, Madame's entrance routine hadn't changed either. She still wowed clients by popping in through a trapdoor. A round of applause quickly followed a chorus of oohs and aahs from the group. Taller than Rick and toothpick thin, Madame inclined her head in greeting and slowly turned in a circle acknowledging everyone by name. She paused when she reached Mackenzie and Rick.

"Thank you for joining us. Tonight you are family." Madame's voice wasn't remarkable, but the intensity of her gaze was. Mackenzie's heart eased out of neutral and accelerated. The effect lasted until Madame moved on and completed her greetings and finally settled on a cushion in the center of the floor.

"Let us begin," she said.

What followed didn't qualify as a séance in Mackenzie's mind. No one channeled the dead or rapped on the floor, but the experience was remarkable and Mackenzie was transported. It was a first-class meditation that banished worry and embraced peace. This was better than a vacation. This was a quickie stress-buster that was worth every second in that cold folding chair.

"And open your eyes," Madame finished.

More oohs and ahhs as people stretched in their seats and Mr. Orange Shorts adjusted the lighting.

"Would anyone like to share before we break for dinner?" Madame asked. "Hazel?"

Hazel shared. Madame was a pro at guiding Hazel through her anguish and beyond. But Dudley's spirit didn't appear.

Poor Dudley, Mackenzie silently mused. He deserved eternal rest from his wife.

Others shared, but when silence finally reigned, Madame persisted. "Anyone else?"

Mackenzie leaned into Rick and whispered, "Had enough? This could go on all night. I think we can slip out of here without disturbing the group. I can follow up with Madame tomorrow."

Rick didn't respond. He was breathing heavy, his gaze fixed on Madame. The knee beneath Mackenzie's hand spasmed and finally he spoke.

"Help me," he cried out. It wasn't ancient Latin this time, but there was no mistake. It wasn't Rick asking for help. It was Dak.

"Mackenzie Cates's absence this evening concerns me," Jeremy Hargrove announced when Mrs. Bidwell finally opened the museum membership committee meeting to new business.

"Gil" Gillespe, one of the stellar graduate students in his department at the university, was sitting in on the meeting and watching him, dared Jeremy hope, in admiration? Hargrove cleared his throat, a calculated pause that he used on his students before refusing to grant a passing grade.

"And for the record"—he nodded at the secretary recording minutes of the meeting—"I request that it be duly noted. At this crucial hour, when we are addressing membership issues, Mackenzie's presence is essential."

He saw Proctor's bushy mustache twitch. The man pulled off his spectacles, little round wire-rimmed affairs, and polished them with his snowy handkerchief. "Your concern is misplaced, Jeremy. Dr. Cates's presence is not essential to the functioning of this committee."

Hargrove persisted. "Far be it for me to point this out since I am also one of the candidates for the position of museum director. However, as a committee member, I would be negligent if I did not express concern. Her failure to consistently support our efforts indicates conflicting priorities. Membership is our bread and butter. This Pompeii exhibit is interesting, but serving our constituency and honoring our loyal and generous benefactors is paramount."

Several committee members conferred in whispered tones. Gillespe made notes. Hargrove's hands started to tremble with excitement. He picked up his monogrammed portfolio and flipped through the gold-leafed calendar, busying his thoughts and his hands. By all rights, this was his museum—or would be soon enough.

Gillespe shifted in his seat. As the lone outside witness to the regular monthly meeting, he looked bored and singularly unimpressed. And Hargrove knew well that impressing the lad could further his career enormously. Gillespe was a golden boy, well-placed in society and endowed with old money. Those were two things Hargrove prized almost as much as besting his rivals.

Mrs. Bidwell tapped her gavel. "If Jeremy is concerned, we should do something, shouldn't we? Perhaps it should be noted in the minutes," the matriarch of the Bidwell crude oil dynasty proclaimed.

Hargrove nearly allowed himself a smile. He rarely

smiled, but this was too easy. His plan was working. This seed of doubt would be enough to upset the status quo and eliminate Mackenzie as a serious contender for the position he so coveted. Few, if any, suspected his crisis. He needed the directorship. The university administration wanted him gone. They couldn't fire him, of course; they'd tried for the last five years but didn't have sufficient proof. He'd covered his tracks in the thesis scandal. All except for the research he'd stolen from Mackenzie Cates. Damn her. She was the cause of all his problems.

He'd wrung what little prestige he could from the university job in spite of the administration's efforts to bury him in obscurity. To distinguish himself further, he needed to move beyond academia, and the museum directorship was the perfect place to land. Also, it offered the bonus of displacing Mac Cates.

Yes, succeeding Proctor was essential. And, thanks to old Biddy Bidwell, his mother's cousin, he had some influence.

"This is the membership committee, Mrs. Bidwell," Proctor explained. "Discussion of subjects beyond the purview of this body are not included in the minutes." He turned to the secretary. "Make a note that, for the benefit of all committee members, staff reviewed function and purpose of the museum membership committee."

Proctor donned his spectacles and glared at Hargrove—almost daring him to challenge his authority. Hargrove fumed, but he dared not protest further. Proctor was an obstacle he could ill-afford to alienate at this stage of the selection process.

Hargrove nodded in Biddy's direction. "If there is no further relevant discussion, I suggest, Madame Chair, that we conclude the meeting."

Biddy acquiesced. "Very well," she said, and brought down her gavel with a limp effort. The committee members began to push away from the conference table.

Proctor, the old fool, gathered up his notes, conferred with the secretary, and generally ignored him. But Jeremy concealed his loathing and contempt for the little man who resembled Teddy Roosevelt in all but breeding. He accepted Proctor's ill regard with his practiced air of irritation born of three generations of wealth and privilege—something Proctor would forever lack. Soon enough, the man would be collecting severance.

Biddy Bidwell was in his corner, but Proctor was another matter entirely. Mackenzie Cates might be Proctor's current favorite because she'd acquired the Pompeii exhibit for the museum, but Hargrove was going to ensure her downfall. All of his troubles were her fault, and she was going to finally pay.

"Get along, dear," he urged with masked impatience as Biddy, befuddled as usual, required his assistance to collect her belongings and depart. "I'll give Mother your best."

Catering to a dotty old woman was a small price to pay for support. However, it irked him all the same. He detested the need to garner support for what should have rightfully been his due. He turned back to have a word with Gillespe and found the boy in a heated conversation with Proctor.

"I'll see what I can do, Gillespe," Proctor concluded. Hargrove advanced on the twosome.

"Well," he forced a hearty chuckle, "what's all this about? Not me, I daresay."

"You're right about that, Jeremy. It has nothing to do with you," Proctor returned.

Hargrove felt his ears burn. He prided himself on being sensitive to the subtle shifts of opportunity. He had worked long and hard to ingratiate himself with the plebian Proctor—to pave the way for a smooth transition from the old to the new—so long as he was the new director and not Mackenzie Cates.

"If it is museum business, it concerns me. I hope Gillespe isn't troubling you with something best left to me or one of your staff. You take too much of the burden on yourself, Proctor," Hargrove said. "As always, I offer my assistance. Just ask and I will make time."

Gillespe started to say something, but Proctor waved him off. "And as always, Jeremy, your offer is too generous."

They were in the hall. Hargrove paused beneath his portrait, making a show of checking his portfolio and patting down his coat pockets until he'd recovered his Mont Blanc fountain pen. It always served to remind Proctor just who had clout and who didn't.

Hargrove cleared his throat again, pleased that Gillespe could witness the exchange. Proctor had overstayed his welcome as museum director. It was high time to clean house and install new leadership from the ground up. If Gillespe played his cards right, he just might get added to the museum staff once Jeremy was named director.

"I am well aware of how important this exhibit is to you and Mackenzie Cates, however, we must not lose sight of our primary charge. If you should need me in that capacity in the days and weeks ahead, I am at your service."

It was enough but not too much, he decided. A gentle reminder to Proctor and everyone connected to the museum that a shift in power was under way and he was assuming control bit by bit.

He pulled out his car keys, the leather Porsche key tag discreet but unmistakable. Subtle displays of affluence were his trademark.

"Can I give either of you a lift?" he asked. It never hurt to remind people who really was in the driver's seat.

Chapter Eighteen

Rick groaned and scrubbed his face with his hands. The front porch of Madame Beefcake's Victorian seemed like the safest place to regroup until the last of her clients departed. He leaned against one of the porch columns, feet crossed, arms folded, and stared into the night. Peaceful little Waxahatchie, a shooting star, a kid on his bike racing home to Mom—all were signs of nice normality that tangled his unruly thoughts. The séance was over. And, although Dak had become still and silent again, he wasn't gone for good.

Rick's insides felt like the frontlines in a battleground where the real estate changed hands day-to-day or hour-to-hour, as he wrestled his invisible opponent for control of his body. The séance had provoked the last contest. Thankfully it had been brief. He'd done it. Alone or with help from Madame and her Séance and Supper Club crowd, he'd won his body back quickly. Only problem was, he knew Dak's alien presence would soon stage a rematch.

"How do you feel?" Mackenzie asked when she and Madame joined him on the porch.

"Never better," he snapped. The tumbler of whiskey Madame handed over improved his humor—a bit.

"I wish I could offer you more than a temporary fix and a dose of Johnny Walker," Madame said. "Unfortunately, your little problem is out of my league."

He nodded. What else could he say? His little problem was out of all of their leagues, and he didn't have a clue what to do next.

Mackenzie didn't share his concern. She looked radiant, sassy, and just a little too sexy for him considering his unhappy state.

"Thanks for letting me borrow these," Mackenzie said. She shifted the stack of books and baubles Madame had supplied.

"I want you to take this too," the woman said and handed over a prism dangling from a neck chain. "It's a gift and a reminder to keep the faith."

"Thanks," Mackenzie replied and slipped the necklace over her head.

Rick bit back a growl when he spied several of the titles. Oh no! Not more physic games and parlor tricks! They hadn't done any good so far.

Madame smiled. It probably didn't take clairvoyant powers to guess what he was thinking.

"I suppose I should thank you," he said graciously, downing the last of his drink. He couldn't think of anything else to say. After an awkward pause, he handed her the empty tumbler.

If Madame was offended, she didn't show it. Nodding in Mackenzie's direction, she added, "Don't thank me, thank *her*. If anyone can help you dispossess your spirit, she can."

Rick glanced at the lovely Mackie, luminous with delight over the stack of treasures she cradled in her arms. "Thank her? Yep, that's top on my list."

Madame shook his hand. "Good-bye, Dr. Mason, and good luck."

"Thanks, I think I'm going to need it," he returned. And, grabbing Mackenzie by the arm, he spun and walked away from the psychic without a backward glance.

Mackenzie gulped. The stubborn set to Rick's jaw didn't bode well for the long ride back to Dallas.

"Just what did all that prove?" Rick asked the moment she started the engine and pulled away from the curb. "Now, in addition to you, I've got a gaggle of folk who think the renowned Pompeii archaeologist is a K-double-O-K kook!"

"Research, Dr. Mason, research. I've got my material, and first thing tomorrow we're getting to work. Foremost on the list: Find an exorcist."

"A what?" Rick blustered, fumed, and finally exploded. He rolled the window down in the Willy and stuck his head out and yelled. Mackenzie tried it too.

"What are you doing?" he shouted.

Mackenzie pulled her head in and grinned. "Feels pretty good. Releases all that junk inside."

"No, I mean what in the heck do you think you're doing? An exorcist! Good god, woman, if any of our peers or bosses get wind of this, we'll both be pitched out on our kooky behinds. I've got my reputation on the line. And you do too. We need to back up and regroup." He paused, shook his head then continued. "Let me rephrase that. I need to back up and regroup. This is *my* problem, not yours. No sense in both of us tanking our careers over it."

"Bull hockey! You need me." She grinned again and turned on the radio full blast to drown him out.

Rick glared at her but didn't touch the dial. Thank goodness for Trisha Yearwood! Mac joined in on the chorus and ignored the pouting Rick until the next exit sign and promise of food triggered an unmistakable flip in her stomach.

Food? She was famished again, and that was a good sign.

She didn't know why she suddenly felt so fabulous and energized, but she did. Everything had just turned topsy-turvy in her life, but Madame Beefcake had said to have faith. Granny Moon had chanted a similar axiom all of her life. And maybe Mac had finally taken a step in that direction. She was tired of being at war with her instincts and trying to reconcile them, without success, with textbook reasoning. Faith was liberating.

She muted the radio and nodded to Rick. "Hey, are you hungry? I couldn't eat a thing back there after Dak cut loose, but now I'm starved."

"Hungry?" The unmistakable male voice was Rick's but huskier. Looking at him she saw a total shift in demeanor from ex-lover and heartthrob to a predator on the prowl. She smelled brimstone cologne. A blast of body heat nearly singed the baby-fine hairs on her arm and then sent shivers rocking and rolling up and down her spine. These were clues she couldn't ignore. It wasn't Rick beside her any longer, but the freeloading Dak.

Mackenzie kept both hands on the wheel and managed a controlled crash into the parking lot of the nearest well-lit establishment—the Snake Pit bowling alley and lounge. It seemed like a sane option even though she'd suddenly lost her appetite. With a few extra Texans available to help out in a pinch, she might have a chance to try out one or two things Madame had suggested.

Mackenzie cut the engine, faced the stranger and held out her hand. "It's time we're formally introduced. Just call me Mackenzie. And you are Dak, I presume?"

Chapter Nineteen

Earth's Core: Day 234

Maude felt the sunlight warming her face. Traces of a dream lingered but the increasing warmth roused her. She stretched and blinked. Rested, content, awake. Her surroundings seemed familiar. The back of the white-coated man seemed familiar. So did the aroma.

Hamburgers? She sat up suddenly, her forehead narrowly avoiding a contact burn from the sun lamp positioned above her pallet.

Hamburgers sizzled on the grill. Steaming fries heaped in a clear serviette glistened under a heat lamp.

"Charlie?"

He spun around and grinned. "Good, you're back."

Maude couldn't focus on Charlie's bio-queries. The image of food blotted out everything else. Fresh Bermuda onions. Sliced dills and beefsteak tomatoes. Lettuce too, and cheese. Her eyes teared and she swiped at the moisture with the back of her hand. A beautiful sight, within reach. Her stomach growled loudly.

"Hungry?" Charlie held out a tray laden with comestibles. The variety of solids and liquids he offered astonished her. She managed to nod. Food. Real food.

"I downloaded all this data from your recon mission. I've got that hot chocolate too, but the color's not quite right," he said. He slid one of the plump patties into a bun and held it out to her. Nothing, she assured herself could taste worse than Charlie's liquid nutrient. She took a big bite. Condiment-free, the burger soared in her regard. She took a moment to load it up with extras before relishing the rest. Clearly, Charlie could cook.

She finished devouring her second burger and drained a frosty root beer before she paused long enough to take in her surroundings. Charlie's lab. That was odd, she shouldn't be here. Reacclimation chambers were located far off in the north wing of Core's Scio-society headquarters.

Still, she wasn't alarmed. Waking up at Charlie's felt good and comfortable, similar to finding herself on the spare lounger at a friend's house. His lab really was a home away from home for her. She'd started her career as a novice-class Rogue in this very chamber approximately one thousand rotations ago—when she'd been offered a chance to forever change her life. A routine population scan had singled her out as something more than a gene-pool anomaly. Charlie had called her gifted, Dak had called her a natural Rogue, and she had called them both friends. Orphaned and rootless, her search for home had ended.

"Is my reacclimation complete?"

"Yeah." He rolled his stool over beside her pallet and checked her vitals. "You're in the clear now. The Scios nearly lost you on the sixth rotation so I brought you over here to finish the process."

She swallowed hard. "Lost me?" She set down her half-eaten cherry turnover, her appetite evaporating. "I thought reacclimation was foolproof thanks to guys like you. What happened?"

"Nothing's foolproof—certainly nothing that allows us to scramble our atoms and send them back and forth across the Continuum." He finished thumping her knees for reflexes and pushed aside his table of instruments. "Deviated septum and right knee scar tissue. Want me to fix them?"

"What?" She looked down at the leg in question. The poorly knitted gash across the top of her knee as well as her broken nose predated joining the Time Rogues. It never occurred to her to request repair solely for cosmetic purposes. Neither aberration hindered her life.

"No, I guess not. Dak once told me to treasure the differences between us and to not value perfection."

"That sounds like Dak, all right. He's anything but perfect," Charlie said.

"I wanted to ask you about that. How did he cause the time rift?"

"A plus B equals C. He initialized his emergency transit beacon in a no-transit zone and triggered a catastrophic time rift."

"Too simple. What *really* happened?" she asked.

Charlie raised one of his bushy brows. "You want to know all this?"

Maude folded her arms and glared. "Yes!" Charlie shrugged his shoulders and complied.

"The transit beacon linked with Foxtrot transit substation, which couldn't process the priority command and overloaded the receptor signal and blew circuits and backups. Then it looped through the safeguard protocols—they clean and sort commands. It was redirected to Zed, the powerhouse for processing difficult commands. Zed processed it, deciphered the no-transit zone origin and executed a system shutdown, but it was too late, the damage couldn't be contained. The mainframe was affected. The subsequent cascade corroded the command paths. Energy reversals flooded with random and conflicting codes surged back along Dak's original signal."

Thankfully, Charlie paused long enough to grab some of her leftover fries. She couldn't fake interest or understanding much longer. Why, oh why, had she insisted on asking for details?

"And that caused the rift," Maude finished. She scraped the last dollop of cherry filling off her serving tile with her finger and popped it onto her tongue.

Charlie nodded, his mouth stuffed with fries. He chewed twice, swallowed, and immediately choked on the wad.

"Wash it down with this," Maude fussed and handed him one of the root beers. "Are you so hooked on nutrient supplements that you've forgotten how to eat? You've got to chew!"

Charlie's eyes watered and he looked chagrined. "I'll try to remember that. Where were we?"

Uh-oh. She'd been half-listening and half-thinking ahead, strategizing on how to convince Charlie to let her transit back to Dallas. Did she remember anything about what he'd just said?

"The time rift," she supplied after rifling through her short-term memory. "Foxtrot and Zed."

"You were listening. I'm impressed."

Maude's pulse raced. Charlie was impressed. Now, that was progress.

"I'm not just another Rogue, Charlie," she said and sat up straight. "I've been trying to tell and show you that since my first mission. I'm serious about wanting the rescue assignment."

"I don't doubt your sincerity, Maude. But understanding Scio stats on transit beacons and time rifts isn't a prerequisite for that mission."

"What is?"

"I'm not going to let you have it, Maude. I need the best

Time Rogue we've got for Dak's rescue. It's going to be a tough job and risky as hell."

Maude grinned and hopped off her pallet. "Novice or not, I'm good. Admit it. I'm a natural."

"You've got a gift for getting under people's skins. And not much else!"

"Thanks, I think."

Charlie snorted. "Rogues. You're all alike."

"Okay. Now we're getting somewhere." Maude climbed aboard one of Charlie's rolling stools and tucked her knees up under her. "On the remote chance that you'll change your mind and give me the assignment, what would I really need to know about Dak, time rifts, and no-transit zones to do the job?"

Charlie unrolled one of the map films and pointed to the blank auto screen. A red smudge appeared when he tapped the surface with the makeshift pointer.

"This is the no-transit zone where Dak triggered the rift. The zone isn't just a spatial location; it's a timeframe too. There's more than one. We've mapped them throughout the Continuum and buffered them to block transits on either end of the timeline.

"You've got to understand that 'no-transit' isn't just a caution or a warning label—it's a prohibition. Within the zone, transit isn't possible. I don't make the rules—well, not this one anyway—it's just the way things are." He stopped to laugh at the face she made.

"Bear with me," he said, and continued. "Certain environments compromise our transit technology. Some natural disasters do, too—volcanic eruptions and seismic events. High concentrations of volatile elements, chemical compounds, as well. Like I said, we've mapped the known environments, buffered them with time and space, and labeled them no-transit zones. And A.D. 79 Pompeii is one of those zones."

"How did Dak get around the buffers?"

"Dak? He could slip past a wormhole blindfolded." Charlie drew a circle around the red smudge. Beyond the circle, he tapped the screen and made a blue smudge. "His initial transit was authorized for a secure location. Once on site, he obviously reprogrammed his transit protocols, removed the safeties, and literally walked in." Charlie connected the red and blue smudges with a straight line.

"He's the worst kind of Rogue, a lover boy with a hero complex. He thinks he's invincible. Dak met Falah on an earlier mission, went back to get her before Vesuvius erupted, and didn't make it out in time."

Charlie eyed her closely and cleared his throat. "I'm to blame as much as he is. I guessed something was up and didn't do anything to stop him. If I had realized it was something stupid like this, I would have pulled his transit authority. And if he survives the rescue and returns to Core, I'll have to ground him permanently. Dead or alive, his Rogue days are over."

"If it's just because he went into a no-transit zone, Charlie, that's harsh!"

He rolled his eyes and pushed her toward one of the numerous viewscreen stations. "Access the Rogue files on time rifts and cross reference it with emergency transits in a no-transit zone." He tapped his foot while she complied.

She scrunched her brow as she scanned the data. She still didn't understand.

"Dak's expanding time rift caused a lot of damage while you were in reacclimation. His SOS triggered the rift because his emergency protocol activated and locked up the Foxtrot transit pad."

"Because . . . transits are impossible from a no-transit zone," Maude added.

"Precisely. Foxtrot's lockup drained servers, blew circuits, launched shadow protocols, terminated lives, and scrambled transit records for others. We've still got folks out there somewhere. And we can't bring them home because we don't know where they are."

"So it's bad," Maude said.

"It's catastrophic for time-travelers. The de-molecularizations on re-entries are the latest mess we're trying to clean up. Reacclimation problems like yours, another. We may have to suspend deep downloads and hard mission preps."

"But your plan will fix it?"

"If it works, it will keep it from ever happening."

"So, I need to save Dak."

Charlie scowled for a half-second. "A Rogue needs to save him or prevent him from activating his emergency transit beacon."

"What you're really saying is that I might have to kill him."

"You can't do it, Maude. It's a big jump from scout to assassin. I want a seasoned Rogue who can make tough decisions about life and death."

"I can, and *will*, to save lives!"

Charlie pressed his fingertips together; a telltale sign that his brain was shifting gears. Would he change his mind?

"I'll tell you what I'm going to do," Maude said. "If Frank hasn't established the link, I'm going to Dallas and attempt to contact Dak directly—his data will determine whether I'll have to kill him or not. When I get back, we'll talk about the mission."

She glared at him. She wasn't a bit of fluff to be dismissed with a pat on the head. She was a serious contender for the job. "I'll probably agree to do it on one condition."

Charlie raised one brow. He looked interested. "What's your condition?"

"Stir up an inoculation or give me an immunity booster for the hives," she said. "They don't itch all that much but I'm not a pretty sight."

"It's not a high priority, Maude. I'll be concentrating on refining the mission to get you in and out alive," Charlie said.

"But you'll try. Right?"

Charlie's grin could light up a dark cave. Maude blew him a kiss.

"Thanks!"

Chapter Twenty

"*Angelus*. My angel," Dak said, and brought her hand to his lips. She looked like a woman of her times, he concluded—strong, independent, passionate, and brave. If anyone could help him, she could. She was aware of him, but not as a man. And, though it seemed crazy, he wanted to change that fact just for a moment and remember another time, another woman, and the love that still burned within him. He'd wanted that since he first sensed Mackenzie Cates.

"Help me," he whispered.

"Wait a minute, just wait," she cried.

She was shaking with fright and plastered against the door of the vehicle, blindly fumbling for the latch. A moment later she was outside the Willy and pointing something small, black, and dangerous-looking in his direction.

"Where is Rick?" she hissed. She wagged the black thing. "What'd you do with him?"

"He's in here," Dak replied and thumped his chest. Actually, he didn't know where Rick was at the moment, but he wasn't going to tell Mackenzie that. He needed to communicate with someone if he was going to ever get back home to Core. Mac was ideal.

She didn't seem to agree. She flipped a switch on the black thing and it started humming.

"Get out of the car," she said. "Slowly."

Dak closed his eyes and concentrated. Nothing. The effort drained him. "I can't," he said.

She leaned in and looked him over. "Try! Try real hard!"

He tried again, willing his thoughts to remember how to flex and extend muscles. That helped a bit, but something or someone was holding him back. Was it Rick? If it was, he was getting tougher to control.

"The mind is willing but the body isn't."

She scrunched up her nose and sniffed the air. "Can't move? Ha! I'd be a fool to believe that, wouldn't I?" She eased back behind the wheel and flipped on the interior lights. "Just keep yourself over on that side of the truck, buddy, or I'll stun you senseless."

The snout end of the black device was pointed at his chest. At this range, Mackenzie couldn't miss hitting him even if she closed her eyes.

"What are you exactly?" she asked. "Rick's split personality or alter ego? A ghost, poltergeist, or demon?"

What indeed? Dak looked down at the hands of Rick's body. He could control some movements, see, and hear but very little else. The limitations of Charlie's stasis lock still troubled him. Was the lock degrading? If so, he was as good as dead.

"I guess 'ghost' fits me better than anything else," he finally answered.

She tilted her head and sniffed the air again. "This smell. I associate brimstone with demons."

"I can't explain the smell," he replied, "but I assure you I am not a demon."

She muttered something about a Granny somebody and a curse before she cleared her throat. “Ghost? Okay, I’ll go with that for now—it’s too bad Granny Moon’s gifts didn’t include a built-in ghost-o-meter. But, that doesn’t explain everything. You’re not from A.D. 79. Dead Romans from Ancient Pompeii don’t speak English. And don’t try to tell me you’re a quick study.”

She didn’t look frightened anymore, and that pleased Dak tremendously. His heart might belong to Falah but Mackenzie was just his type of woman. She was a beauty with brains, of course, and she was also elusive and intriguing—characteristics that baited him and lured him in from afar. Mackenzie took risks. She dared to consider the improbable and impossible. If he were still recruiting for the Rogues, he wouldn’t hesitate to make her an offer.

He could tell her the truth. What did it matter if he broke another Time Rogue edict? Mackenzie was bright. He was sure she could comprehend and accept time travel. But he doubted she would understand what he failed to understand himself—why he had disregarded Core parameters for the chance to be a hero and ended up a fool.

“I can’t explain,” he finally said.

She stared at him for the longest time. “God help me. Am I going crazy?” she whispered. “How is all this happening?”

“You aren’t crazy,” he replied, “and it’s happening because you touched me.”

“I’m responsible for this?” she wailed. “Oh, no!”

“Only for giving me hope, angel,” he quickly returned.

He flexed the limbs of Rick’s body, since he could move them now, and sucked in air and blew it out. He was learning how to command the borrowed body but couldn’t enjoy the full use of it. Maybe the sense of taste and touch and smell would come later. Sight and sound sufficed for now. It was enough. They allowed him to reach beyond the grave and communicate with another soul.

"You can help me," he whispered. "Will you?"

She shook her head. "I want to help Rick. I'm not sure it's the same thing. Is it?"

"Yes," Dak replied. "Trust me. It is."

Trust a ghost? Not bloody likely. Mackenzie wagged her stun gun again. He was moving his legs. She could zap him senseless and cross her fingers that Rick would take control again. Or, she could pitch him out into the parking lot and take off. Just how dangerous were possessed ex-boyfriends anyway?

The flashing arrow above the Snake Pit Bowling Alley's main entrance offered her a compromise. "Let's go inside," she demanded and backed out of the truck. Dak followed suit, and when he rounded the front of the vehicle she waved him ahead and pressed the stunner to his back. "Ghosts first."

Thank the good Lord for bowling leagues. The crowded lanes offered Mackenzie a sense of security that allowed her to pocket the stun gun for now. She grabbed one of the tables in the smoke-filled snack area and ordered two tall RCs and a basket of greasy curly fries. Funny, a face-to-face with a ghost hadn't hampered her appetite.

Dak was taking it all in like a tourist from Siberia. He cautiously sampled the food and drink until suddenly he shuddered with obvious delight.

"I can taste food!" Dak cried.

"Don't get comfortable in there," Mackenzie warned him. "That body belongs to Rick."

Dak licked the salt from his fingers after polishing off two-thirds of the fries. He finally finished and laughed. "It's very good. Thank you."

That did it. She needed to put a stop to this charade. "Who *are* you?"

"A fool." He looked away from her and laughed, this time with bitterness. "It was a mistake. I shouldn't have been in Pompeii, I shouldn't have died that day, but I did."

Bells and whistles sounded above the snack bar. Over the loudspeaker, the league winners were announced.

"I'd like to try that," Dak said and pointed to the nearest lane where the Gutter Gals were celebrating their victory over the Ball Belles.

Mackenzie choked on her RC. "Not so fast, Dak. Don't change the subject. You stole Rick's body and I'm going to make sure you give it back."

The noise level in the bowling alley masked most of their conversation from the other customers, but Mackenzie was noting some curious stares. She lowered her voice to a hiss.

"You want my help? You want me to trust you? You better start talking or I'm going to get the whole Second Wednesday Séance and Supper Club to exorcise you right into Hades."

Truthfully, Dak couldn't explain all of it even to himself. This ghostly state of affairs might even baffle Charlie. Flashes of life were brilliant and brief. Core. Transits. Charlie and the Time Rogues. He'd planned the clandestine mission to get Falah out of Pompeii and broken rules to do it. And he could only imagine the full extent of the damage he'd unleashed.

"I am dead," he started. That wasn't entirely true—yet. However, if the stasis lock significantly degraded, he would surely cease to exist.

If Charlie's simplest transit tools baffled him, the stasis-lock prototype fell into the category of a complete conundrum. How he'd come to exist in this limbo with his mind and passion intact was a mystery. He told her that much and watched her grasp it, accept it, and move on.

"So, what's next and how can I help?" Mackenzie asked.

Dak needed to buy time until the Rogues could make

contact and rescue him in the past. And he was willing to twist the truth just enough to dangle a bit of bait in front of Mackenzie's nose.

"I'd like peace. Knowing what happened to my beloved Falah would grant me that peace."

Mackenzie chewed her lip. "That's a tall order, but maybe it's not impossible. I'll need some specifics."

"I can give you some."

"Meanwhile, you've got to stop popping in and out of Rick's life."

Dak remained silent. He wasn't sure he could control that—or if he wanted to. Possessing Rick's body was motivating Mackenzie to help him.

"Tell me about her," she demanded, catching him off guard.

He felt the borrowed body seize up, and for a moment he felt a heart beating again—not his but Rick's. The man's passion for Mackenzie was like his own for Falah. It would live beyond the grave.

"I bought her freedom. She was carrying my child in her womb. We were happy."

Images of Falah swamped him with emotion. And Rick's body reacted. Was Rick seeing and feeling all of this too? Were they beginning to share his senses? If so, eventually there would be no secrets between them. Rick would know about Core and the Rogues, which would violate his oath to protect the knowledge.

"Was Falah with you in Pompeii?"

"I can't remember," he said. More of the past was crowding his thoughts and pushing images of Falah aside. Core dictums. *Do not interfere. Do not procreate. Do not alter the past.*

"It was a mistake!" A silent scream flooded his newfound senses and he crushed the fragile cup in his hand. Ice chunks and fizzy dark liquid squirted through his fingers.

Mackenzie blotted the table, his hands, and herself. And she was wiping back tears too.

"I'll try to help you, but you've got to let Rick go," she whispered.

She looked frightened. She obviously loved Rick. He'd seen the same look in Falah's eyes just before he'd returned to Core that first time. It was the look of love, and it had changed everything for him. He'd been a diehard Rogue with a new woman with each new mission until he'd fallen in love with that slave girl in Ancient Pompeii.

"If she survived, she would have gone to Misenum," he told her.

Mackenzie nodded. "I'll find her. And then you'll go?" she asked and sniffed back tears.

Dak nodded. "I promise. This isn't my life. My life was with Falah and our child. And, with your help, I hope I'll be free at last to join them."

Mackenzie smiled even as her eyes filled with more tears. "I'll do my best."

"Thank you, angel," he said. Then he pulled her fingers to his lips for one last kiss.

Rick muscled Dak's persona to one side and regained control of his body. There was a knack to it, a bit like tripping someone from behind when something or someone distracted them. And Mackenzie had distracted Dak.

"He's got a crush on you, Mackie," Rick said, suddenly aware that he was jealous, defensive, and pissed off. "And I don't like it!"

"Rick!" Mackenzie choked back a sob. "Thank God! You're back."

Her shift from sadness to joy was palpable. And in that unguarded moment, he saw love. She still cared!

"Glad to see me?" he asked. A chuckle rumbled through him like a seismic shimmy.

"That's an understatement. How do you feel?" She grinned and wiped her eyes with the back of her hand.

He didn't dare answer that. His libido bucked like a rodeo bull in the chute. His tethered restraint was about to snap. And if it did?

He sized up their surroundings. The tables were filled with rowdy league bowlers, but the presence of an audience wouldn't deter this cowboy!

"I'm hungry," he growled.

"You just ate nearly a whole basket of fries and chugged a huge RC," she protested.

"Not for food, Mackie." He tugged her out of her chair and onto his lap. He groaned with pleasured agony as she wiggled against him.

A few Snake Pit customers looked over, cheered and hooted. Rick waved and gave them a thumbs-up.

"Hey, what are you doing?" Mac cried and grabbed hold of his neck.

"Taking you up on your offer," he returned. "Didn't you request a kiss last night?"

"Yeah, but . . ."

"Does it still stand?"

She looked stunned but she hadn't said no or decked him yet. That much was in his favor. Dak was currently AWOL—for how long, Rick couldn't guess—and Rick was going to take advantage of the situation and press his suit.

He tipped her back and kissed her soundly, without giving her another moment to protest. Damn her rules. Damn Dak and the peeping Toms in the bowling alley. And damn the consequences of yielding to this urge. Nothing mattered except tasting Mackie's heat again.

She didn't fight him when he pressed into her, sucking the sweetness from her lips. She opened to him. Welcomed him. He was coarse, rough, greedy, and on fire with need. And she answered his need with her own.

Their hot, wet mouths slapped together and pulsed with

a primal rhythm—tongues tangling and teasing soft slick flesh till they were both breathless. They slid apart and a moan escaped Mackenzie's lips.

She'd been arguing with her subconscious for the last twenty-four hours. She wanted more than a taste of the man. She wanted the whole enchilada. Damn the past and future. Her body was on autopilot and she lacked the will to restrain her desire for the sake of pride. Rick was a man. She was a woman. And all she could think about was finding a bit of privacy to explore the differences between them.

"Let's get out of here," she whispered against his mouth.

Rick didn't answer with words; he scooped her into his arms and set her soundly on her feet. "Hand over the keys, I'm driving tonight."

Outside, they found an obstacle barring their way. Were the heavens against them?

"It's a class six gully washer," Rick said. Several smokers were standing under the awning with them.

"I've seen worse," one of the smokers remarked, "but this is pretty bad. Wouldn't set off till it passes."

Mackenzie and Rick exchanged glances. She shrugged her shoulders when he jangled her keys. The torrential downpour was a minor annoyance for a woman in lust. "I'm game if you are," she said.

Rick grinned, tucked her under his arm and dashed out into the storm. They were soaked to the skin and laughing like kids by the time they reached the truck.

Inside the Willy, with the thunderous rain pounding the roof and sheeting over the windshield, the rest of the world faded away. The Snake Pit's pink-and-yellow neon sign washed their refuge in a fanciful light. And, while Rick cranked the engine and set the heater on meltdown, Mac crawled to the rear and searched Bubba's stockpile for supplies.

"Bingo," she cried. She produced a package of jumbo-sized tee shirts and tumbled back into Rick's embrace. The heater blasted their soaked bodies, but it was Rick's touch that eased her shaking and ignited an inferno.

"We could be stranded for hours," Rick said. "And your vehicle isn't designed with creature comforts in mind." He stripped off her strappy pumps and toweled her legs dry with one of the cotton tees.

"No, it's strictly utilitarian. A tin can with bucket seats," she replied between little gasps of pleasure when Rick's hands strayed off course. It was exquisite torture.

"But I'm a resourceful guy," he said and settled her closer.

"I have a few ideas myself," she whispered against his throat and licked the water from his skin.

It was a magic moment—the steamy windows, two heartbeats trying to tango, and Rick kissing her till her toes curled. It was the start of something luscious and unmistakably decadent. They definitely had chemistry. Like two natural elements linked in a compound, they realigned ideas, moods, and needs to accommodate the other. It was a chain reaction sparked by a kiss and fueled by passion. Apart, they were inert. Combined, they were explosive.

"Mackie," Rick groaned against her tender lips. "You're the reason I live and breathe."

Mackenzie didn't want to hear it. "Don't complicate this, Rick," she managed to reply. "This is about sex and nothing else."

It was a lie, like the others she'd been telling herself. But he didn't need to know that.

Rick paused and groaned. As suddenly as it had begun the rain had stopped, and by the sound of it, the Snake Pit patrons were exiting in droves.

"Don't try to fool yourself. This is about as complicated as it can get between males and females. But I agree that makeup sex between boxes of salsa and a gear shift is a bad idea," he said. "And I'm not wild about a bunch of bowlers peeping in the windows while we get it on. How about you?"

Mackenzie frowned. "I'm still mad at you, Rick Mason. And I don't trust you entirely either."

"Okay," Rick replied again, then kissed her senseless in zero to sixty seconds before maneuvering the Willy out onto the highway home.

No, Mackenzie conceded. Stalled outside the Snake Pit wasn't a likely setting to rekindle a romance with a possessed ex-boyfriend. But somehow it had done just that.

Twenty minutes later, Rick pulled into his motel's parking lot and cut the engine. Breathing was nearly impossible. The windows were still steamy, his armpits dripped sweat, and a furnacelike blast of heat spiraled between his legs. He was all male at the moment with a single objective: Mackenzie, in his bed, now!

Only, Mackenzie wasn't cooperating. She faced forward and didn't move. In profile she resembled the Sphinx. Unsmiling, with her gaze fixed on the stuccoed motel beyond, she seemed to have severed her connection to him with a bulwark of silence.

"Remember, it's just chemistry, Rick," she said suddenly and spun to face him. "Sex."

She folded her hands, which wasn't a good sign. His big motel bed was less than a hundred feet away but it might as well be a hundred miles. The fire that he'd sparked in her only minutes earlier had cooled considerably.

"Don't lie to yourself, Mackie. It's more than 'just sex' between us," he said, but he could see she wasn't listening. She'd buried her feelings again behind the wall he'd help build five years ago. Distrust and anger bolstered the barrier, and it would take more than one feverish night between the sheets to demolish it—it might take two.

He laughed out loud. His libido wasn't willing to give up without a fight. He decided to admit that to her.

"I'd like to cart you up to my big bed and plunder you till dawn."

"But?" She looked him in the eye. He didn't see what he wanted to see.

It was killing him to do this. His libido was in overdrive and to pass up this opportunity sans Dak to make love to Mackenzie was insane. But, it really, really, *really* wasn't about sex. Loving her was all about earning her trust. And damn it, there was only one right way to do it.

"But it's been another long day. Possession, psychic, séance, *and* sex? I'm going to have to pass." He handed over the keys and climbed out of the truck.

Seeming a little relieved, Mackenzie laughed and slid over behind the wheel. "Okay. But I want a rain check, Rick Mason."

He didn't even bother to suppress his groan. He was already regretting the decision to let her go. He slapped the lock down, slammed the door, and walked away before he folded.

"You've got more than a rain check, Mackie," he said after she'd driven away. "You've got me."

Chapter Twenty-one

Dallas: Thursday morning

"So far so good? No reoccurrence of your little problem?" Mackenzie asked. She cradled the phone and munched bacon from Mrs. Jay's breakfast. She slapped Bubba's hand as he tried to grab the last piece.

She marveled at how good it felt to talk to Rick. She'd gone to sleep frustrated but happy, and had woke up craving the sound of his voice. For all these years—trust hadn't been lost entirely, it was just misplaced. And forgiving herself for the countless mistakes she'd made while running away from love was helping her pick up the pieces of their shattered relationship. At worst, they would become friends again. At best? She'd just have to wait and see.

"No, I slept like the dead," Rick replied. "Do you think—is Dak on hiatus or did you use one of Madame Beefcake's spells to exorcise him?"

"I made a deal with him. I said I'd try to find out what happened to Falah if he agreed to stop borrowing your body. But, just in case he can't keep his promise, I'm still checking the yellow pages for an exorcist."

Oops. Bubba glanced up from the want ads. She didn't want a loose cannon like her cousin zeroing in on Rick's problem. She pushed her half-eaten breakfast over to his side of the table in an effort to distract him.

"Falah? No kidding? That explains a few things," Rick said.

"Really? I'd like to hear about it, but not right now. Your lecture is at seven tonight. Meet me this afternoon and you can fill me in."

"Oh yeah, the lecture . . ."

"You're not backing out, Rick. You're going to do it," Mac snapped. "And if Dak doesn't keep his promise . . . He will, of course, but if he doesn't, I'll cover for you."

Rick didn't reply immediately. Mac bit her lip and held her breath. It was a tall order. Could she deliver? Could she cover for a ghost?

"Okay, Mackie," Rick finally replied, and chuckled. "It's a date. See you then."

She hung up the phone, topped off her coffee, and tried to ignore Bubba's stare. "Again, it's not what it sounds like," she finally cried.

"Bull crackers!" He was gloating. "It's just a matter of time. You two are perfect for each other." He sopped up the last bit of egg with a buttery chunk of biscuit.

Whew! He hadn't picked up on the "borrowed body" line. She stretched in her skin. It was a new day and a new world.

"Don't rush me," Mackenzie said, but she couldn't help but grin. "I've got a lot of things to resolve with Rick." The small matter of a ghost, for one!

"Everyone has things," Bubba announced. He tore out one of the want ads and jammed it in his pocket. "They get married, have kids, and work it out. Time you joined the crowd."

* * *

Researching Falah was a challenge. Near the end of the day, Mackenzie slipped into the museum's small library with its Internet access to primary resources. A stolen hour away from the demands of the Pompeii opening was all that she could spare for the time being. But, when her wrist alarm sounded sixty minutes later, she hadn't made much headway. Her sketchy notes amounted to nothing better than guesswork. Falah's fate was as elusive as ever.

She logged off the computer and reread her notes, scowling as she bent over the pad.

"That bad?" Jeremy Hargrove asked.

The interruption startled her, which was deliberate. Hargrove stood at the entrance to the library, a noiseless, colorless creature devoid of much presence. For all his wealth, her nemesis lacked style and wore gray exclusively. It matched his watery eyes and the pallor of his paper-thin skin.

"Dr. Hargrove," Mackenzie said in measured tones. "Are you looking for someone?"

They weren't friends or colleagues, not after the witch-hunt, but by all standards they were peers. They were on opposite ends of their circle of acquaintance, and Mackenzie allowed the gray man wide berth whenever they came into contact.

"You've been reading my book, I see," Hargrove replied.

Mackenzie frowned and took in her surroundings. The prop for her notepad, chosen purely by accident, was Hargrove's book. It lay open beneath the pad and index cards that had fallen from her lap.

"You are mistaken," she returned. She didn't bother to explain. Words were wasted on the man. His ego couldn't absorb challenge, rejection, or explanation, any more than flat-out "no."

Hargrove leaned into the library—not really stepping in,

but hovering. It was close enough for her taste. She folded her arms and waited.

Oblivious, he continued. "I'm flattered that you picked up my book. I'd be glad to sign your copy."

Perhaps Hargrove couldn't help the leer. Muscles in his face tugged in odd ways and hinted at dental problems; root canals or bridges or both. Still, a leer was a leer.

"How may I help you?" she persisted. "I'm busy, as you can see."

A man carved from stone would have taken the hint. Unfortunately, Hargrove wasn't stone; he was made of denser stuff. He didn't back off or excuse himself. Instead, he advanced into the room, first with his long thin leg and followed by his lanky body.

It was futile to remind him that he was in a staff-restricted area. He moved at will, often without regard for others, always with purpose. This encounter wasn't accidental. He had sought her out.

Mackenzie calmly collected her notes and stood up. She didn't trust the gray man. What was he up to?

He circled the library table, easing past chairs and book stacks like a silent storm cloud. He'd penetrated her buffer zone—something she'd survive, she hoped—and pressed forward almost within reach.

Mackenzie had two choices: stand her ground or retreat. Retreat wasn't an option, not for a true daughter of Texas.

Her favorite pen slipped out of the papers she clasped to her chest and hit the carpeted floor with a dull thud. It landed between them, in no-man's land as far as she was concerned.

"Allow me," Hargrove said, his hand sweeping forward, ready to scoop up the pen and deliver it.

"No, thank you," Mac snapped with the crisp finality of a Marine. It was an old joke among the female grad students: *Watch out for Hargrove.* Having heard the stories and now imagining his imminent lame attempts to cop feels and brush flesh against flesh, she was well warned.

She kept watch and kept clear. She held her ground. Hargrove froze just inches away from her hand.

But he hadn't been stalled by her firm rejection; something else had triggered alarm in the gray man—something or someone that all sane mortals feared. An enraged and powerful male.

Shadowed and surly, the shape loomed behind Hargrove in the doorway. Its low growl warned off the world and set Jeremy Hargrove trembling.

"Touch her and you're a dead man," the shape said.

"Mason?" Hargrove cried. He spun around, collided with a wall of books, and squeaked with pain. "Something amiss?"

"Step away from her. Now." It looked like Rick standing in the doorway but it didn't sound like him.

Mackenzie realized in a heartbeat that something was amiss, all right, and they were in big-time trouble. Even dense Hargrove was picking up something on his scanners. She didn't say a word. She just moved, fast, stepping between Hargrove and Rick before the personality possessing him took action that warranted a string of assault charges and jeopardized a professional relationship.

"Look at this, Rick. Bedouin artifacts." Mackenzie thrust her sheaf of notes into Rick's hands. "Pots and tools unearthed in the twenties." She was babbling, thinking quick and making it up as she flipped through pages of her scribbling and stabbed at some text halfway down one page. "Part of the French expedition. I've noted the source."

The room reeked of brimstone. Rick, or rather Dak, circled Hargrove like a lion cornering his prey.

Fortunately, Hargrove was too distracted to notice. Mentioning a fake project had intrigued him, had appealed to his penchant for scooping other academics. This was something he hadn't heard anything about. His mouth hung open.

"Bedouins? Another project, Mason? Something you'd like to share?"

"It's mine, really," Mackenzie interrupted. She stabbed at the paper again, forcing Rick or Dak or whoever was in his body at the moment to look away from Hargrove. "Maritime, Rick. Anchors, keels, and casks."

Her voice shook, threatening to betray her ruse. She was bad at lying and worse at the spur of the moment tactics she was attempting, but they seemed her only hope. Yeah, artifacts. That was the ticket. She was relying on Rick's single-minded obsession with artifacts to rouse the real Rick Mason and displace the ancient Roman in his body, intent on bodily harm to Jeremy Hargrove. As much as she would secretly like to see bodily harm to Jeremy Hargrove.

"Ship keels? In Turkey?" Rick asked. "Not Savaion's Black Sea excavation. He's a damned fool if he's pushing that Bedouin theory again."

Whew! Mackenzie had reached him and stirred him to action. She nearly fainted with relief.

"Take a look. He might have something this time," she answered, and tugged him into the other room. Brushing past Hargrove in the process, she shoved him into the books quite by accident. Hargrove yelped again.

"You'll excuse us, Jeremy?" Mackenzie called over her shoulder. "I need to show this to Rick before the lecture."

"Certainly, certainly," Dr. Hargrove replied. He backed out of the library and rubbed his arm. "If you'll promise to share your impressions of my book when you finish."

Mackenzie smiled her most charming smile, the one she used for driver's license photos and to impress her dentist. It was a vapid smile of toleration.

"Shut the door on your way out," she said. Her tone finalized the exchange.

Hargrove cleared his throat and backed out, focusing on her rather than Rick. It was a minor victory for Mackenzie.

She sighed and turned to Rick. "That was close," she said.

Rick grunted. His index finger traced the text in her notepad. "What does this have to do with Savaion?" he asked.

Mackenzie grabbed the corner of the notepad, wresting it from of Rick's grasp. "Nothing. These are my notes on Falah."

"Eh?" he said. "They're pretty interesting."

"Forget it for the moment," Mackenzie cried, and punched his shoulder. "Are you in there?"

He nodded. "Yep, and alone again for the time being. What'd I do, by the way? I wanted to slug Hargrove, and he looked pretty nervous as he left. Did I hit him?"

"I wanted you to slug him," Mackenzie replied. "But, no, you didn't."

"I won't promise to be so smart next time, if he pops back in here."

"Me either," Mackenzie returned. She picked up Hargrove's book, hoping to charge the subject. "Heaven help us. He's in print again."

Rick shrugged, looking unimpressed. "Guy's got clout, a following, and full tenure at North Texas—something rare these days in academia."

"You know, he wants the job as museum director when Proctor retires," she explained. She scowled and grabbed her pen where Hargrove had left it, and clipped it to her notes. "I don't have much of a chance against him, I suppose. That's the part I don't get. He came in here to harrass me for some reason, but why? I'm cloutless."

"Not when it comes to succeeding Proctor," Rick said. "You're the top candidate. My guess is Hargrove's just trying to buy you out. What's your price?" he joked.

Mackenzie took a wild swing at him and Rick dodged it neatly. "Watch out, you don't want to get Dak's blood up again, do you?" he warned, grinning.

"Heavens, no! You've got the lecture tonight." Mackenzie checked her watch and yowled and raced to the door.

"Look at the time! I've still got to run home to change and pick up Mrs. Jay."

Rick whirled her into his arms and flipped the lock. "We've got time for *this*."

Surprising herself, Mackenzie didn't struggle. Her head and heart were still in conflict, but she didn't see the point in arguing with Rick when he was right. There was always time for one heart-stopping kiss.

Pete Proctor set the scene for the special lecture. The crowd attending the private opening of the exhibit was primed and Mackenzie was shaking like a leaf, but not because of the museum event. Rick would have that under control; even possessed, he was a pro. Mackenzie introduced him and slid away from the lectern. Gillespe followed her as she backed down the ramp and paused by the light and projector controls.

"I've got it, boss. Don't worry. I ran through the slides this afternoon. All he has to do is push the button and talk into the mike. It's a piece of cake."

Uh-huh. A piece of cake. Mackenzie didn't think she'd ever take anything for granted again. Still, she felt a ton of gratitude to the kid for bolstering her optimism.

"Thanks, Gil. I really couldn't do any of this without you."

"Is something wrong?" Gil was a little too perceptive tonight. If she wasn't careful, she'd have more than just the ghost and Jeremy Hargrove to worry about.

She said, "No, not really. Rick just mentioned he wasn't feeling well. I'd like to stay alert just in case he needs something."

"Really?" Gillespe watched Rick for a few minutes. "He looks and sounds fine to me."

He did, damn him. He looked fantastic, and she was a mess. Just great!

Mrs. Jay waggled her fingers and smiled. She'd made it! No hint of her recent foot disorder was apparent. Front and center, elegant in coral lamé, she looked like she was enjoying herself. Mackenzie silently prayed that the woman would still be enjoying herself after the night was over!

The house lights dimmed, the first round of slides cast odd shadows on Rick's features, but so far Mackenzie hadn't smelled brimstone or heard Dak's husky voice. Could she relax yet? No, not until the mike was off and Rick was on his way out the door could she abandon her vigil. She couldn't quite twist her trust around the ghost's promise. The sudden pop-in visit that afternoon hadn't exactly bolstered Dak's credibility rating in her estimation, even if it had been to help her out.

Gillespe slid down into one of the seats in the back row and listened to the presentation. Mackenzie couldn't manage it herself. She stood ready. Waiting for something that thankfully never happened.

Forty-five minutes later, plus or minus a minute or two, and Rick wrapped up the presentation. Mackenzie roused herself and nodded at Gil, who turned up the house lights. It had been a success. Nothing to worry about. A piece of cake. Right?

Right.

Mackenzie stepped out of Hargrove Auditorium, leaned against the credenza beneath the loathsome man's portrait and composed herself. Dak had kept his word for the evening. And, thus unfettered, Rick had presented a clearly entertaining and visually arresting survey of the Pompeii project. It had been professional, enlightening, and pleasurable for everyone save herself.

But next was the tour of the exhibit. This exclusive presentation and tour for the select membership was her final exam for the Pompeii project. There was no middle ground. It was pass or fail. Either they would love it or not.

Mackenzie groaned. She didn't want to go on. Feedback was important, but she really didn't have much doubt that it would be a positive experience. So, why was she nervous? Rick, that's why. Rick and his damned ghost!

Covering for Rick was costly. She knew she couldn't keep it up without someone, either Gillespe or Proctor, noticing she'd turned certifiably wacky. She didn't doubt that Hargrove was trolling for flaws or weaknesses, too—any evidence that the management of this Pompeii exhibit had taxed her beyond her capacity.

A quick glance at her reflection in the glass partition wall revealed a red blur. That's how she felt too. Hopefully her effort to disguise her discomfiture worked. Her sleek crimson sheath dress fit like a glove. And her new satin mules and the long single strand of pearls on loan from Mrs. Jay's cherished collection bolstered her morale.

As the audience spilled out into the foyer, Mackenzie mustered her best smile. Leading the crowd was Mrs. Jay, her arm linked through Proctor's, her flushed cheeks and twinkling eyes clear signs of delight.

Mackenzie ushered them all to the entrance of the Pompeii exhibit and held her breath. This was it. This was the first official tour. Tomorrow, the grand opening for the public would resemble a circus. But tonight was special. Never-wracking. Intense. *Intimate.* Rick slipped his hand under her arm and squeezed.

"Don't worry. They're going to love it, Mackie," he said as they followed the tour through the exhibit.

And they did. No one, not even Hargrove, complained. Everyone gathered around the elegant candlelit buffet after the tour, sipped champagne, and praised and applauded the staff one and all. Proctor preened. Rick gloated, answered questions, told stories, and grinned. Gillespe looked like a proud papa. Hargrove looked gray. And Dak looked absent.

It all pleased Mackenzie to no end. She excused herself from Mrs. Jay's conversation with Biddy Bidwell about silver patterns and sororities and slipped quietly to Hargrove's side. She waited until he'd tucked a cheese puff into his mouth before she cleared her throat.

Hargrove choked on the pastry. Mackenzie resisted the urge to pound him on the back.

"We didn't get to finish our talk this afternoon. Though, of course, this is not the time or place to discuss business," she said.

Hargrove stiffened. He glanced around the room; maybe he wanted an ally or a quick escape. She didn't give him a chance for either.

"How much?" she asked.

"Pardon?"

She turned and forced herself to look into his watery eyes. "How much do you want the directorship?" she asked.

Perhaps her directness stunned him. He didn't speak for a moment. At one time he had held her fate in his hands and nearly squashed her dream like a sad little bug. She could never forget his clever allusions, misdirected efforts, and the idle gossip that had spun a curious idea into a suspicion of grand theft.

"Is it for sale?" Hargrove hissed.

Mackenzie laughed loudly for the first time that day; it felt good to release some of her pent up energy. But the situation wasn't funny. Nothing connected with the man could ever be remotely amusing.

"It may be for sale, Hargrove," she replied. "But, in spite of your low opinion of me, I'm not. One of my friends seemed to think you wanted to buy me off. They were right. How sad."

Hargrove tried and failed to look unaffected. He tugged at his French cuffs, adjusted his tie, and managed a sneer that would have cast a shadow in a dark room.

"Everyone, including you, Mackenzie Cates, has a price. I'll find yours."

He pointedly turned on his heel and left her standing alone in the crowd. It was intended to be a grand gesture, but she inwardly chuckled; no one noticed or cared.

Fat chance, Hargrove, she silently said. Five years of suffering his snubs and jibes had inured her to them. Jeremy Hargrove might not ever respect her or regard her accomplishments with anything but disdain, but so far his opinion hadn't ruined her prospects or her career, either.

Gillespe skirted the table with the ice sculpture, balancing two goblets of champagne and a plate of delectables. "What did ol' Jeremy say to you?" he asked as he handed off one of the goblets and offered up a slice of smoked salmon and dab of goose paté.

"Nothing important," Mackenzie returned. And it wasn't important, she realized. She wasn't the same green grad student who had once hoped to earn back the trust and regard Hargrove's witch-hunt had eroded.

Gillespe swirled his glass of champagne and nodded in Rick's direction. "I wanted to let you know that I believe Hargrove's got it in for you. The thing is, I can't imagine why. It's like he truly doesn't like you."

"It's a story from my grad school days," she said and sighed. "Hargrove's got a long-standing grudge against me. But thanks to this job at the museum, he can't hurt me now. I've got Proctor on my side."

"What's going to happen when Proctor steps down? Are you going to get the promotion? Will you take it if it's offered?"

"Or let Hargrove buy me off?" Mackenzie retorted. Gillespe looked shocked. She mused, "Good question. If I believed Hargrove, he could do it."

"He can't," Proctor interrupted as he and Rick joined her and Gillespe. "You're one of the few people I can trust not to sell out to him." The museum director leaned in and kissed her cheek. "You'll keep this museum focused in the right direction. I'm sure of it."

Mackenzie blushed and nodded her thanks. "That's the nicest thing you have ever said to me, Pete. After tonight's success, it's like the cherry on the top of my sundae."

Proctor smiled and nodded. He tapped on his glass until he got everyone's attention, then began his toast. "There are a few people I want to thank for making this special event possible . . . ," he said. He didn't miss a single contributor, staff member, or friend of the museum. It wasn't one of his usual long-winded speeches, but by the time he'd finished and pushed Mac into the center of the room, she was more weary than grateful.

Mrs. Jay blew her a kiss, and everyone drank a toast to her. Mackenzie smiled. She had passed the test. It was her moment. But, even as she savored the acclaim, her thoughts were not entirely settled. She raised her hand and the crowd grew quiet.

"Thank you, Dr. Proctor, for your kind words. But I would like to thank someone else to whom I believe we owe an immeasurable debt of gratitude for truly making this exhibit a success." She looked over at Rick and grinned as she lifted her glass. "A toast—to the victim of Vesuvius, Mr. Pompeii. May we find out everything there is to know about him."

Rick winked and was the first to empty his glass. He wasn't alone at that moment. She didn't need the smell or a husky voice to confirm it. That faraway gaze was all Dak. And so was the smile of thanks.

Chapter Twenty-two

It was finally Friday. Tonight the exhibit officially opened to the public, but Mackenzie felt like she'd already won her Oscar and was indulging in the afterglow of a job well done. Three-dozen yellow roses had been delivered that morning, and two mixed flower baskets arrived at noon, but it was the bouquet of violets hand-delivered by Rick that touched her the most.

The two of them had taken advantage of their day off, and if the cool shade in Mackenzie's backyard, and had made a small picnic out of the fried chicken and cole slaw he brought.

Mac fingered the violets she'd used as a centerpiece on the cedar picnic table and laughed. "Hey, stop encouraging him," she said.

Both Rick and Sam her cat seemed to possess selective hearing. The cat had found the food spread out on the table to his liking. And Rick continued to indulge the beast's frequent requests.

"Hope you got some rest last night," he said as he

scratched Sam's head and sipped a tall glass of iced tea. "You'll need it."

"I'll be on automatic tonight," she returned. "I could guide those tours in my sleep."

"Well, I'd rather not make love to an automaton, so take a nap or something."

"Excuse me?" Mackenzie cried. "Is that an invitation, or a foregone conclusion?"

"Both. A little crass, but I'm sincere. Are you interested in cashing in your rain check?" He tossed a chunk of chicken to the ground and Sam chased it, abandoning his lap.

Mac scowled. "That's romance for you. How could I resist such a tempting proposal?"

"I've done better, if you'll remember. You don't always respond well. I'm just sending out a test balloon. Are we to the forgive-and-forget stage?"

She hugged her knees to her chest and closed her eyes. She didn't have to search for the answer. They hadn't talked about it together, yet; but she'd been talking to herself plenty. She'd forgiven Rick for past transgressions—and herself as well.

"I hear that makeup sex is pretty good," she said. She peeked between her lashes to check out Rick's reaction. It was good. The guy could flip a switch and turn dreamy and dangerous-looking in a heartbeat.

"Really? How about a sample?" he asked.

It wasn't slow or tantalizing. Rick punched the accelerator on her pulse with his first touch. The guy could kiss better than anyone else on the planet. Not that she wanted to test that theory anymore. He was everything she remembered, and a whole lot more. And this shady spot in her backyard now felt like it was a hundred and ten degrees and rising.

"Want to cool off in the shower?" she whispered against his lips.

"Thought you'd never ask," he returned.

"Last one in is a rotten egg." She danced away from his grasp and dashed inside the back porch, letting the screen door slap shut before he could catch up with her.

"Woo hoo," Mrs. Jay called from her yard. "That you, Mackenzie?"

Rick raised one brow and Mackenzie nodded. She poked her head out and hollered back. "Yes, ma'am. How are you today?" It was a formality, a southern thing one said without thinking. Mackenzie bit her lip but smiled, hoping the conversation wouldn't run too long.

"Oh dear, you have company," Mrs. Jay said as she rounded the corner with a basket of cut flowers. "I won't keep you. I just wanted to bring over my jet choker and earbobs as promised—they'll be perfect with your linen outfit—and ask a small favor. But I can come back . . ." The woman looked a bit disappointed.

Rick, the Devil incarnate, was tempting Mac with his eyes, his mouth, and his body to grab the jewelry and run. But, good manners and the image of Hell freezing over quashed the urge.

"For you, Mrs. Jay? Anything. Come on inside. I'll make us some fresh iced tea and you can tell me what I can do for you."

The invitation didn't ruin the afternoon, quite the contrary. Mrs. Jay's favor was simple enough to accommodate—Proctor's phone number. Mackenzie's old mentor, widowed for nearly a decade, was about to be added to the woman's list of eligible seniors. Rick nodded in approval. And while Mac made the tea, he and Mrs. Jay found common ground with their love of Italy and all things Italian.

"You wouldn't know it to see me now," Mrs. Jay said, "but at one time I was a globetrotter. I toured Pompeii probably before you were even born." She tapped her ringed fingers against the side of her tea glass and puzzled the actual date aloud. "Summer of 'sixty-nine or 'seventy. There was a quaint little pension near the Herculaneum Gate, and my room had the north light—great for painting."

"I've got a small apartment in an old hotel near there. It might be the same one!" Rick said. They compared notes, exchanged descriptions, then decided it didn't matter.

"I think I like him," Mrs. Jay said to Mac, and nodded in Rick's direction.

Rick returned the compliment. "If you get the itch to visit Pompeii again, Mrs. Jay, promise to give me a call. I'll set you up in my lodgings and give you the grand tour."

It was a casual comment, but it hit Mackenzie hard. There it was, the biggest obstacle to rekindling a romance with Rick. Trust—misplaced or displaced—was still at the heart of her grievance.

Rick was based in Pompeii. A long-distance relationship was impossible for her when one of them lived a half a world and umpteen time zones away. They could work together to resolve the bad business that had torn them apart five years ago, and the great chemistry between them helped, but nothing could shrink the ocean that would separate their lives. It was a fool's paradise to think that falling in love with Rick again would be easy or smart.

"Good gracious. Look at the time. I've still got to run to the market and bake some brownies for tonight," Mrs. Jay said. "It's my turn to host our weekly poker game. I'll make an extra batch and bring them over tomorrow," she promised as she hurried out onto the back porch.

"Whew!" Rick said after the woman was gone. "That lady's a whirlwind. A lot like you." He pulled Mackenzie into a quick embrace and kissed her nose.

Mackenzie rested her cheek against his chest. "What are we doing, Rick? It's one thing to kiss and make up. But there's no future for us. Not really."

"Since when did you get practical?" he returned. "It's not impossible, you know—other people have worked their problems out."

She pushed away from him and shook her head. “We’re going too fast, Rick. I need to think about this.”

“And maybe you don’t.” He cradled her face in his hands. “Look at me. Don’t analyze this. Just let it happen.”

This time, Rick’s kiss severed access to all reason. Mackenzie melted into him as he pulled her against his body. She wrapped her arms around his neck and hung on for dear life. She was slick with sweat and fainting with want. This time, they would surely make love.

But then, far off down the street, she heard Bubba’s rust-bucket Chevy backfire. Good old Bubba. Was he the answer to a prayer or a bad omen? At the moment, she felt he deserved to go straight to Hell for showing up on time for the first time in his life.

“Damnation, is that who I think it is?” Rick groaned.

Mackenzie nodded. “I can’t get rid of him either. He’s paying me back for some things with home repair projects.”

“Something quick, I hope.”

“Afraid not,” she said, and forced herself out of Rick’s embrace.

By the time her cousin had parked his noisy beast, climbed the back steps, and poked his head into the kitchen, she’d squelched the desire for murder. Rick was standing far, far away at the kitchen sink, dousing his head under the cold water spigot.

“Hey, Rick.” Bubba tossed his work belt on the kitchen counter. “You in the mood to pull up carpet and refinish floors?”

Rick groaned. “I had other plans, actually.” He gave Mac’s cousin a dark look.

Bubba’s jaw dropped open. He glanced back and forth between her and Rick. “You want me to take off, Mackenzie? No problem.”

Mackenzie was mortified, and she felt a blush spread lightning-fast from her head to her toes. “It’s opening night for the exhibit, Bubba. We’re both going to be busy!”

"But I can still come back another time." Bubba checked his watch. "I've got to run get the rest of my tools, and that'll take a couple of hours."

"No!" Mackenzie closed her eyes and counted to ten. She peeked. Both men were looking at her. "I'm going to soak in a bubble bath. Alone!"

Chapter Twenty-three

The circus atmosphere at the exhibit opening was a celebration Mackenzie could enjoy. She felt like she was floating on air. Nothing could pop her bubble of happiness. Dak wasn't possessing Rick. Hargrove was absent. And Proctor's praise was generous.

After her third guided tour in a row, she took a break and let Proctor do the honors.

"They love it—especially that strange female you gave a ticket," Harry said from his post by the metal detector.

"Maude's here?" Mackenzie asked. Rick had set up that pre-Opening tour, so . . . "I didn't give her a ticket. How'd she get in?"

A flicker of worry must have been visible in her expression, because Harry stiffened and quickly surveyed the immediate crowd. He suggested, "Rick must have let her in. They're over in the corner." He felt for his slimline walkie-talkie. "Is there a problem? Do I need to alert the other guards?"

Mackenzie watched Maude for a solid minute before

she shook her head. "No. The exhibit isn't in danger." But, she wasn't so sure Rick was entirely safe.

Maude still missed the mark on appropriate attire by a wide margin. A curve-hugging shiny blue bodysuit with countless zippers gave her a Lara Croft tomb raider look that Mackenzie instantly envied and despised. She hated the wig too, a jet-black ponytail with a three-foot mane that Maude tossed around like a bullwhip.

"Stop glaring at the poor girl, Rick's only got eyes for you," Harry said, and chortled under his breath.

It was small comfort for someone endowed with a smidgen of Granny Moon's instincts. Mackenzie inched her way over to the intense Ms. Kincaid and Rick, and was upon them before either noticed.

"Dr. Cates," Maude cried and jumped back from Rick. "Good to see you again. The exhibit is a success. I knew it would be."

The girl was babbling. Rick looked dumbstruck. And Mackenzie's bubble of happiness quivered as if it had bumped into a cockleburr.

"Ms. Kincaid." Mackenzie linked arms with Rick, intent on sending a clear message to her statuesque rival: *Off-limits. This man is mine.*

"I'm glad you could make it for opening night," she added. "I need to borrow Rick for a moment. Will you excuse us?"

Mackenzie tugged Rick beyond earshot. She fumbled with his tie and leaned close. "Watch out for her, Rick. I think she's after your research."

Actually, she didn't. Mac had eliminated that once she'd realized Maude was fixated on Rick, not data. But damned if she was going to let him think she was jealous when she wasn't. And she wasn't. Right?

Rick stayed her hand and pulled her palms together. "Hello again, angel," he said.

"Dak?" Mackenzie snorted and waved her hand in front of her nose. "Your brimstone cologne is a dead giveaway. What are you doing here? You promised you weren't going to keep borrowing Rick's body. Get lost before somebody notices!"

She glanced over at Maude, who was trying hard to blend into the crowd but failing: Neon blue jumpsuits just didn't blend. It had successfully attracted Gillespe, of all people. Mac made a mental note to warn him about strange females in skin-tight outfits.

Dak said, "Don't worry about Maude. She can help. And if you take me to Pompeii, I can help you research the records for Falah."

His aroma was attracting some attention. She backed him into a corner and tapped his chest with her finger.

"Negative on both counts. I'm not letting anyone in on Rick's secret ghost, especially Maude, and I don't need to go to Pompeii to research Falah. Besides, I can't go anywhere for the next six weeks, and neither can Rick. It'll have to wait."

"I can't wait," Dak replied. His eyes clouded. "I'm running out of time."

"It's the best I can do, Dak."

Dak looked past her and growled. Mackenzie turned and saw Hargrove. He'd just arrived, and was working the room like he already owned the place.

"If you blow this for Rick or me, all bets are off!" she whispered in his ear.

"Take me to Pompeii," he countered. "And let Maude help."

Mackenzie stared at him. Was he threatening or bargaining? With Hargrove in the room, she couldn't afford to take a chance on pissing off the ghost. She wrinkled her brow as if she were seriously considering it.

"Help? Are you sure about that?" she asked in her most diplomatic voice.

"Relax, Mackenzie. We're sure," Rick replied. It was his voice again.

Mackenzie gasped. The abrupt shift was enough of a shock to stop and start her heart. "Damn it, Rick. I'd appreciate it if you guys could work out a system. Can't you get him to ring a warning bell when he comes and goes?"

"Sorry. Next time our two personalities pass in the night, I'll ask him." Rick laughed. "Deal?"

Mackenzie shook her head. "Do I have a choice?"

"Just one. Your place or mine?"

"Yours. Let's go."

Chapter Twenty-four

It was a nice room for a motel. They wouldn't be interrupted. And they were consenting adults. But Mackenzie felt something was very wrong with the picture.

"So you're getting more comfortable with Dak inhabiting your body. Just how much information do you and he exchange when your personalities . . . bump into each other?" she asked.

Rick handed her a tumbler with an inch of golden liquor. "Enough. He likes you a lot."

Mackenzie sipped the liquid fire, one of the finest tequilas. It mellowed the edge of her worries and reminded her that a room with two queen-sized beds afforded ample space to stretch out and relax. She kicked off her shoes and said, "He's not too bad either. A little preoccupied with Falah's fate, and there have been a few transgressions, but otherwise he's someone who is basically keeping his promise. And now that we've launched the exhibit, I can try to keep my promise to him and find out what happened to her."

"What are the odds that you're going to find anything?" Rick asked.

Mackenzie had to shake her head. She didn't like saying they were slim to none, but that was how it seemed at the moment. Ancient Roman census records or histories weren't going to help. If personages weren't leaders, heroes, or notorious scoundrels, their lives and their deaths were lost to the ages.

"I really don't know where to start looking. My Italian is abysmal, and my ancient Latin—forget it. I've been able to translate some of the primary accounts of the day, but females are little more than a sidebar and often referenced only as 'second wife of Claudius Maximus' and never by name."

"So, you're not optimistic. Maybe we should take him to Pompeii and let him help, as he suggests."

"Don't worry, we've got other options. That's why I'm also working on our backup plan."

Rick groaned. "Not the exorcist!"

"You better believe it. I'm checking one out tomorrow and, if it looks good, I'll schedule a meeting for you."

Rick scrubbed his face with his hands and made a few choice remarks that she ignored. "You've got to stop this," he said. "Do the research but drop the rest. An exorcist? You're going to jeopardize your career."

"Like I said before, it's my choice."

Rick glanced at her. That dark look, the one that hinted Dak was in for business or possibly cruising the outer limits of the conversation, was apparent.

"You like him—Dak—don't you?"

Mackenzie didn't have to think about it. She nodded. "Yeah." Admitting it didn't change anything. She was still going to do her damnedest to exorcise him.

She watched Rick prowl around the room. He was flat-out wonderful to watch. If she could put music to the movements, it would stir up every beast in the jungle. It mesmerized her, called to her, and lured her deep into his lair.

"You can tell us apart?" he asked.

Mackenzie chuckled. "Most definitely. He's smelly, serious, and very, very mysterious."

Rick shook his head. "That's just great."

Mackenzie blinked. He was jealous? "Something wrong?" she asked. She reached out and stayed his restless pacing.

"Nothing that a little honesty can't clear up." Rick's jaw flexed like he was chewing tough leather. His eyes flashed like a stormy night. Heat sizzled from every pore, as though he'd harnessed the fury of a prairie fire.

Calm, cool, and collected, Rick was a force to be reckoned with. Enflamed by jealousy, lust, or both, he was capable of tearing away every shred of her reserve with a glance.

Mackenzie craved the man. Wanted to call him her own. Wanted him to call her his. This was the fear she'd toyed with each moment since he'd returned to her world. She couldn't play with this fire and remain unburned. To know Rick Mason was to love him.

Mackenzie backed up. She needed air to breathe. She needed time to be reasonable and deny her lust, to deny her love. Because if she didn't, she would lose her heart completely to the man.

"I want you," she admitted. Was that giving in? A one-night stand didn't mean commitment. She'd said that before, though she hadn't acted. They still had issues. Still, she wanted him, ached for him, and no amount of reasoning was going to satisfy her craving to finally dance one more time with this danger.

"You love me, Mackie. I know it," Rick said, but he didn't look too happy about it. Maybe he was reconsidering whether he wanted a second chance with her. Was it simply because she'd said she liked Dak?

"Maybe I do and maybe I don't," she returned. "You might have let me say it first."

"I've waited five years to hear you say it again," he said and held out his hand to her. "That's long enough."

Mackenzie was all he wanted in a woman. Steamy and sassy, prickly and funny, she'd proved she could roll with the punches and come up swinging every time. He wanted a lifetime to get to know her and love her. But because of one damned ghost, he couldn't even get to first base.

He'd tried to muscle Dak out of the picture long enough to intimately convince Mackenzie he was true blue and earnest. But Dak never checked out for long enough, and never when Mackenzie was around. Dak lurked, horned in, fouled up his moves, and drove him crazy!

Here she was at last, waiting and willing and he couldn't have her. Not like this. Not at this price. God, were they running in circles?

He'd invited her touch, but when she slipped her arms around his neck and pressed her soft curves into his heat, it was as if she lit the fuse to a bundle of dynamite. Her breath tormented his flesh, her throaty laugh unleashed a flood of desire, and her lovely sweetness—the pool of pleasure that she offered with every glance—was an oasis for his thirsty heart. But he wasn't alone. He could sense Dak, and that was enough to temper his ardor.

"Mackenzie," he managed through clenched teeth. "I've got company." He pulled away from her body, though regretting it immediately.

"Rats! I'm not keen on the idea of a ménage à trois," she said. "Can't you send Dak out to the movies or something?"

"No, damn it, I can't. He's only lurking right now, not trying to inhabit me. Maybe his outing at the museum drained him. But he could also be sandbagging." He tapped her on the chin. "You know . . . he's got designs on you."

"I don't like the sound of that, Rick. I like him, but . . . Can't we do something with him? I'm going to call that exorcist and—"

"We can take him to Pompeii," he replied. "The sooner, the better."

"If that will get rid of him, I agree. But we can't go now. We're both committed for the duration of the exhibit."

"Six weeks? I'll never make it. I've been taking cold showers since that first night at the Rib Joint."

Mackenzie laughed. "Sorry. I'm not laughing at you."

Rick knew all too well what she was laughing about. After all these years of waiting, two consenting adults couldn't consent because of an ardent ghostly chaperon. He'd be laughing too if he wasn't aching in all the wrong places with no recourse but another deluge of icy H_2O.

Mackenzie groaned and seemed to come to a decision. "Can't wait? Neither can I," she said. She unwound his tie, tugged on his shirttail, and pushed him down on the bed.

To Rick, this wasn't the start of anything new between them; it was the second act, the middle ground. The only problem was, he didn't yet know whether it was going to be a comedy or a tragedy. Too much about his plan to win her back waited upon expelling his ghost.

Mackenzie had pulled off his shirt, loosened his pants, and made her intentions known. When Mac made choices, she didn't do it halfway. If she was in for a penny, she was in for a pound. And that was the rub. His wonderful and deliciously daring lover was flawed.

In grad school, he'd gone nose to nose with her and never known her to back down. She wasn't going to back down on exorcising Dak. She wasn't going to back out on him. Sure, he appreciated that fierce loyalty, unswerving devotion, and relentless optimism. But those things came at a price that he refused to pay. It was simple enough: Mackenzie lacked common sense. She put herself in occupationally dangerous situations. At a certain point she put her heart over her mind. And if he really loved her more than he wanted to win her body and soul, he needed to leave her the hell alone.

No, as long as Dak leased space in his body, his career was at risk. As was the reputation of anyone fool enough to help. Exorcism? Damn the woman. If Hargrove got wind of it, her career would be permanently on the skids. Who would want a museum director who believed in or practiced exorcism.

"Are you paying attention? Or are you going to try and give me another damned rain check?" Mackenzie cried.

She looked magnificent. But he loved more than her packaging. She was an amazing creature who sang a siren song to his mind, heart, and body that no other woman could. And she was too damned wonderful to deserve a sorry-assed guy possessed by a ghost. Until he dumped Dak, he had to put her off. For her sake. And he didn't know how long that would be.

"I'm sorry to say, it's rain-check time," he managed. It was the first time he'd ever lied to her. He was saying goodbye—for how long, he didn't know.

He pulled her off the bed and into his arms for a kiss that was so hot it nearly scorched the wallpaper. It was torture to kiss her, and torture to put her off. And when she moaned and pressed into his body, his resolve allowed room for compromise.

Just a few minutes more, as long as Dak remained out of sight and totally under control, he could savor what he craved like water in the desert: Mackenzie, loving him again. And, for now, that would have to be enough.

Her kiss was a drug. Her dark velvet mouth opened to his questing tongue, and tempted both the saints and the devils battling within him. His resolve snapped. Kindling sparked, igniting a pyrotechnic extravaganza that rivaled the Aurora Borealis. The smell of brimstone filled the air.

"Hey, knock it off, Dak!" Mackenzie cried. She planted a fist firmly in Rick's gut and shoved.

Rick's eyes flew open. He could see annoyance in her face. "Damn," he mumbled, and backed away until she was beyond his reach. "No more fooling around, babe. Get me an exorcist!"

Chapter Twenty-five

Earth's Core: Day 235

"Dak and I have it figured out," Maude said between gasps. She'd just finished Charlie's stress test and chugged two flasks of his nutrition supplement without complaint. "He's going to get Rick to take him to the Pompeii ruins. We need to give him two or three days to get Rick there. Then I'll transit in and he'll show me exactly where he was and what he was doing the last couple of hours before the volcano erupted."

She clawed at her blotchy skin. Her body had finally adjusted to frequent time travel, and most of the usual temporary maladies no longer troubled her except for hives.

"It just might work," Charlie's assistant said. He unhooked her leads to the vitals monitor and handed Charlie the summary report. "A dry run will give her all the information she'll need for the actual rescue."

"Dak's idea is good," Charlie said. "We'll use the information you collect and download it into the Rogue who will take the mission."

"You're not going to give it to me?" Maude's breathing had eased a bit, but now it sped up again. She collected her empty nutrient flasks and stowed them in the service cart. She kept her eyes lowered, concentrating on the task and trying to manage the disappointment that tugged at her emotions like a weighted anchor.

"Look at her vitals, she's in great shape. I've never seen a Rogue recover so quickly," Charlie's assistant said.

Charlie glanced at the report and tossed it aside. "You're a great scout, Maude." He laid his arm across her shoulders and squeezed. "But you're not a killer. Dak's one of our own, and it's not going to be an easy assignment for any of the Rogues."

She shrugged off his arm. "We're not going to have to kill him, Charlie. Dak's plan will work."

"I sincerely hope so. But will you be able to terminate him if it doesn't?"

"You asked me that before, Charlie," Maude snapped. She wagged a finger at him. "Do you grill all the Rogues this way or just me?"

"Just you." Charlie grinned and held up a tiny purple tablet. "Stick out your tongue."

Maude frowned but complied. The tablet dissolved on contact, and within seconds her hives were in swift retreat.

"You did it!" she cried and hugged his neck. "Thanks."

Charlie's fair features pinkened with embarrassment. "It could be a temporary fix or permanent. It's not my best work, but you gave me a condition for doing the job. I'm holding up my end of the bargain. See if it works after A.D. 79 Pompeii."

"You mean it? It's my mission?"

He nodded. "It's yours if you want it."

Did she want it? Of course she did. She nodded, hugged him again, and swiped at her eyes.

Charlie's grin flagged. His buoyant personality seemed

on half-power and she guessed the full weight of saving the future was finally taking its toll.

"What's wrong, Charlie? Is it the rift?"

"Class-ten rifts are nasty," he replied. "It's tough staying ahead of them, compensating for errors, sending Rogues out half-prepped." He paused, swallowed once and cleared his throat. "It's tough losing Rogues, too."

She shook her head. "Dak's not lost. You'll see. I'll bring him home."

He nodded and sighed. "If it can be done, Maude, I believe you'll do it."

Chapter Twenty-six

Dallas: Saturday morning

Mackenzie curled her hands around a steaming cup of coffee and sipped as she scanned the online facts in her search for Falah. The early morning chill would soon burn off, but for now she savored the feel of the soft, nubby, oversize sweater she'd tugged on after her shower, and the warmth of the purring cat snoozing in her lap.

Her night with Rick hadn't ended with a romp in the hay. But she wasn't complaining. Rick's safe compromise had been a healthy dose of brain sex. They'd ordered pizza, a pay-per-view movie, and talked through the night about everything and anything including the Savaion expedition and Hargrove's penchant for gray. All the while, Dak had continued to lurk like a wedding guest who'd overstayed his welcome.

Finally, at dawn, Rick had thrown in the towel and dropped her off at her house. It was a break in the action, a breather between rounds, but she needed it so she could handle her top priority of the day: locate and check out available exorcists. Unfortunately she'd have to do it without Rick; his obligations at the museum included conducting another lecture in the series.

Another less-pressing priority was keeping her promise to Dak. After tossing and turning for a few hours, she'd given up all pretense of sleep and started this fresh search for Falah.

A database that included Misenum and Pompeii records had produced some possible hits; vague references to prominent females equaled progress in her book. She sighed. Dak was right. Ideally an on-site search would produce better results. But with the exhibit in full swing, a trip to Italy was out of the question.

The smell of bacon and eggs wafted into the study. Great day in the morning, Mrs. Jay could cook! Mackenzie scooped up Sam and dashed down the back stairs to greet Mrs. Jay and Petunia. While the dog and her cat managed a standoff, Mackenzie hugged the spatula-wielding Mrs. Jay.

"Can you join me for breakfast?" she asked and shook Petunia's leash.

"Oh thank you, no, dear," Mrs. Jay said. "I won the pot in poker last night, so I'm treating the crowd to breakfast at IHOP."

"Congratulations." Mackenzie toasted her neighbor with orange juice, and since the pug was leashed and eager, she started out the back door.

"You better marry that boy quick, before he runs off back to Italy," Mrs. Jay called after her.

Mackenzie glanced into her peaceful backyard. Birds swooped, a gentle breeze stirred the feathery leaves of the giant willow tree, and her morning glories were turning their blue faces toward the rising sun. It looked the same, but she wasn't. Yesterday she might have settled for one night with Rick. Today, she wanted more.

"You think he's a keeper, do you?" Mackenzie called back.

Mrs. Jay banged the spatula on the side of her skillet and flipped some bacon. "Don't wait for him to ask you. You're a smart girl; you've got him hooked. Time to reel him in."

It wasn't impossible. Was it? Mackenzie chewed her lip. "I think I might just do that," she replied.

With Gillespe's help, Rick was setting up the slide show in the Hargrove Auditorium when Dak bowled him over with a demand. *Pompeii! Now!* The urge to drop everything and comply was overwhelming. He staggered to one of the seats and sat before he fell down.

He glanced over at Gillespe. The kid looked like he'd seen a ghost; his mouth moved but no words came out.

"Are you all right?" he finally asked. "Boss said you haven't been feeling well."

Rick tried to laugh it off, but Gil didn't buy the lame jet lag story. He'd been back in Texas too long for that excuse to fly. "I've been feeling a little out of sorts since—"

"It's the statue. I guessed as much. There's something weird with it. Possession beats out the split personality theory I was working on. I've had some experience with this, actually I should have figured it out sooner. I dated a card-carrying channeler a few years ago."

Rick didn't deny it, but he wasn't quite ready to confirm the boy's guess. "Have I been . . ." He didn't quite know how or what to ask.

"Acting strange?" Gil finished for him. "Yeah. Boss, too. She's been covering for you, but that stench is hard to ignore."

"Brimstone?"

"Gawd, yes!"

Rick groaned and closed his eyes. The secret was out. How many more knew or suspected? He should have split for Pompeii that first night, and then it would have been only his reputation on the line. Now Mackie was involved, too. Damn!

Gillespe glanced to the back of the auditorium. "We're alone for now, but you're going to have to be careful. Hargrove's a snoop. This is just the kind of thing he's looking for. He can twist it and roast both of you—Proctor too, probably—and then offer to step in as director and save the museum from scandal."

"I can't let that happen," Rick said. He suddenly stood up and collected the loaded slide carousels.

"Unfortunately, this will be my last lecture," he said as he sorted through his notes on the podium and stowed them beneath the lectern. "I've been called back to Pompeii."

Gillespe nodded. "Sorry to see you go. How fast can you clear out?"

"As soon as possible after tonight's lecture," he replied.

Gil nodded again and offered his hand. "Good. Don't worry, I'll do what I can to help cover. But, maybe the boss shouldn't be here tonight. In case something happens. Try to keep her from coming."

Rick shook Gil's hand. He was a good kid. Loyal. Mackenzie was lucky to have him.

The exorcist wasn't a complete bust, but the fact that Ms. Lucy Skydiamond recognized her blew Mackenzie's plan.

"The exhibit is wonderful. And so realistic," Lucy cried. Her ethereal demeanor, a high-pitched voice with a breathless quality, and her drifting gaze were all a bit disconcerting at first. But when they got down to the discussion of exorcisms, Ms. Skydiamond proved to be a wealth of information.

Mackenzie made notes, asked questions, and kept the inquiry at a purely academic level. "So the nature of the haunting dictates the form of exorcism used," she repeated. "Take possession, for example. Would a general, all-purpose exorcism work?"

"In some cases, yes, most definitely," Lucy tittered. Her veil sparkled with each movement of her head. She listed several forms and general categories for exorcism, cross-referenced a variety of haunting, manifestations, and possessions, and supplemented the data with healing incantations and a recipe for a preventative tea.

"Is the afflicted dangerous?" Lucy asked.

Mackenzie pondered the question. It was one thing to conduct research; it was quite another to get right down to specifics—unless the possession posed a life-and-death threat to Rick.

"Can they be dangerous?" Mackenzie countered.

"To themselves and others," Lucy assured her. "But not every possession is evil."

Mackenzie nodded. Evil was something she hadn't really considered. "And if they are?"

Lucy sighed. "Then they are beyond my help." For a moment, her ethereal quality dimmed, and she fixed her gaze on Mackenzie.

"Take care, Dr. Cates. If this spirit is evil, you cannot exorcise him alone. Not even with pure love."

Rick had told her cousin that he'd help fix up her house, but Mackenzie found him and Bubba playing hooky in her backyard, lounging under the willow and listening to a ballgame. Next to a pile of carpet remains and cans of stain and shellac was a cooler full of iced beer.

"Hi, guys," she said, and dropped a lingering kiss on Rick's brow.

"Top of the seventh inning," Bubba said. "Rangers are ahead."

She nodded and fired up the gas grill. "Wash your hands at the seventh inning stretch and I'll give you some dogs and burgers to burn."

She stepped inside the cool kitchen and, pausing to lean against the door frame, watched Rick. Was he dangerous? Rather, was Dak?

Her visit to Lucy Skydiamond had raised the stakes. If

Dak didn't leave peaceably, she'd have to resort to drastic measures—something not easy to keep under wraps. Her life up until now had been an open book. People walked in and out and pretty much knew her business down to the last detail. So, a leak was possible. And if anyone suspected that she and Rick were dabbling in the occult, both their reputations would be toast in academic circles.

She sighed. Am I more of a handicap than a help, at this point? she asked herself. She shook off the possibility, and pulled out the meat and seasonings for dinner. Ridiculous. Rick needed her.

"What else did she say?" he asked.

After the barbecue dinner, their brief nap on the hammock had recharged Mackenzie's energy. But Rick still looked drained and surly.

His chest pillowed her head. She watched the lazy clouds drift above and told him about Lucy's recommendations.

"We'll need to use the appropriate remedy for the specific affliction," she added.

"This isn't necessary, you know," Rick said.

Mackenzie glanced up at him. She spoke as if Dak were listening. "If Dak doesn't leave soon, of his own accord, we'll kick him out."

"Courtesy of Ms. Skydiamond, no doubt," Rick snapped. He sat up suddenly and the hammock swung. He grabbed her by the shoulders and held Mac fast. "We're not going to sacrifice everything over this, Mackenzie. Not you. And not me. This has got to stop!"

She nodded. "Exactly! That's why I talked to the exorcist."

"No! Listen carefully. It stops here. It stops now. Or else."

"Or else what, Rick?" She didn't like the look on his face. Wrestling Dak for control of his body had taken a toll. The guy was exhausted.

"Nothing. Forget it," he said, and brushed a damp curl

away from her temple. "Tell Bubba I'm sorry I can't help finish the floor. I've got to get back to the museum for the lecture."

"Want me to come?" Mac asked.

"No."

She almost sighed with relief. She explained, "It'll give me some free time to look over the exorcism rites I bought."

Rick growled and shook his head. He stopped her mouth with one of his breath-stealing, heart-stopping, toe-curling, drug-addicting kisses. Then he suddenly set her away from him and stood up. He looked delicious and dangerous, and her heart flipped at the sight. Dak? Which one of them had just kissed her? Rick or the ghost? Good golly, she couldn't be sure; it had happened too fast. But she only wanted Rick.

"See you later tonight?" she asked, afraid he'd say no but half-praying he would. She couldn't handle being denied again.

"It's not a good idea, Mackie. But I'll call you before I turn in for the night."

She nodded and sighed. "Another rain check." This time neither of them laughed.

It was late. He'd waited to call her until after he'd booked a flight and packed. Her voice was husky with sleep, and he ached to join her in her big brass bed. Who knew how long they'd be apart this time? He didn't. It could be five days or five years.

He said good night and turned off his cell phone. No more calls. He couldn't risk it, not until he'd put a thousand miles or more between them.

He'd left her once, fool that he was. Promised himself he'd never do it again, no matter what. Now, his bags were at the door because of love. He loved her too much to stay.

Chapter Twenty-seven

"Mackenzie Lou," Bubba yelled from the kitchen door. "Get your butt down here, and *fast*!"

Mackenzie rolled over in bed, checked the clock—it was damned early—and searched for some sign of Rick. Nothing. Of course not; he hadn't stayed over last night. She only wished he had.

Grumbling, she grabbed a robe, hopped over the sticky hall floor and joined Bubba in the kitchen. Her frown evaporated with one glance at her cousin. Bubba's notorious scowl, the very one that scared babies and offensive linemen, was fixed in her direction.

"What happened?" she asked.

"He's gone, and I want to know what you're going to do about it." Bubba seemed to fill the entire kitchen. Hands on hips, broad shoulders squared, he was looking bigger than a side of beef. And the scowl. It all added up to bad news of a different sort.

"Who's gone, Bubba?" Mackenzie's gut twisted; she knew the answer even before she finished asking the question. "It's Rick, isn't it?"

"Who else? He was supposed to go to the lumberyard with me this morning, and when he didn't show, I called his motel. He's checked out."

Mackenzie grabbed the edge of the table and lowered herself into a chair. "When did you call?"

"Fifteen minutes ago."

Mackenzie dabbed her eyes with the sleeve of her robe. She remembered the night, the passion she'd felt, the joy and hope that had rocked her soundly to sleep. "Rick Mason!" She spit it out like it was coated with soap. "Damn your hide, you need me!"

Bubba's scowl disappeared. He pulled out a chair and straddled it. "Hell, honey, what happened? Everything was just great yesterday."

"And everything was hunky-dory last night!" Mackenzie snapped. "Except that he didn't bother to say good-bye."

She stood up suddenly and her chair fell over. She didn't bother picking it up. She didn't have time. She wagged her finger in his direction. "Don't you dare move a muscle. Give me five minutes to pack a bag and find my passport."

"But . . . ," Bubba called after her. She didn't wait to hear the rest. Eleven minutes later she was back in the kitchen and nearly ran into Mrs. Jay. The smiling busybody held out an egg sandwich and a post-it note.

"His flight leaves at ten-thirty-two. Here's the flight information."

Mackenzie blinked and absorbed the transmission in a flash. Bubba grinned and jangled the keys to her truck. "Ready?"

"Go on now; don't worry about a thing," Mrs. Jay said, and shooed them out the door. "Call me when your plane lands."

Inside the Willy, Mackenzie allowed herself a deep breath. She checked her watch as Bubba maneuvered the vehicle out of the driveway. "Stop by the museum. I've got time and I need to leave Proctor a note."

Her cousin nodded and switched lanes. "There's something else going on," he said, but kept his eyes on the road, "and it's not that old business between you two, is it?"

Mackenzie nodded. "Yes. But I can't tell you about it."

He reached over and squeezed her hand. "If you need me, Mac, promise you'll call."

She looked over at the man. He was the salt of the earth, a good guy, and a friend. This was what kept her in Dallas: Family. Any one of them would say the same, back her up, and hold her hand when times got tough. These were her roots, strong and deep, and the source of her faith that everything was going to turn out okay.

"Thanks, Bubba." She smiled at him. "I promise."

"I absolutely forbid it," Proctor railed. His mustache twitched and his barrel chest nearly doubled in girth. "This exhibit is for all the marbles, Mackenzie Cates. I won't be able to smooth it over with the board or keep Hargrove in check if you run after Mason. You can kiss your chances at my job good-bye."

"I don't have a choice," Mackenzie replied. "It's personal. And Rick needs me."

"Mackenzie," Proctor called as she turned away. "Come back here!"

She didn't dare stop. She raced back through the maze and paused at Gillespe's study area. She owed an explanation to the kid; she might have just tanked her promotion and possibly even her job, and she couldn't go without leaving Gil a note. She scribbled one and taped it to his computer.

"Mornin', boss," Gillespe said as he wandered in, balancing a fresh cup of coffee and a stack of books.

"Don't you ever take a day off?" she scolded. "This is

Sunday. Go home. Play, sleep, reclaim your life before you burn out."

He shrugged his shoulders. "Too late, this *is* my life now. What's up?"

"Read the note." She spun away from him, calling back over her shoulder as she raced down the hallway, "And don't worry about a thing."

Don't worry? Ha! Mackenzie silently answered herself as she climbed back into her truck and Bubba hit the gas.

"How'd it go?" her cousin asked.

"I might have just burned a bridge or two."

Bubba let off of the accelerator. "Are you sure about this, honey? I mean, Rick's a great guy and all, but are you really sure?" he asked.

It wasn't too late. She didn't have to do it this way. She could wait until the exhibit closed, take a leave of absence, and schedule a nice little trip to Pompeii to kick Dak's butt and stick a ring on Rick's finger.

"Yes," she said. "I need to settle something once and for all with Dr. Rick Mason. And if I get my way, I'll bring him back home to Texas permanently."

Bubba hooted and honked the horn. "That's my girl. Go get him!" He stomped on the accelerator again and Mackenzie held on for dear life.

Rick wasn't glad to see her when she checked in at the gate. In fact, he was downright ugly.

"What the hell do you think you're doing?" he barked as she settled herself in the waiting area.

"You know what I'm doing! I'm trying to save your hide."

"You're blowing it, Mackenzie. I'm doing this for you! This is bad news. I'll be lucky to salvage my own career."

"You're not going through this alone. That's my final word on the subject."

When airport security approached them and asked if there was a problem, Rick finally backed off. He was pissed, all right. But she was more pissed. Imagine, running off to save her!

Rick finally cracked a smile—he didn't want to laugh at the absurdity of the situation—but he laughed all the same. He laughed till he broke through Mac's own foul humor and she joined in.

By the time the flight was boarding, she and Rick had made up. And Rick had persuaded the gate personnel to juggle seat assignments and relocate them to the empty back row.

"You sure he's coming with us?" Mackenzie asked. She checked her seat belt again.

"Hmm?" Rick replied. He lifted the edge of one earphone. "You say something?"

She could hear the noise from his earphone. Count Basie compressed into a thin wire and squealing with static. She dug out her own earphones and plugged them into the socket on her armrest. "Are you sure he's coming with us?" she repeated.

"Oh, Dak's with us," Rick replied. "The message to get to Pompeii has finally stopped flashing on and off in my brain, but I'm sure he's around somewhere."

"I'd hate to make the trip without him," Mackenzie said. She tried on the earphones and flipped through the channels, frowning as she scanned the selections.

"You okay?" Rick asked. "Is it the flying? I thought that didn't bother you."

"It's not the flight." Mackenzie's face cleared and she nodded. She tried to change the subject. "I found it. Try channel nine. It's the link to the cockpit."

"No thanks, I'll stick to jazz." Rick reached out and took her hand. "What is it, Mackie? What's troubling you? If you want to back out, it's not too late."

Mackenzie closed her eyes. She started to shake her head but stopped herself and tugged off the earphones. "What's wrong? Okay, here's the shopping list: What happens to your job if the Pompeii museum catches wind of this? Is Dak being square with us? What does Maude have to do with everything? Did I bring the right clothes? And I'm not sure if I paid the power bill."

"That's it?"

Mackenzie raised an eyebrow and ruminated in silence. "Yep, that's it. But cross off the last one. I remember I paid the bill."

Rick grinned. "What about conducting an exorcism? No doubts about that? I imagine you brought the stuff—just in case this trip fails. Remember, you're not attempting to remove a spot off one of my suits."

Mackenzie extracted a sheaf of notes from her carry-on bag. Itemized and color-coded, the mode—or rather modes—of exorcism were prioritized and annotated.

"I've got all my bases covered," she said.

"You're kidding." Rick blanched at the sheer volume of research the pages of text represented. Mackenzie wasn't smug about the effort; in fact, she felt rather sheepish. "I only got a chance to do one dry run with Lucy Skydiamond," she explained.

"Ah yes, the bonafide exorcist." Rick struggled to keep a straight face and failed miserably.

Mackenzie confiscated her notes from Rick's clenched fist and tucked them away. "She's a third-generation exorcist. Madame Beefcake recommended her because she's also a past-life regressionist." She paused in her tucking and nesting and glanced over at Rick. "What?"

Rick looked stunned. "How do you do it? Is there any unturned rock, overlooked theory, or banshee or spirit guide you failed to contact?"

"Well, certainly. I had to be selective. No sense in fooling around with ectoplasm studies and the like. I narrowed the field to purges, extractions, and protective blessings and blisters."

"Blisters?" Rick must have swallowed the wrong way. His fit of coughing prevented any further exchange of facts for a few moments. When the wheezing finally subsided, she patted his hand.

"Don't worry, Rick. If I have to, I can do it. I'll make Dak an offer he can't refuse."

"Just answer me one thing," Rick managed to croak between gasps. "Will I have any dignity left when you're done?"

Mackenzie's grin must have triggered a relapse. She rolled her eyes and slapped Rick on the back several times.

"Pardon me." A man shouldering an oversize backpack down the aisle tugged off his shades and grinned. "I believe that's my seat." He pointed to the vacant spot next to Mackenzie.

"Gillespe?" Rick snapped between gasps for air. He didn't move to accommodate the youth. "What the hell are you doing here?"

"I believe it's obvious," Gillespe replied. "Excuse me, won't you? They won't push away from the gate until all the passengers are buckled up."

"You're not going with us," Mackenzie returned. "Three's a crowd, Gil. Go home."

"Sorry, boss. Can't oblige you at the moment." Gillespe stowed his baggage in the nearest available overhead bin and climbed over knees and feet to settle into the window seat. "Get comfortable," he said as soon as his fanny hit the seat cushion. "It's a long flight to Rome."

Rick and Mackenzie exchanged glances. "What do you want to do?" Rick asked. "Ditch him here or in Rome?"

The plane jerked as the DC-10 pushed away from the gate. "I suggest Rome," Gillespe said.

Mackenzie groaned. She was on a mission, and nothing and no one was going to foul it up.

"I take it Pompeii is our final destination." Gillespe said.

"You're not invited," Mackenzie returned. She folded her arms and looked straight ahead, focusing on the air-crew's safety briefing.

Gillespe shook his head. "I beg to differ," he said. His countenance darkened a bit as if a storm cloud passed overhead and sobered his youthful exuberance. "By the way, just who is this Dak character I'm hearing so much about?"

Chapter Twenty-eight

Rome: Monday afternoon

"I don't trust him. He's a wild card," Mackenzie whispered. Just why she whispered, Mackenzie couldn't say. Both Rick and Gillespe leaned in to hear.

The corner restaurant afforded a view of the midday sun and traffic, both foot and motorized. Noise bounced off every surface. Dishes in the kitchen, boisterous patrons at neighboring tables, horns honking, music, and Gillespe's constant chatter drowned out all normal speech. Mackenzie's whispers were lost in the wind.

"Who?" Gillespe asked. "Me?"

Mackenzie cast a furtive glance to her left and right. "No. Well, yes, I don't trust you. But, no, I'm not referring to you at the moment."

Gillespe grinned. "I knew this would be a blast. What's up? Who are we dodging? Dak?"

"I agree," Rick added. "I don't trust him either. Why did he invite Gillespe?"

"Dak?" Gillespe repeated.

"I've got a few ideas on that score," Mackenzie replied.

"I do too," Gil said. "I've seen the *Legend of Hell House* seventeen times. And one of my old girlfriends dabbled in the black arts."

Mackenzie rolled her eyes and groaned. She twisted more pasta around her fork and levered it into her mouth, then chewed. She wasn't even hungry. A bottle of house Chianti and two platters of linguini filled every hollow in her body, but the act of chewing occupied her mouth. She didn't dare say more in front of Gillespe or Dak. Not yet. The flight, the meal, and her out-of-sync body clock complicated her ability to reason. Instinct and emotion ruled for the moment. And she wanted to hit Gillespe with the nearest weapon. She eyed a basket of bread and considered pelting him with the contents.

Her wicked smile must have hinted at the mischief stirring within; Gillespe grinned again but said no more. He filled his platter with more pasta and applied himself to the task of refueling his well-toned physique.

"Wise move, Gillespe," Rick commented. "Keep out of this for the time being, and I might convince her to spare you for another day."

"Ha," Mackenzie returned. "Maybe another hour, but that's all I can commit to for now."

"Where is he, Rick? In, out, malingering or lurking?"

"Haven't got a clue," Rick replied. He seemed to struggle with his thoughts as though sifting through data. He shook his head. "Haven't sensed his presence since our plane landed. But I'm tired. We're all tired," he announced. "I suggest we get some shut-eye and digest the meal before we catch the night train to Pompeii."

Mackenzie sighed and nodded. Gillespe shrugged and bit into another meatball.

"Good. We've got a plan." Rick sounded relieved.

"Don't wait on me, I'll catch up," Gillespe said. He kept eating. "Night train to Pompeii, right?"

Mackenzie stood up. She looked suspiciously at the intern. The smell of brimstone filled the air. "Wrap it up. I'm not letting you out of my sight."

"What's the problem, boss?" Gil asked. "First you want to dump me, and now I'm on a short leash?"

"I'm not talking to you, Gillespe. I'm talking to Dak."

The youth smiled then—not the innocent, brash, toothy grin of a senior grad student but the seasoned smile of the dead guy with a penchant for prowling.

Mac clenched her teeth. "Explain it to him, Rick. Tell him he can't use Gillespe's body."

"Excuse me?" Gillespe choked on his meatball, seeming to come back to himself. "What's she talking about, Rick?"

"I don't know how he managed to swap bodies, Rick, but I don't like it. Gillespe shouldn't be subjected to this. It's dangerous."

"Handle what?"

"Quiet, Gil," Rick said.

"Hey, what's going on?" Gillespe's mouth hung open. Rick picked up another meatball and popped it in.

"You sure?" Rick asked.

"Same look in the eye. I think I'd recognize Dak in a German shepherd. And the smell is the clincher."

Rick sniffed, then stood up and tugged Gillespe to his feet. "She's the boss, Gil. We're sticking together for now."

In their hotel room, thick drapes blocked Rome's late afternoon sun. The hiss of filtered air from a contraption anchored to one wall provided white noise, enough to allow Rick, Gil, and Mac to snooze for a few hours without distraction from the Eternal City. Rick, the last to succumb and the first to rouse, willed himself to adapt. Travel across time zones hampered some skills and heightened others, Rick realized—such as, talking to a ghost.

"Leave him alone, Dak," Rick said. "I'm warning you."

"What are you telling him?" Mackenzie asked from her prone position across one of the twin beds.

"To knock it off."

"Good idea. Also, remind him that we've got a deal—and it doesn't include borrowing another body."

"I'll tell him, but Dak's got a mind of his own."

"What do you mean?" Mackenzie returned. She propped herself up on one arm and looked over at Gillespe. Sprawled over the stuffed lounger, the intern snored, his face untroubled and innocent for the moment.

"Dak's on his home turf," Rick said. "He may abandon us altogether and take off on his own."

"That's great for you and Gil, but it means we've unleashed a libidinous ghost on an unsuspecting population." Mackenzie half-groaned.

Rick watched stress settle on her features like a permanent frown. "Come here," he said and held open his arms.

Mackenzie settled herself against him. They were both operating on depleted energy reserves. They needed rest if any plan of theirs was going to work.

For the briefest of moments, Mackenzie gave in to the pleasure of welcoming Rick with every cell of her being. She savored the sweet taste of passion. Twisting and turning, she warmed her flesh with his heat. "This feels great," she whispered against his lips. "But, not with an audience."

Gillespe's snores intervened, and they both glanced in his direction. Mackenzie smiled. A pretzel looked more comfortable.

"How can he sleep like that?"

"Youth. Not too long ago we did the same thing," Rick replied. "Remember pulling all-nighters at the library prepping for the orals and trying to catch a few winks on the floor?"

Mackenzie laughed. "How'd we live through it? No

sleep, lousy diets, and lots of attitude. How'd we do any of it? The dissertation? The doctorate?"

Rick chortled. "You pulled me through. I had to save face. Couldn't let a female out macho me."

"We did it together," Mackenzie replied.

"Yeah, we did," Rick said. "Thanks, by the way, Dr. Cates. You saved my bacon back then."

"Ditto, Dr. Mason."

Mackenzie stretched and pulled herself erect. She looked over at Gillespe. "What do we tell him, Rick? Everything?"

"He's a bright kid. He'll figure it out."

"This isn't a course for credit. I need to cut Gil some slack. Forewarned is forearmed."

"Ignorance is bliss."

"Will you two give it a rest?" Gillespe asked, one eye open and fixed in their direction. "I know about the ghost in me. We're hitting it off."

Rick hooted. "I told you he'd figure it out."

Mackenzie frowned. "Are you okay, Gil?"

Gillespe snorted. "It's not too bad, but I'm not interested in offering a long-term lease."

"Good." Mackenzie relaxed a bit. "I've got a plan."

The intern looked interested. He unfolded his body and sat up. "This, I'd like to hear."

"It stinks in here," Gil said later that night. He glanced out the window, staring at nothing but a reflection of their train compartment. Inky darkness swallowed the Italian countryside as they sped toward their destination.

"That's just Dak's signature perfume. It'll fade in a minute," Mackenzie said. "What else did you pick up on when you switched bodies?"

Rick raised one brow as he watched the youth. Gillespe had been experiencing the state of possession differently than he had; except near the end when Rick had been seeing bizarre things too. Like a strange tunnel with white-coated scientists, and glimpses of Pompeii.

The intern's fair features furrowed as he bent to the task, struggling to recall any of the memories the experience had given him. "I don't know. It felt really hot. It was dark. People were screaming." Gillespe grinned suddenly and looked over at Rick. "And Falah. No wonder Dak has a crush on you, boss."

"I beg your pardon?" Mackenzie dropped her pen and stiffened her spine.

Rick nodded. He'd seen Falah himself. "That's true, but let's stick to the events immediately preceding and during the eruption. Did you pick up on what Dak was doing or where he was going?"

"Was Falah there?" Mackenzie asked, and turned to Rick. "If she was with him, she probably died during the eruption."

Gillespe shrugged. "I don't know. It's all a jumble.

"By the way, boss, you don't look just like Falah," Gillespe added. "But, Dak's got strong feelings for both of you."

"Thanks. She already knows all about that, Gil," Rick interrupted.

"I can't explain the similarity between you, but it's there," Gillespe continued. "It's one of the reasons Dak jumped into Rick's skin that first time. And it's probably why he's borrowing mine now. He wants you to keep your word."

She cleared her throat. "Trust is a two-way street."

"And then there's the other reason," Gillespe added.

"Which is?"

Gillespe looked to Rick, and Rick looked elsewhere. Neither man spoke and Mackenzie fumed.

"Don't everybody talk at once," she snapped.

"Mackenzie," Rick said quietly, and he took her hand in his. "He's borrowing Gil so we can have some time alone."

"Oh," she said. It was all she could manage.

Gillespe tried to whistle, study his fingernails, and blend in with the upholstered couches in the train compartment. Rick entwined his fingers with hers and squeezed.

After a moment, she cleared her throat. "Is there anything else, Gil?"

"Dak is getting weaker," the intern replied. "Maybe jumping into my skin zapped him, or maybe there's a time limit on his ability to interact with us."

"A time limit? Madame Beefcake didn't cover that. In fact, none of the exorcists I consulted mentioned that possibility," Mackenzie returned. She chewed on her bottom lip while she gathered her thoughts. "But Dak's distance from the exhibit and those artifacts might cause his weakness. Or maybe it's the first step in letting go—freeing his soul."

Gillespe shook his head. "I'm not an expert, but I don't think it's the same thing. Not if we're talking resurrection in the Judeo-Christian sense."

"Stick to the facts, Gillespe," Mackenzie replied.

"What facts, Mackie?" Rick returned. "You obviously exhausted the primary documentation on the subject, a great starting place but it's not the whole enchilada. There are going to be gaps. We're flying by the seat of our pants now. We've got to be open and let our observations and experiences guide us."

Mackenzie sighed. "Okay, okay. Start at square one. Remind me, what's our objective here?"

"To get rid of a ghost," Gillespe supplied.

Mackenzie circled it on her notepad. "Why?"

"Because he keeps borrowing mortal bodies," Gillespe answered. "And if we succeed, my guess is that he'll be heaven-bound. He thinks he's done unforgivable stuff but, heck, who hasn't? I bet he's a shoe-in upstairs. He seems like a basically good guy."

Mackenzie laid down her pen. "Good grief, Rick, whatever made me think this would work? I'm struggling to apply the scientific method. I can't dignify a boondoggle with graphs, charts, outlines, or hypotheses. I'm a damned fool for trying."

"Relax, Mackenzie." Rick squeezed her hand again and released it. "It's a leap of faith. We've come to where Dak wanted us. And you've convinced me that if anyone can motivate him to pack up and move on, you can."

"I thought I could too—until he complicated it by swapping bodies," Mackenzie returned. She glared at Gillespe. "Now there are two of you to worry about."

Gil held up a hand. "Hey, I was invited. Maude said that something was coming up, and that I might want to join her in Pompeii in a few days."

"Maude?" she cried. "I knew it! Dak's brought her in on it and now you're involved too."

Rick shrugged his shoulders and tried to laugh. "It's done now, Mackie. And I'll have to do some fancy damage control to keep my colleagues from getting wise, but I'm sure I can swing it."

His lips twitched. Mackenzie frowned. "Something funny?"

"Let's all relax," Rick returned. "We've been at it for hours. Put away your notes, Mackenzie, and give it a rest."

"You're up to something," Mac shot back.

Rick shook his head, then nodded toward the windows. "Ready or not, we're here. Somewhere in all that night is Pompeii. We've flown halfway around the planet to get here. But, I think we deserve a little R & R first."

"Great idea!" Gillespe chimed in. "Where's the bar in this choo choo?"

"Lead the way, Gil. We'll be right behind you," Rick said. He held out his arm to Mackenzie. "Angel?"

Gillespe didn't need further encouragement. He slipped out of the tight compartment without a backward glance.

The intern's departure didn't register with Mackenzie. She slapped at Rick's outstretched hand. "Get lost, Dak, I belong to Rick."

"Thanks for admitting it, but it's me. If he's anywhere, Dak's still with Gillespe." Rick chuckled and pulled her into his arms. "By the way, the kid's right—Dak is getting weaker."

The news lightened her load a bit. However, there was an odd tugging at Mac's heartstrings. Dak's cooperation wasn't a guarantee and she had to be ready, willing, and able to fight him for every inch of turf that rightfully belonged to Rick.

"Knowledge is power," she muttered like a mantra. It might not function like one, but it was a great reminder. Clean out the cobwebs. Shine light into the shadows. Her foundation was solid; she had a method for chopping down Goliath-like problems that never failed. Knowledge. One pebble at a time. She filled her imaginary sling with the first pebble.

"I think Dak's using Falah as a smokescreen. Why does he care what happened to her? They're both dead. Whether she died with him in Pompeii or twenty-plus years later shouldn't matter to a ghost." She stared straight ahead and tried to focus on the faded plaid in Rick's chambray shirt. Her throat felt dry.

"I agree," Rick said.

"So, what is he not telling us? It's something big. Don't you have a clue?" Mackenzie asked.

"I . . . It doesn't make sense, Mackenzie."

"So there *is* something," she yelped. "I knew it. You've been holding out on me, Rick. It doesn't make sense to you so you're dismissing it. It could be crucial information."

Rick shook his head. "It's too fantastic."

"Try me."

"What if Dak isn't from the past but the future?"

Mackenzie rocked back on her heels. *Nope.* Her mind wouldn't allow her to absorb that one. Of course, it might explain Dak's language proficiency. But a guy from the future dying in ancient Pompeii? Impossible!

"See?" Rick said. "Fantastic. It doesn't make sense."

Mackenzie shook her head. "Maybe not right now. But I'm beginning to believe that Maude is the key to this mystery."

"Which mystery?"

"What Dak was doing there that day."

Chapter Twenty-nine

Naples: Tuesday morning

Fortified with espresso, thick buttered bread, and slabs of succulent roasted meat, Rick, Mac, and Gillespe stepped out of the station café and squinted at the sun. Nothing ancient rose among the constructions surrounding the hub of rail traffic. This was a thoroughly modern city, and even at this early hour vehicular traffic polluted the air with noise. Mackenzie shook her head, bemused by the fact that rush hour existed here, too.

"Let me drive," Gillespe said as they waited for the garage to deliver Rick's car from long-term parking.

"Not on your life, kid," Rick returned when the sleek black Fiat pulled up to the curb. A stunningly handsome Neapolitan attendant handed over the keys.

"Buona fortuna, bella donna," he said, and helped Mackenzie into the front seat with all the gallantry of a subject for his liege lady.

"Get *him*." Gillespe grunted from the backseat as Rick pulled into traffic.

"Get used to it," Rick replied, and blasted his horn several times. He sawed the wheel to accommodate a moped. "Italian males love women, and women love the attention."

"What sane woman wouldn't?" Mackenzie said with a huge grin. Warm and content, the little bit of admiration from a handsome stranger had boosted her ego a notch or two. Sincere or not, Mackenzie adored the custom. "I'm not going to create an international incident by rebuffing hospitality," she added.

"He made moves on you, boss. Aren't you offended?"

"I'm getting used to it, thanks to Dak. He's a pro. Besides, when in Rome . . . ," Mackenzie began. She swallowed the rest of the quote and smiled at Rick's abrupt display of male pique, or driving finesse, or both.

Rick stomped the accelerator to the floorboard. His little car shot through the thick of traffic with both Mackenzie and Gillespe hanging on, grins plastered on their faces. Eventually, the vehicle emerged unscathed on the outskirts of modern civilization with the occupants breathless and laughing.

Rick slowed the car and downshifted. The vista silenced all in the car, ensnaring them at first sight.

Vesuvius. Quiet and serene. Lush with growth. Aproned with vineyards, it rose above the plane of humanity and welcomed them home.

"I feel like I've been here before," Mackenzie said. Her breath came in short gasps. "Wow, this is weird."

Lovely. Bucolic. A vacation mecca two thousand years ago. A vacation mecca now.

"Pull over," Mackenzie cried, even as Rick acted on a similar instinct. "Where is it?" she asked as the three got out and stood shoulder-to-shoulder, looking at the scene.

Rick pointed to an indistinct clump of color woven throughout the terrain. "Dak died there." He lifted his gaze and nodded in the direction of the harbor. "He could have escaped either by sea or on land, south toward Stabiae."

From their current vantage point, nothing revealed the

ancient carnage wrought by Vesuvius. Fertile soil had healed the landscape and nurtured new life both plant and animal. Later, farther along the roadway, other vistas would yield the heart of death where layers of time peeled back by generations of looters and scientists exposed the ruins of old Pompeii. But, for the moment, evidence of nature's awesome power to restore life humbled the adventurers.

"Where do we go from here?" Gillespe asked. "How do we do this, boss?"

Before Mackenzie could refocus and formulate a reply, Gillespe shifted gears and personalities, literally. He let out a great whoop, scrambled atop the stone wall separating the roadway and the sloping fields, and bellowed. Arms stretched wide, he turned his face to the rising sun.

"Pompeii," Dak cried. "Thank you!" He gestured for Mackenzie and Rick to join him on the wall. The guy was passionate. It was getting under Mac's skin, which was not entirely a good thing because she needed to keep her priorities clear. She was first and last Rick's advocate. Still, it was hard not to want to do everything possible to help this lost soul find peace.

"Hope we can help him," Gillespe said after a long silence. Mackenzie glanced at her intern, who was himself again. He was handling the ghost shifts well.

"We'll do our best," Mackenzie said.

"Time's running out," Gillespe returned, and glanced over at Rick.

"I know," Rick replied. He faced the distant horizon. Silent determination filled every cell of his body. He extended his hand and Mackenzie caught hold.

"We'll make it," she said.

Mackenzie hung out the window of Rick's apartment, leaning far beyond the thick sill and clinging to the ancient wooden casement as an anchor. "Rick, come look. Is that the Herculaneum Gate?"

"Just a minute," Rick hollered from the neighboring chamber. "I've got damned few modern conveniences in this joint, but hot water is one of them. I'm going to wash my face."

Rick's rooms at the pension were small and sparely furnished, but he had clearly marked his lodgings with his personal style and as a result the space exuded masculinity. Odors of leather, wood fires, and sandalwood permeated it. Books lined the shelves. A ticking mantel clock was mounted above the freshly laid hearth. Rick's stained and dusty excavation garb and tool belt hung from pegs on the whitewashed walls. There wasn't a flowered spread or cushioned seat anywhere in sight. And, thankfully, no hint of temporary or permanent female occupancy.

Mackenzie sighed with relief. Rebuilding trust took time and effort, but this was a huge step in the right direction. They were on Rick's home turf and this was her first glimpse into the life he'd created without her. She didn't belong in this world—yet.

The sound of moaning pipes and splashing water reached Mackenzie's ears. Laughter bubbled up inside her. She was delighted with the lack of modern intrusions. Doing without in old Pompeii inspired romance, stuff she desired when it came to the fine art of seduction. It was time to savor each moment alone with Rick. That was, if Rick ever got his butt back close enough for her to attack. They'd managed to ditch Gil and the ghost, and, she wasn't going to dink around with unpacking, checking lists, strategizing, or anything else that had to do with the rest of the world. She'd waited too long already. She had a plan for romance, and all she needed was Rick and a big fat mattress.

"Pompeii," she whispered, and hugged her shivering body. Leaning still farther out the window, she took in more of the city of mysteries.

Outside the small pension, the sky still wept with the sudden deluge that had been unexpected by all but the seasoned tourists and locals. Sheets of rain had effectively stopped all outdoor activities and forced friend and foe alike to seek refuge. Some huddled under umbrellas in the piazza, waiting the weather out and getting soaked in the process. Others fled indoors, to food, a delightful alternative to the inclement situation; *amore*, another. Rick and Mackenzie had done just that.

Gillespe and Dak were out there somewhere. Just where, indoors or out, Mac didn't care. When they'd checked the intern into a room down the hall from Rick's, she'd dropped broad hints and Gil wasn't stupid. He'd stay lost, hopefully for the entire night if he valued his life. All fear regarding Dak's motives and Gillespe's welfare no longer concerned Mackenzie. As Gillespe had pointed out more than once since arriving in Italy, he could and would take care of himself.

"Mackie," Rick roared. He lunged for her and hauled her back into the room. "You little fool." His hands skimmed her body in a quick assessment of her welfare.

Mackenzie grinned. Drenched and giddy, she felt no pain in spite of the fact that Rick's rescue had embedded wood slivers into her palm. Rick growled and removed the splinters with studied efficiency, saturated her wounds with peroxide and blew on the flesh till the tingling pain ebbed to a mild ache.

"Thanks," she whispered. She swiped at her dripping hair and soppy clothes with the thick towel he forced into her free hand.

Rick nodded. His eyes, serious and watchful, assessed her progress. "You're not making much headway with that," he said. He turned his attention away, suddenly intent on blotting his own wet figure.

She wrung out a sleeve. "This is hopeless."

"Need some help?" he asked.

Boy, did she! She nodded slowly, and Rick seemed to size up the situation and her intent without difficulty.

"You need to get out of those wet things before you catch cold," he suggested.

"So do you," Mackenzie returned, her tone husky and low, matching Rick's.

Rick chuckled. His emotions were visible. Nothing was impassive, detached, or even controlled about the light in his eyes, the rhythm of his breathing, or the blood pulsing through the vein in his neck.

"Don't want you to catch cold either," Mackenzie echoed. She tugged on one sleeve then the next, shrugging out of her sodden sweater. She dropped it between them. It was a gauntlet thrown down. A challenge.

Rick laughed aloud and reached for her. "Catch cold? Not a chance. I'm hotter than a volcano."

"Care to prove that?" Mackenzie returned.

She shivered as his palms slid over her bare flesh and skimmed her back, pausing long enough to flick the hook on her damp bra and release her breasts. Rick groaned but held himself in check. Caution? Restraint? Whatever stopped him, it was a tantalizing puzzle that fueled Mac's appetite for the man. His body couldn't lie. He wanted her. His jaw twitched. His eyes flashed. His fists balled into white knots of flesh and bone. Yeah, he wanted her.

Rick sucked in a breath. "Great day in the morning, you're gorgeous," he said. His lips twisted as passion flooded his features and filled his every movement.

"Thanks. Mind warming up this gorgeous body a bit?" she asked. Slow and purposeful, Mackenzie unfastened the buttons on Rick's soggy shirt and pushed the fabric aside. His chest radiated heat, steam heat. Mac moved against him and sighed deeply.

"Not a problem," Rick mumbled. His lips scorched her brow. If more words were said, they were incoherent. But

Mackenzie didn't care if he'd lost the power of speech; she was sick of words. She demanded action from this man.

"More," Mackenzie cried softly when he pulled back.

"I take it a soak in a hot bath can wait?" Rick asked as he nibbled her lips. He palmed her bottom and hitched her up against his manhood. Nothing disguised his desire, not even the thick soggy jeans they each wore.

"Later," Mackenzie returned. Pure emotion. Magic. Nothing mattered beyond this moment in Rick's arms. Not ghosts or possessed interns or mysteries.

Rick laughed again and twirled her in his arms. "I spent five years in exile in this apartment. You don't know how many times I imagined you here like this."

"Five years is a long time," Mackenzie returned. "We've both changed."

"I know." Rick raised a brow. "You got married."

Mackenzie nodded. "You bet I did. I tried everything to get you out of my system."

"And did you?"

She laughed and shook her head. "What's your guess?"

Rick's voice hummed with intensity. A deep growl reverberated from his soul and sliced through the words Mackenzie wanted to add. His gaze plucked at her heart.

"So you still love me?" he asked.

Mackenzie grinned and shook her head. "Not so fast, cowboy. You're going to have to woo me to win me."

Rick sobered. "That's the thing. I can't promise you a future while a ghost keeps borrowing my body. That's why I left Dallas."

Mackenzie kept the smile on her face, but a chill crept into her body that she couldn't shake. She was risking more than her job to be with this man. She was risking her heart. But she had no choice. Some risks had to be taken.

"I don't care about tomorrow," she said. "I only care about right now."

Rick stopped smiling. The jokes were over. This was

Rick the man; hard, lean, and hungry. And Mackenzie matched his ardor.

"You do love me. Don't you." He wasn't asking. He was telling.

Yes, she loved him, but her throat tightened around the admission. It was one thing to admit the guy curled her toes, but saying more would complicate everything.

"No," he said at last, supplying the answer himself. "I guess I haven't won back your trust," he said.

Mackenzie reached out and touched his bare shoulder. A few words between them and everything would change. She needed to savor the sensations and move slowly into this place of no return.

"Almost," she whispered as she pushed herself into his gentling embrace and touched his cheek with her lips.

"One day I will," he promised.

The second of silence between them seemed like an eternity. Mackenzie met Rick's fiery gaze with her own look of fevered intensity, and then they fell together in a violent embrace, their lips searching and meeting in a frenzied kiss. Their hands explored each other's body; hard, eager fingers skimming over offending clothes and slipping beneath to stroke tender flesh.

Mac ran her fingers across his abdomen, and under the edge of his jeans, and thrilled to the feel of the warm skin that flexed from her touch. She discarded every hindrance to contact, kicking aside blue jeans and modesty with reckless abandon.

"Now. Love me, Rick," she whispered. She led him to the bed and fell back against the mattress.

"I do," he returned. The darkness of his tone slid between them. He knew this wouldn't completely win her back; his eyes told her he knew.

Still, he was aroused by the sight of her willing, waiting. He eased his body down on hers. It was a torturous pace that maddened Mackenzie's thirst for his claim.

"But?" she returned. She gave a gasp of surprise when he finally pressed her down into the deep hollow of the bed, the length and weight of his body molding to her.

"But, I think I'll sustain permanent damage if I keep letting you stir me up without jumping your bones. I need you now."

Mackenzie laughed softly. "Live in the moment, Rick."

He groaned and shifted his weight.

A ripple of delightful sensation raced through Mackenzie's body. Her banked passions flamed bright. She writhed beneath him. Her legs trembled. Her loins heated where he pressed against her, throbbing with a need that matched her own.

Rick reached for a foil package and tore it open with his teeth. Mackenzie shook her head. Rick ignored her protest.

"You're not ready, babe. I'll not bring our child into this world," he said. His voice was a soft growl edged with passion and pain. "Not yet."

She watched his eyes. The pain there was deep and of her own doing. It mirrored Mac's own. Her grief was short lived, though. Rick captured her lower lip and gently teased the flesh with his tongue.

Mackenzie moaned. Heat spiraled through her from her core. She opened her body to him. Her wetness met his weighted member as he pressed against her flesh. Poised. Ready.

For Rick, this wasn't rekindling romance or reacquainting two lovers. This felt like the first time. He'd known women, known Mackenzie too, but this wasn't simply sex or lovemaking. This was like climbing to the summit of Everest and jumping off.

And Mackenzie was his guide. Slow and easy didn't suit her.

"Rick," she cried out.

"Open your eyes, babe," he growled.

Tormented and wild with need, she opened her eyes.

Rick drove hard into her body. Mackenzie bucked beneath him. They cried out in unison—a groan of intense pleasure, a moment of shared bliss.

Mackenzie's gaze held firm. Rick met it with a fierce hypnotic stare of his own, drawing her deeper into his soul, urging her to follow him. He eased out his breath and moved within her. Slow, deliberate strokes.

Mackenzie thrashed beneath him. She clawed at his buttocks, wrapped her legs about his waist and took him deep within her. She moaned each time he retreated, screamed each time he buried himself to the hilt and claimed her anew.

She pushed at him, rolling him over on his back and straddling his hips. "Touch me, Rick," she hissed, and pressed his hand to the soft heat between her legs.

Ah. Her soft moan, when the tip of her breast slipped past his bristled jaw, bent him to her will. Rick reached between their bodies, seeking and finding the honeyed juncture.

Rick thrust his rock-hard member upward, sheathing himself in her soft, hot body, again and again. And with each stroke, she shuddered with pleasure and pulsed against his fingertips, straining to meet his touch.

"God, babe," Rick groaned. "I love you."

The rumble in his lungs matched Mackenzie's gasps for air. Her cries, her nails biting into his flesh as she rode him, urged Rick to keep pace. Her thrusting hips, her pulsing core slick and hot—Rick rose up to meet her, matching her desire.

The heady scent of passion swirled about the room. Rick's groans responded to Mackenzie's own. Intoxicating cries of need, wrung from the deepest parts of their bodies—mated, harmonized—gave voice to the white-hot pleasure mounting between them.

Mackenzie stopped. Seized by a stunning climax to their

furious joining, she hung there, breathless, near pure bliss. Rick joined her. In one final blinding stroke he plunged them both over the edge and into a whirlwind of ecstasy. She fell against him, her limbs liquid, her body spent and satiated.

She opened her eyes and met Rick's brilliant gaze. They touched fingertips and laughed, sharing in that single moment of unfettered peace when two hearts could bond as one.

"Now *that*'s what I call great make-up sex," she finally said when she found the energy.

"So, we've made up? I'm forgiven?" He watched her and waited.

She shrugged and grinned. "Sure looks like it."

The truth was, this was everything she wanted. She'd fought it so long. But now, trust or no trust, Mackenzie couldn't and wouldn't deny the completeness Rick brought to her soul. And if they couldn't make it work out between them—if he left her life and world forever, for whatever reason—Mackenzie accepted that she had invited and allowed this man to possess her. And he would possess her until the end of time.

"I'm not convinced," Rick mumbled against her neck. "Let's try again until I am."

Mackenzie laughed. And, for the rest of the day, she applied herself to the task with diligence.

Chapter Thirty

Pompeii: Wednesday morning

They sat around the table and stared into their steaming cups, silence and companionship bonding them in the center of the busy café. Each face was flushed and bright-eyed with life. Well-exercised, well-rested, and now well-fueled with the delights of prosciutto and oven-fresh bread, the three adventurers leaned on their elbows and savored their thick black espressos.

"Well, say it," Gillespe demanded. "Get it over with. Chew me out."

"You're doing fine on your own. Keep going," Mackenzie suggested. "If you feel it's necessary."

"Of course it is," Gillespe said, looking from his boss to Rick and back again. "Isn't it?"

Rick lifted his cup and sipped. He raised a brow in Mackenzie's direction.

"Thanks for not sending out a search party," Gillespe admitted. "I told you I could take care of myself." After a moment, a low chuckle rounded out his statement.

Mackenzie busied herself with dabbing at a fresh spill in her saucer. Rick contributed his napkin when she sloshed the remaining contents of her cup a few seconds later; her fingers having gone suddenly slack and rubbery from a slight brush of his thigh against hers. Her skin heated where the soft weave of her silk sweater teased her wrists. Her pulse jumped when Rick covered her hand with his.

"Want another?" he asked. He might have meant another coffee, but it didn't matter. The casual query triggered an explosion of desire within Mackenzie. Yes, she wanted *another*—another night in his arms, another kiss from his lips, another taste of the passion that fed her ravenous soul.

"I do," Gillespe spoke up, and he waved fingers at the curvaceous beauty behind the serving counter. "Gina. *Caffé per favore*."

Mackenzie shook her head and reluctantly slipped her hand from Rick's. "I better not, I'm already beyond my limit for the week."

"We're living dangerously. Remember?" Rick said. "When in Rome . . ."

"Exactly," Gillespe chimed in, and ordered three more shots from the buxom Gina.

Gillespe introduced the waitress like they were old friends. Mackenzie guessed that in many ways they already were, even though Gil hadn't been in the country long. There was an easy familiarity to their interaction.

And, lush in all the right places, Gina flaunted her endowments, something the males at Mackenzie's table appreciated in silence. They turned to watch every roll of her hip and swish of her skirt as she returned to the counter.

"Boys?" Mackenzie said and cleared her throat. "Hello?"

"Wow. She looks even better in daylight," Gillespe said as he turned back. He chuckled again.

"Don't even think about sharing the intimate details," Mackenzie said. "I don't want to know."

Gillespe blushed. "It's not what you think, boss. We went out together last night, but I didn't *do* anything." He managed to assume a modicum of innocence. "And I'm pretty sure Dak didn't either."

Mackenzie held up a hand. "Not another word."

Rick grinned and folded his arms across his chest. "If you 'didn't,' and 'Dak didn't,' what in blazes were you just about to confess, Gillespe?"

"You thought I meant *that?*" The intern hooted and slapped his leg, nearly tipping over his chair. "Well, we tried—at least I did—but didn't get anywhere. Then Dak wanted to go back and . . ." Gillespe stopped and shrugged his shoulders. "I couldn't think of a reason not to go."

Mackenzie swung around on Rick. "Gillespe is a talker, if you haven't already guessed. He might benefit from one of your lectures on clear and concise communication." She heaved a great sigh and wagged a finger at Gil.

"Get to the point but spare me the details. Where did you go?"

"To where he died."

"To the dig? You went into the dig site alone?" Mackenzie asked.

Rick waved off the question. "What happened?"

Gillespe shrugged his shoulders again, but his eyes seemed brighter, awash with excess moisture. "Weird stuff."

Mackenzie reached out and touched the boy's arm. "You shouldn't have gone alone."

"He was there, you know. A copy of his body cast. Your mold is good, Rick, it looks just like the original." Gillespe paused and cleared his throat. "I've seen death masks before, but not with the ghost of the guy looking back at me. Dak got spooky. I got spooky. Guess I didn't know exactly who was who anymore, at least for a few minutes. I might have blacked out, and I think that's when he took off."

"Took off? Where?" Mackenzie's grip on Gillespe's

arm tightened. Could it be as simple as that? Had he only wanted to come back here? Had all her preparations for an exorcism been unnecessary? She hoped so.

But what about Falah?

"I don't know," Gillespe replied.

Rick shook his head. "I haven't picked up any vibes from him."

Mackenzie released Gillespe and folded her arms about her shoulders, hugging herself as if suddenly chilled. Damn, this was a surprise. She'd wanted him gone—hadn't she?

"You think he's permanently gone?" she asked.

Gillespe laughed out loud. "Not a chance, boss. I'm pretty sure he'll be back. He wanted to give you two some space, remember. I thought it was a good idea too, what with all those hints you were dropping. Three's a crowd."

"Good grief," Mackenzie groaned. Embarrassed from head to toe, she accepted a fresh cup of espresso from Gina and focused on bringing it to her lips without spilling again.

"Thanks," Rick added.

Not a sign of regret plagued his features, something that eased Mackenzie's discomfort somewhat. She could almost look at him a full minute without going numb in her left brain. He made her think of sex, sex, and more sex, with only blips of rational thought.

"No problem," Gillespe said. He glanced over his shoulder. Another customer was getting a little too friendly with Gina. "Back in a sec," he said, and headed toward the circle of admirers around the girl. The curvy spitfire was holding her own with a local lothario.

"What do you think?" Mackenzie asked after a moment.

"I'm still not thinking," Rick replied. "My brain is stuck in neutral with my libido in overdrive. I want to lose the kid, the ghost, and jump your bones again, lady. It's been five years without you. A couple more days in the sack might take the edge off my ardor, but I doubt it. You're a drug."

Mackenzie laughed. "Glad to hear it. So are you."

Rick leaned across the small table and took possession of her lips, blocking out the rest of the world for a dozen heartbeats. Then he whispered against her mouth, "If I haven't mentioned it in the last five minutes, I want you."

Mackenzie's blush spread throughout her body and heated her to the tip of her nose. "Damned fine time to bring it up," she complained. "But tell me again."

Rick did more than that. He pulled her into his arms and tipped her back, settling a hungry kiss at the base of her throat. A roar of approval accompanied the move, clapping and cheering from several café patrons endorsing the act.

Gillespe returned, flipped his chair around and straddled it, his chin resting on the back of the seat. "So, you guys want me to cut out for another day, or what? I could spend the day with Gina and practice my rusty Italian."

Rick pulled back from Mackenzie's mouth. "Yeah, get lost for about a century, will you?" he said. He gave the kid a grin.

Mackenzie reluctantly pushed out of his arms, negating the decision. "Hold that thought, Dr. Mason. If Dak's still hanging around, we've got some unfinished business with him before we can get on with our lives. Time to visit the dig site and try a little exorcism. We're going to see that this guy goes on to the afterlife."

The sunny spring weather was warm enough to warrant shorts and sunglasses. Mackenzie had tucked paper, pens, and her Lucy Skydiamond notes into her shoulder bag. Still, it wasn't quite how she'd envisioned her first exorcism.

Rick led them through one of the staff entrances near the Nuceria Gate—the most direct route to his archaeological dig site, he said—but their journey was stalled by numerous encounters with coworkers and site guides. Mackenzie didn't protest. It gave her a chance to gawk. She might be on a venture to eliminate a ghost, but this was also her first visit to the ancient Pompeii excavation and she was as overwhelmed with the experience as any neophyte tourist would be.

"Wow!" she repeated for the umpteenth time as they stopped again, this time at the intersection of Via di Nocera and Via dell'Abbondanza. She had memorized the maps of the ancient city, seen countless pictures of the excavated structures, and created an exhibit that simulated a streetscape on the day that Vesuvius erupted. Yet she was unprepared for the full impact of standing in the midst of the ruin itself. Left to right, ahead and behind, were countless buildings restored to their former splendor.

It was more than the gradual ascent over the deeply rutted basalt road with Mount Vesuvius looming in the background that left her breathless. It was the journey through time that her mind had taken; seeing the streets and reconstructed villas, baths and shops not filled with tourists but with the lost victims themselves. And with Dak.

"It's amazing," she cried as Rick concluded another greeting and took the lead again.

"You should have seen it at night," Gillespe confided in a hoarse whisper. "Really spooky."

Rick snorted. "I don't know how you managed this maze in the dark."

"I had help," Gillespe said, a little winded from exertion. "But I don't now."

Mackenzie stopped. She looked first at Rick, then Gillespe. "Still no Dak?"

Both males responded in the negative. Mackenzie stifled an urge to grumble. If the ghost had departed peaceably, left both Rick and Gillespe intact, she shouldn't protest the *faux pas* of his not saying good-bye.

"We're here," Rick said, and stopped at an entrance on the north side of the Via dell'Abbondanza labeled number six. "Ready?"

Mackenzie nodded.

"Lead the way," Gil added.

Mac slipped off her shades and stepped through. It was as if she'd crossed a portal of time and transitioned back to A.D. 79.

Once a thriving bakery, the first rooms they entered were thick-walled and gloomy with grindstones and baking ovens. Mackenzie paused and allowed her eyes to adjust to the light. It gave her other senses a chance to dominate. The smells of limestone, plaster, and mortar filled her nose. And, sounds—the muffled voices of other tourists passing by outside and the echo of water from the cistern in the courtyard—echoed in her ears.

Beyond the bakery was the "House of Chaste Lovers" and finally Rick's open-air archaeological dig site, from which the remains and artifacts had all disappeared save one. Dak.

The sudden sunlight was blinding, and the copy of Dak came into focus slowly. Vesuvius a gray silhouette behind him, Dak's stark white figure looked nearly aglow. As before, his mid-stride, mid-breath, caught in time body looked not quite claimed by death but no longer alive.

"Wow," Mackenzie said.

"And how," Gillespe seconded.

Mackenzie circled the ancient statue much as she had the first time she'd seen it. Taking in the details. Absorbing the wonder and the horror of a dead man she now knew as Dak.

"Rick," Mackenzie whispered. "You sensing anything? Is he here?"

"Oh, he's here, all right," Gillespe answered. "Can you feel him, Rick?"

Rick sniffed the air. The smell of brimstone was present.

"Yes, he's here," he said. "And I was wrong. His death wasn't easy or brief."

Gillespe shook his head. "It was like he was frozen in place."

Mackenzie and Rick exchanged glances. Dak was a riddle in more ways than one. A guy from the future dying in the past? Was that more believable than an ancient Pompeiian dying upright? No. But only one thing mattered now—freeing his tormented soul.

"That was supposed to work, boss?" Gillespe howled with laughter. "I've seen better hocus-pocus when my kid sister has a sleepover and they get out the Ouija board."

Mackenzie bristled and nearly christened him with her half-eaten ice cream cone. At the site of Dak's death, she'd conducted one of Lucy Skydiamond's classic exorcism rituals, not a raucous affair but something quiet and simple. And utterly ineffective.

Now, half an hour later, they were sitting in the amphitheatre, one of the many groups of tourists contemplating the pit designed for gladiatorial games, and combat was about to erupt in the stands if Gillespe didn't stop laughing!

Rick had managed to keep his own mirth under control, but his grin was irrepressible. "Let's give her a break, Gil, before she clobbers one of us," he said, and finished his double-dip chocolate gelato.

"That was just a warm-up, Gil," Mackenzie said. "The official exorcism is at dawn."

"Dawn?" Gillespe cried. "I have a hot date with Gina tonight. I'm hoping not to get *in* till dawn."

Mackenzie ignored him and continued. "Well, exorcism isn't our only option. If it fails, I've got a long list of other spirit-removing techniques. Plus, we might as well continue researching Falah's fate."

"Ah, research," Rick said, and chucked her under the chin. "That's my niche. And I know just where to start."

"You think it's a link to Falah?" Mackenzie asked. One of the other researchers looked up from his books and scowled. Libraries the world over were the same: Quiet reigned supreme. And the rare collections library in Naples was no exception.

Rick nodded. He held his fingers in three places in the old leather dictionary. Translating key documents had taken most of the afternoon, but by some act of random fate, a reference to a spouse of Claudius Maximus of Misenum had appeared hopeful.

"Dak seems to think so," he said quietly. "Just what it means isn't clear but Dak thinks we're on to something."

"Is he here? Is this enough?" she returned in a hoarse whisper.

"Yes, he's here. And it's not enough to send him on his way but it's a giant step forward," Rick returned. He closed up the materials and stacked the books.

Mac relaxed and rubbed the bridge of her nose. She'd been squinting at small fonts and fading texts for hours. And her grumbling tummy reminded her that their last meal had been a hurried affair she'd forgotten to taste.

"Come on, let's get out of here. They're going to kick us out anyway if you can't keep your stomach quiet," Rick said.

Mackenzie didn't wait to be asked twice. She packed up her notes and followed Rick downstairs.

"What's the plan?" she asked once they were in his Fiat and zipping back to Pompeii.

"Dinner, a good night's sleep, and a dawn exorcism, I believe," Rick replied.

"Oh yeah, the exorcism. Dawn. I said that, didn't I?" She groaned.

"I take it the hour is crucial?"

"And so is Dak's presence. Do you think you can get him to show?"

"Definitely," Rick replied. He slowed the car to take a sharp curve and glanced over at her. "He's inside me. And he agrees. But if I can't find Gillespe and pawn him off, he's going to complicate our sleeping arrangements."

Back at his lodgings, one whiff of brimstone and Rick knew Dak was in him for the night and he was fresh out of options. Gillespe had already been and gone and left a cryptic note telling them not to wait up—the hot date with Gina was obviously panning out. It was late, and the feather bed looked inviting. If only Dak would oblige him and get lost.

"Three's still a crowd?" Mackenzie laughed her slow, husky laugh that said more than words and weighted the atmosphere with promised passion.

Rick planted his palms against the small of her back and tangled his fingers in the soft fabric of her dress, pausing a heartbeat to master his desire. He failed.

"Mackenzie." He breathed her name. In and out. He said it again and again, absorbing it like a life force and spinning it out between them—the sound, the feel, and the taste of it weaving their atoms together.

Rick let air slip between his clenched teeth. It wasn't a simple task to make love to a woman with a ghost breathing down his neck, damn it. Possession wasn't too bad when Dak cooperated, but when he couldn't or wouldn't, Rick found it truly a pain.

Just how much space Dak occupied when in residence changed. But certain areas of anatomy and thought were definitely shared. It was inescapable. Dak knew about Mackenzie breaking Rick's heart. And Rick knew about Dak's passion for females—and that he'd finally found true love with Falah. It seemed at best a trade-off of memories.

He knew other stuff about Dak, too. He'd seen glimpses

of a future world, with concepts like time travel, people called Rogues, and rules to protect humanity. One rule in particular, "Protect the future from the past," seemed vital.

Did any of it matter? Could he use any of the information as leverage to expel Dak? He didn't have the answers, yet. But, he sure as hell hoped he would soon. The ghost had definitely overstayed his welcome.

"Lock the door behind me," he growled, and forced himself away from her. "Dak says he won't try anything, but . . ."

Mackenzie seemed to understand, and she didn't object when he grabbed a blanket and camped out on his sagging leather sofa in the next room. But, in the last moments before sleep claimed him, Rick cursed Dak for every moment stolen from Mackenzie's side.

Chapter Thirty-one

Pompeii: Thursday morning

They tried Lucy Skydiamond's official exorcism ritual at dawn. They burned candles. Rick stood in the center of a pentagram. Gillespe echoed the chants Mackenzie read from the sheaf of notes. Two hours later, they regrouped over coffee and laughed till their sides ached.

"Well, we had to eliminate it," Mackenzie said. "Lucy didn't think it would work either, but it's the old standby."

"Third-generation exorcist? Ha!" Rick said.

"She's more familiar with demonic possession," Mackenzie said. "Dak falls outside her immediate area of expertise."

"Non-demonic possession? Subtle difference I suppose," Rick said.

"Most definitely. None of the *Rituale Romanum* apply if Dak's not Satan in disguise."

"Okay, what's next?" Gillespe asked, and leaned in to take a look at Mackenzie's list.

"I'm suggesting we skip some of the rituals Madame

Beefcake recommended—for the same reason," Mac said. She ran the tip of her finger down the page, flipped to the next, and about halfway down stabbed at one of the terms highlighted in Day-Glo pink. "Here they are. Past life therapy and spirit releasement therapy, or PLT and SRT," Mackenzie announced. She lifted her face to look at Rick. "Just the ticket, I believe."

"At least we're not down to purges or blisters yet," Rick replied. "I may have to draw the line before we get to those."

Gillespe looked back and forth between the two of them. "Blisters? Nobody said anything about blisters."

"They may be necessary, but only as a last resort," Mackenzie said. "Now, listen up. There are six steps for SRT. The first step . . ."

Gillespe just shook his head and shook with laughter.

Later that morning, the fun and games ended when Rick spied Hargrove in the piazza. Two days of ghost-busting hadn't produced results, and he didn't have any assurances that two dozen more would either. And now that Hargrove had followed them to Pompeii, a new type of trouble was brewing, which all focused on Mackenzie. With her enemy obviously on her tail, if he had to trick, bribe, or hog-tie her, Rick had to get Mackenzie—God love her—back home to Dallas and to forget all this ghost business.

But first he wanted to confront the gray man and level the playing field. He left the unsuspecting Mackenzie and Gillespe worrying over another batch of translations he'd downloaded, and slipped out of the pension. Without much trouble he located his quarry and followed him into ancient Pompeii.

"I'm surprised to see you here," Rick said as he joined the man on the wall near the Nuceria Gate.

If Hargrove was taken aback at seeing him, he didn't

show it. He removed his sweat-drenched cap and mopped his brow. "Mason," he wheezed. It seemed to be all that he could utter at the moment.

Rick shook his head. The man could sweat—that was something he'd never seen before, even on the hottest days in Dallas. And Hargrove's hue had shifted from gray to an odd lavender.

"Your sudden departure—and Mackenzie's—piqued my curiosity," Hargrove finally said. "I thought it might have something to do with your research on the Savaion expedition."

"Savaion?"

Hargrove raised an eyebrow. "Don't play coy, Mason. You and Mackenzie were discussing it just last week in the museum library."

"Oh, that." Rick made a great show of stroking his chin as if in deep thought. "No, I was called back. It was unavoidable, as I explained to Proctor."

Hargrove stopped fanning his face and looked at him. "And Mackenzie too? No, no, my boy. You two are on to something."

Rick shrugged. "Just doing my job."

"Very well," Hargrove said and winked. He patted the leather camera case beside him on the wall. "And I'm just here taking in the sights. Your artifacts and the exhibit inspired me."

Nothing had ever been simple between them. The jealousy was still palpable after all these years. It oozed out of Hargrove with every carefully spoken word, and it made every gesture and glance suspect. Rick never doubted that Hargrove had been behind the thesis debacle that barely failed to destroy Mackenzie's career. And he didn't doubt the failure still obsessed him.

He looked out on the vista afforded from the point on the wall. The southern district of the excavation site spread out before them. Rick nodded in the direction of the site. "If you're staying a couple of days, I'd be glad to give you a guided tour myself."

Hargrove's chuckle sounded more like a viper's hiss. "I might just take you up on your offer," he said.

"Good. Take my number and address," Rick said. He jotted the information on a scrap of paper and handed it over.

Rick believed in the adage, keep your friends close and your enemies closer. Until he got Mackenzie on a plane back to Texas, he wanted to keep Hargrove very, very close.

When Gil returned from the café with a tray of food and drink, he acted sheepish or guilty or both. Mackenzie rocked back from her stack of translations and smothered a giggle. Gil's left cheek looked scalded—or rather, it looked like he'd been slapped.

"Problems in the romance department?" she asked.

"This? I owe it all to Dak!"

Mackenzie's smile froze. "Oh, no. Please don't tell me what I think you're going to tell me."

"Gina just met Dak," Gil said.

She groaned. "I told you not to tell me!"

Gil continued on without a hitch. "He popped in at an inappropriate moment, so to speak. And Gina knows a possession when she sees one—her cousin is the local witch."

Mac shook her head. "I don't believe this."

"Don't worry, boss. Gina thinks her cousin can help us."

Mackenzie covered her ears, squeezed her eyes shut, and started humming "Yankee Doodle" as loud as she could in an effort to block him out. She was on overload. No more. Not one bit or she honestly believed she'd pop.

But after a moment, she couldn't stand it. Her curiosity

got the better of her and she peeked at Gil. She couldn't help but laugh at the comical expression on his face. She dropped her hands from her ears.

"Okay." She took a deep breath and nodded. "Tell me about the witch."

"You did what?" Rick stormed. He looked furious, and if sounds could kill, his tone was lethal. Mackenzie tried to ignore him while she collected all the necessary items for the newest, late-night exorcism.

"It's a *local* exorcist this time. A real one. Gillespe talked to Gina and she set it up with her cousin. It's all hush-hush, Rick. Your coworkers won't know a thing. And if it works, we'll finally be rid of Dak. Hopefully he'll go off wherever he should already be."

It sounded simple and easy, but nothing about evicting a ghost could ever be totally hush-hush and she knew it. It was a risk that she'd taken without consulting Rick, and she was pretty sure he'd be mad for a long time even if it worked.

"So Gina knows," Rick raged.

"And Gina's cousin, of course," Mac added.

"Of course. And what about Hargrove? Did you invite him too?"

"Hargrove? Jeremy Hargrove is here in Pompeii?" she asked. Her hands started to shake. She tried to ignore them.

"Yes, here. We're not invisible, Mackenzie. People take note of our odd behavior. And with Hargrove in town, anything you do can be front-page news in Dallas with one phone call.

"It'll be the end of your legitimate standing in the museum field," he continued, shaking his head. "You may as well hang out a shingle like Madame Beefcake's and stock up on black candles and pentagrams. All your scholarly work will be suspect and rejected. And worst of all, Hargrove will steal your chance for the directorship of the museum!"

Mackenzie fastened her canvas satchel loaded with flashlights and candles and set it by the door. "I don't care," she finally said. "Dak's my priority, especially after last night. He's cramping my love life and I'm pissed. I'll deal with Hargrove after we get rid of Dak."

Her attempt at humor didn't diffuse Rick's anger one bit. He stomped around and packed her bag in swift and efficient moves. "This is over. Now! I'm driving you to Rome and putting you on the first plane back to Dallas."

"Are you open to a compromise?" she asked. She settled herself in the middle of the bed and tucked her knees to her chin. They were both stubborn, but Rick was practical.

"I'm listening," he growled, and slid her packed bag across the floor to her.

"It's late. I'll leave in the morning."

"And? There's always something else with you, Mackenzie. What's the condition?"

"Come with us tonight when Gina's cousin tries to exorcise Dak."

"Absolutely not." He looked at her for a long minute, long enough to scare the pudding out of her that she'd lost him completely with her latest wacky plan. Then he pulled her into his arms and kissed her soundly. Before her teeth could stop chattering and reason returned, he was gone.

Rick hated to bail on Mac, but someone had to distract Hargrove during the exorcism. Short of hog-tying her to the bed, he couldn't stop that headstrong female from conducting another ritual on his behalf—even if he'd wanted to. And he didn't. Not really.

Hell's bells! It might work. He didn't believe in the effectiveness of mumbo jumbo, but he believed in Mackie. It was impossible not to. And he owed her respect, admiration and his full-fledged support, which meant protecting her from the inquisitive Hargrove.

Chapter Thirty-two

Pompeii ruins: Thursday night

Thankfully, Gillespe didn't want to back out. Mackenzie met him in the piazza an hour after sunset to rendezvous with Gina and her cousin.

"I didn't think Rick would go for it," he said. "It's his job on the line. There'll be hell to pay if we're caught inside the excavation site after hours conducting a séance."

Mackenzie nodded, if a little sadly. It was probably better this way. And a few moments later, when Gina and her cousin Mia joined them, the two Italian women agreed.

Mia looked like Gina's twin. The two nodded through the introductions, and with a little cross-translation between Gina and Gillespe the current state of affairs was discussed.

"Mia says if Rick wasn't cooperative, the negative energy would clog the flow," Gillespe explained. "She thinks she can do better without him."

"How about Dak, do we need him?" Mackenzie asked.

Gillespe shook his head. "We've got the next best thing, the place where he died."

The foursome finalized plans, parted ways and half an hour later met up near the Herculaneum Gate. There they crossed into the excavation area without notice.

It was rough going in the dark. And spooky—especially when the half moon rose and cast long shadows, and when each puff of wind from the bay whispered through the ruins like a moaning spirit. Gillespe led the way with Gina and Mia close behind. Mackenzie followed, keeping watch for any of the night guards that patrolled the major thoroughfares of the site. The group made slow but steady progress, threading their way along side streets until they reached Via dell'Abbondanza.

They paused in the shadows at the intersection and listened. Gillespe held one finger to his lips; they had just missed one of the patrolling guards. Shoulder to shoulder, they waited until the echoes of boots on cobblestones receded and Gillespe waved them forward one by one.

Mackenzie rounded the final corner ahead of everyone, and hugged the wall until at last she could slip noiselessly into the dark opening of the building at number six. When the others joined her, she heaved a great sigh of relief. They were in.

Everyone pulled out their flashlights and kept the beams low as they moved beyond the bakery and finally outside to the clearing with Dak's body cast.

Mia clicked her tongue when she saw it. She opened Mackenzie's satchel as well as the small knapsack she'd brought. Laying out objects, she lit candles and then slowly circled the statue, her hands outstretched. Finally, she stopped and faced the others.

"She's ready," Gillespe whispered.

Mackenzie glanced around the site. Their voices carried on the wind. It was another risk but, after so many, Mac was losing count.

She nodded and joined the others in the circle of candlelight, and soon they were in quiet harmony, following

Mia's melodious voice. It left no doubt in Mackenzie's mind that somehow Mia was stirring the mists of time and invoking the dead to come to her.

It worked. Dak arrived in full vigor, and knocked Gillespe flat on his back. The intern picked himself up and staggered toward Mackenzie, but it was Dak rather than Gillespe who possessed his body. She could smell the brimstone in the air.

"Dak," Mackenzie whispered. "Mia is going to help you. Listen to her, she can free you."

Dak laughed and shook his head. He nodded in Mia's direction but focused on Mackenzie's face.

"Falah?" he whispered. "Did you find her?"

"That's a wild goose chase and you know it. It's a trick so you can keep hanging on to Rick. I'm finished making deals with you."

Mia's chanting continued and she twirled about, hissing and spitting. Mackenzie stepped away and gave her room to give him the works—whatever those consisted of.

"Angel, I can't go yet. I must hang on."

"Why? You're dead. Falah—if she ever existed—is long dead too. It's time to move on and free the living."

Dak shook his head. "I must hang on. I can't tell you why. But trust me, help is on the way."

"This has got to stop! You're destroying all of our lives! Rick's, Gillespe's, and mine."

"Just a little longer, angel. I promise."

"I'm not going to give up. I love Rick. And you can't have him."

Dak grabbed her and shook her like a rag doll. "I don't want him. But you don't understand. I *can't* go yet."

"You can and you will! Sic him, Mia," Mac yowled.

The woman chose that moment to blow a fistful of foul-smelling power into Dak's face. And, as Mia continued her chanting and gyrations, he dropped Mackenzie and backed away.

He looked up into the heavens and closed his eyes.

"Trust me, angel. One last time. Only a bit longer. Then I promise, when Maude comes I will go away forever."

Trust a ghost? Two weeks ago she wouldn't have considered it for a second, or even consider that it was a conundrum she would have to face, but damned if she wasn't going to do it. It went against logic and the scientific method. It strayed from the straight and narrow. It rejected the safe and sound. But it felt right, and she didn't have much choice.

She looked up into the heavens too. Granny Moon's gift wasn't weird or strange, but it was magic. And that was the best kind of gift that love could buy. Trust.

Rick checked the time again without breaking stride in his conversation with Hargrove. From their table in the pension's café, he could see both entrances. And, if Hargrove noted his preoccupation with his watch and the patron traffic in and out of the establishment, he didn't comment.

His plan had worked. Hargrove had scheduled a tour for the next day, agreed to meet for dinner, and now sat across from him volleying probing questions and deflecting any of Rick's own. Other than the company, it was a pleasant evening. Music from a street band floated in through the large open windows, and tempered his anxiety.

Given the previous attempts at exorcism, Rick could guess the success of Mackenzie's latest adventure with the occult. Two hours was excessive. So they were overdue.

"Just how long is Mackenzie planning to stay in Italy?" Hargrove asked, his thin voice competing with the chatter and clatter of the café diners.

Rick refocused his attention on the man. Once, long ago, he'd been impressed with Hargrove's ability to extract information. Now it seemed clumsy and pathetic.

"I'm not certain of her plans," Rick replied.

Hargrove had minced his way through dinner like a dainty prince and now wielded a toothpick with precision.

"But you're quite sure it has nothing to do with researching the Savaion expedition?" he asked, and sucked his teeth.

The man was persistent, if nothing else. Rick smiled and lifted a jug of Chianti. "More wine?"

A flash of movement at the lobby entrance, someone dressed in black, caught his attention. A quick glance confirmed it was one of the ghost-busting team, and he suddenly felt like he could breathe easier. No alarm had sounded. Gillespe wasn't in handcuffs. But where was Mackenzie?

"Is anything troubling you, Dr. Mason?" Hargrove asked, his head inclined—attentive, fatherly.

Rick mumbled a reply, filled Hargrove's glass and topped off his own. Good, Gillespe had spotted them. He waved the intern over.

"Dr. Hargrove, what a surprise," Gillespe cried, and pulled up one of the chairs. He was breathless and filthy, but all in one piece as far as Rick could tell.

Genuine shock registered on Hargrove's features. "Gillespe? My boy, what are you doing here?"

Gil grinned. "A little R & R," he said and grabbed a glass from the neighboring table to pour himself some Chianti. After a gulping half of the contents, he added with a conspiratorial wink, "I'm on a mission."

Under the table, Rick kicked him in the shins. Gillespe was a talker, all right! He grabbed a baguette, ripped off a hunk and held it at the ready.

"A mission? Really!" Hargrove said with obvious delight. "Do tell."

Gillespe hooted. "And here she comes. Gina!" He put two fingers in his mouth and gave a short whistle. The luscious waitress obliged Gillespe by blowing him a kiss, but she didn't pause in her journey through the café into the kitchens.

Two down, Rick thought. But this was driving him crazy. Where was Mackenzie?

And then he saw her standing in the doorway, flushed

and winded but alive and well. At that moment, as relief flooded every cell of his body and covered his body in sweat, he knew he never wanted her out of his sight again. No matter what.

Dak had come to realize there might be something to Mackenzie's mumbo jumbo after all. Either that, or his stasis lock had finally been compromised. He couldn't reconnect with either Gillespe or Rick. He didn't even have the energy to locate them. He settled into the copy of his body cast and waited. Maude would come and bring Rick with her. She had to. He needed Rick one last time.

Gone was the heartbeat and pumping lungs he'd shared with the mortals. Nothing of life remained, no sensation at all to measure the force that summed up his existence. As he probed the vast void that surrounded him now—an abyss absent the sweet scent of Mackenzie's skin, the heat of Rick's vital organs, and Gillespe's youthful enthusiasm—Dak considered the finality of death. The silence stunned him. And he recognized at last that this might be his fate, that Maude and Charlie might fail, and he might remained trapped in limbo for eternity.

Could he accept that destiny peaceably, or would he move on—assuming he still could—and borrow one body after another? He'd grown fond of Rick, Mackenzie, and Gil. And, through them, he'd lived again. But would any mortal willingly accept the curse of sharing their life with a dead man? These three didn't entirely enjoy it.

He regretted many things in his life as a Rogue. He resolved to not regret any in death. He'd violated Core dictums that protected the future, treasured the past, and respected humanity. He deserved his just rewards for failing the Rogues and himself. If he'd restrained himself, he wouldn't be dead or a ghost. But . . . he wouldn't have known and loved Falah either.

He still hoped against hope that Charlie could give him

one last chance to make amends for his mistakes. But, after reflection, he would make no excuse for choosing love. If given another chance, he would again return to Pompeii and fight to save Falah's life with every fiber of his being. Damn the cost to humanity and the future. He would never regret what he'd done for love.

"What happened?" Rick asked after abandoning Hargrove and cornering Mackenzie on the stairs.

She looked luminescent, almost as if she'd been transformed. It scared the crap out of him to see her like that. She stared at him, grabbed his shirtfront and pulled him close. "You in there, Dak? Remember your promise."

She sounded more than a little drunk. "I love Rick," she cried and poked his chest. "I trust you to give him back to me."

She turned away and fled, and he let her go. His gut knotted. The ghost was tearing them apart, and they'd had enough of a past to overcome.

"She'll be all right," Gillespe said as he appeared from around the corner. Rick leaned against the wall. "It was pretty rough on her. Mia's a powerful exorcist, but if a spirit is unwilling, she can't budge them."

"And Dak's unwilling," Rick said. "We both know that."

"Yeah, and we both know he doesn't want to hurt anyone either," Gillespe said.

Rick pounded the wall and swore. "Well, it's too damned late for that."

Chapter Thirty-three

Pompeii: Friday, dawn

He leaned over Mac's sleeping form and called to her, whispering her name again and again until her lashes fluttered and she roused. Her smile was like a green light at the Indy 500. His heart took off at a gallop.

"He's *gone,"* he said.

Her smile was tenuous but hopeful. "Are you sure?" she asked. "How gone?"

"Gone," he said slowly. He felt different; not exactly empty, but absent the almost constant pressure that had once swamped his senses and filled his body. It was as if his connection to Dak, whatever it was, had been severed. He flexed his limbs, shouted, and thumped muscles and joints till Mackenzie stalled him. She was looking nervous.

"There's one surefire test. Come here," he said, and tugged her into his arms. He kissed her sweet lips. The warmth wasn't challenged, and the rising passion was his and his alone.

"He's gone. I'm sure."

Mackenzie nodded. A giggle burst free and she clapped a hand to her mouth. "He's really gone?" she cried.

Her smile faded. "What about Gillespe?" She pushed past and scrambled for the door to the corridor, but Rick pulled her back into his arms.

"I already checked. No Dak. He's gone from Gil, too."

He spun her around and laughed loud and hard. He was liberated, freer than he'd ever felt. Joy welled up inside him like a raging sea. It washed over him, beating back doubt and disbelief. He was glad the ghost was gone but . . . if not for Dak, he might never have truly appreciated his right to choose life and love. And, here she was, within his grasp. It sparked a flame of hunger in Rick that only Mackenzie's touch could satisfy.

"You saved me. I didn't have much faith in all that hocus-pocus, but something must have worked last night because he's gone. And, I'm one grateful son-of-a-gun!"

Mackenzie laughed. "I don't think exorcism had everything to do with it. I just reasoned with the ghost and told him I'd never give up."

"You can be pretty convincing, I'll give you that."

She kicked the packed suitcase at the foot of the bed. "Just how convincing am I? Are you still booting me out of here today?"

Rick shook his head and backed her into the mattress. "Not on your life, lady! If you're willing, I've got a few other ideas that might suit your fancy."

Mackenzie crooked her finger and he obliged. Kissing the woman with Dak hovering nearby had felt like a blast from a stun gun. Without Dak, it was like touching his lips to white lightning. She was a mustang, a wild heart, a mystery, and a tease. And she was more than willing to accommodate his ideas and toss in a few of her own.

Much later, when the rays of dawn filtered through the wooden shutters and bathed their spent bodies in a soft golden light, he kissed her brow. "You love me," he whispered.

Mackenzie stretched in his embrace and smiled. "I never stopped. And I never will."

"Want to come along on the tour I set up for Hargrove?" Rick asked after they'd hiked to the rim of Vesuvius and enjoyed the panoramic vista.

Mackenzie could see the difference in Rick. Without the connection to Dak, the edge of danger was blunted from his features and the weight of age-old sorrows erased.

She groaned. "Hargrove, here. I still can't believe it."

She sighed and leaned back against Rick's chest, savoring the solid feel of his arms encircling her. It seemed appropriate that they were celebrating this new beginning with a climb to the top of a snoozing volcano. It was beautiful and serene at the moment, but she knew it couldn't last. They still had other challenges to face and problems could erupt at any moment, like Hargrove. But for now, she was swimming with bliss, and trouble was as distant as a stormcloud on the horizon.

"Yep. And he's up to his usual tricks. He thinks you're here helping me with a new project, and he's hunting around for a piece of the action."

"Ha! He wants to scoop us and take all the credit. Boy, does that sound familiar. I still burn every time I think about the work I put in unearthing Alfred Rudnick's data, only to have him claim it was his."

"I'd like to get even with him for that too. Translating all those Aramaic resources for you fried my brain," he added. He swore under his breath. "But damn, Mackie, I loved working with you back then, every hell-raising minute! I almost wish we were collaborating on something like the Savaion expedition."

"Me too," she replied.

Rick paused, then hooted. "Let's do it!"

"Savaion? Rick . . ." She groaned. "There's nothing to it. The whole thing was a bust. A boondoggle."

"I know," he returned, and eased out a rather sinister chuckle. "But Hargrove doesn't know that. Let's toss him a bone."

"Send him on a wild goose chase?"

"Can you think of another way to get even with the old reprobate? He'll relocate to Turkey, spend big bucks, and—"

Mackenzie took over for him. "And stay out of my hair at the museum. Wonderful! Let's do it!"

They'd started back down the slope to the car when Rick stopped her in the middle of the rocky track. "You know this could backfire on us," he said, and laughed. "With all those dollars behind him, Hargrove just might unearth something of value."

Mackenzie giggled. "It'd serve us right for trying to get even with him. But I don't care if he does. After taking on a ghost, a jerk like Hargrove is insignificant."

Maude heard Rick and Mackenzie's laughter floating up from the pension lobby as they rushed in from the street. She sighed with relief. Rick was back. Good!

"Dr. Cates," she cried as they met face-to-face on the landing. Mackenzie stumbled and nearly toppled down the stairs. She hung on to the railing and scowled.

"Maude?" The woman didn't sound happy.

Maude nodded and tried to keep her panic at bay. Mackenzie Cates had a tendency to unnerve her more than anyone else did. She was sharp, observant, and one of the few obstacles to the success of this mission for Core.

"Can I trouble you and Dr. Mason for a few minutes?" Maude asked. "I promise I won't take much of your time."

Mackenzie looked skeptical and defensive. And Maude

couldn't blame her one bit. She'd popped into this timeline three times in the last two weeks, each time looking and acting very strange. But it wasn't her fault they hadn't hit it off.

"A few minutes is about all we can spare—unless you're wanting to join us for a hike through the ruins," Mackenzie returned.

"Yes, I do," Maude replied.

Perfect. Thankfully, she was dressed for it. Maude had refined her appearance and was garbed for minimal impact. Her lightweight and nondescript bodysuit and gear pack would pass for acceptable attire in a plethora of eras. At this, one of the premier colossal archy dig sites in the world, her tan suit and camie-colored boots fit right in.

Mackenzie didn't look pleased, but nodded in the direction of the lobby. "Rick's waiting for me. Go on down, I need to grab something from our room."

Maude noted with regret the references that branded Rick as taken, off-limits. But she shrugged it off. Sure she had a crush on Rick Mason, but her days of pleasure transits were a thing of the past. Her mission was to enlist Rick's aid to rescue Dak. The bonus of a little romance on the side was just that, a bonus. And it sure wasn't going to happen as long as Mackenzie Cates was on the scene.

"Maude!" Rick cried when he saw her. He pumped her hand enthusiastically.

It made her heart skip a beat when she saw that big grin, but she quickly realized it wasn't solely because she'd stumbled back into his life. It was a blow to her recently acquired self-confidence. Maybe it had been a mistake to reload those emotions.

"Mind if I join your tour?" she asked after they exchanged pleasantries. "Dr. Cates suggested it."

"Not at all. It'll give us a chance to catch up," Rick said.

She opened her mouth to ask him right then and there

about Dak, but Gillespe arrived, followed by the odd fellow with the watery eyes, and finally Mackenzie. Rick's reaction to Mackenzie's return made Maude ache with envy. That did it; she needed to dump these useless feelings. As soon as this mission was over, she would take Charlie's advice and request a complete memory purge.

"So what's up, Maude?" Mackenzie asked once she'd cut the woman from the tour group and isolated her from the appreciative males. The ruins afforded ample opportunities to sit down, reflect, and interrogate—especially anyone so fixated on her man. Mackenzie found just such a place in the House of Venus in the Shell. The small garden in its central courtyard was placid, and Maude was disarmed and distracted.

Dak had kept his word. She'd trusted him, and Maude was here and he was gone—forever? How? Why? And did she want to know the answers?

No. She was done with ghost-busting, and she was keeping her distance from everything associated with Dak—including the copy of his body cast.

Also, Mac was doing her best to keep her claws retracted and to give Maude the benefit of the doubt. But it was tough. If it was possible, Maude looked better than a runway model in her drab flight-suit-like attire. She might have a hair problem that kept her bald as an egg, but the woman was blessed with great bone structure and a fabulous body. And her repeated surprise appearances and fascination with Rick set off a host of alarms. There was more to Maude than a crush on Rick or any of Pompeii's artifacts. Dak might be gone, but he'd left the persistent Maude, and the promise of trouble lingered like a bad smell.

"What's up?" she repeated.

"What do you mean?" Maude asked.

Mac was pleased to note that the girl wasn't altogether perfect; she couldn't play innocent to save her life.

"What do you need Rick for? And be honest. Rick and I don't keep secrets from one another. What you can say to him, you can say to me."

"Not this," Maude returned.

Things were beginning to fall into place in Mackenzie's brain, like tripping the key tile in a dominoes run. "Does it have anything to do with Dak?"

Maude gulped. She bit her lip. She hemmed and hawed until Mackenzie wanted to reach out and slap her flawless cheek.

"What do you know about Dak?" the woman asked.

"He said you could help Rick. But it's no longer necessary. He's gone," Mackenzie said.

All the color seemed to drain from Maude's face. "Gone? I'm too late?"

Mackenzie patted Maude's back with a little extra force. "Suck in some air or you'll pass out."

Maude grabbed her hand and squeezed. "I've got to talk to Rick. He's got to help me! I can't do this alone. He knows all about Pompeii, and Dak, and I told Charlie I could do it but I don't think I can without Rick, and all of the Time Rogues are counting on me."

"Time Rogues?" Mackenzie felt like she'd hit the jackpot in a dollar slot machine. Maude was babbling and probably revealing more than the situation warranted. Such weakness was an imperfection that Mackenzie found endearing.

"Slow down, Maude, and take a breath." The girl took Mac's advice—another endearing quality. Maude's attributes were adding up.

"I think Rick needs to hear this himself."

Mac checked the time. They'd all agreed to rendezvous at five by the Temple of Jupiter in the Civil Forum if they got separated. With a steady pace, she and Maude just might make it there before the others, and had a slim chance of catching Rick without Hargrove. Maybe it was the urgency of Maude's tone or just a crazy inclination to trust the girl. Whatever the reason, Mackenzie didn't want to put off Maude's explanation a moment longer than necessary.

"Okay. Come on, let's go find him."

"I don't see how I can help you," Rick repeated for the third time in a row. He appeared unmoved by Maude's request for help. And Mackenzie couldn't decide how she herself felt.

They'd managed to break away from Hargrove and Gillespe soon after meeting up in the Temple of Jupiter. They'd relocated to a quiet restaurant beyond the Marine gate, where Maude had restated her request. It was dusk, the prelude to enchantment. The view of the shimmering bay from their table beneath the colonnade was breathtaking. The aromas of bubbling Gorgonzola sauce, steamy potato dumplings, and roasted meat was heavenly. The soft breeze stirring the tall trees and the sweet serenade of nightingales was delightful. And Rick, Mackenzie's adored, her beloved, was near enough to intoxicate her with a glance. But the intense Ms. Kincaid's presence robbed the scene of all romance.

Maude gobbled her food as she talked, as if she'd never eaten anything as tasty. Mackenzie watched and listened with fascination. Still, while she wasn't immune to appeals to emotion, entertaining a ghost for a week had dulled her sense of the extraordinary. And Maude's blanket plea was a strange request, nonspecific except that it had something to do with Dak.

Rick threw down his napkin and folded his arms. He was digging in his heels and Mackenzie knew why—Hargrove and her career. Even with Dak gone, the hint of paranormal antics could still cause trouble.

Rick didn't say no aloud, but Mackenzie knew how difficult he could be when he shut out all possibilities. "How about telling us what's really going on?" she suggested.

Maude looked like she wanted to do just that, but something was holding her back. "I don't want to violate a Core directive. Can't you just trust me?" Maude asked.

"Frankly, Dak exhausted my quota for trust," Rick said. "Get honest or get lost."

Maude bit her lip. With a furtive glance at the other restaurant patrons, she fished around in one of her pantleg pockets and pulled out a small chrome device.

Dropping the palm-sized piece of technology on the table in front of Rick was an invitation he couldn't resist. He picked it up before Mackenzie could fully grasp what it was.

"Don't punch any buttons," Maude warned.

"You're from the future too, of course," he said as he carefully examined the gadget. He handed it to Mackenzie.

Maude nodded. "You know? Will you help me?"

"More info," Mackenzie said. "Keep it coming." The numeric register on the apparatus was flashing the current date. Big deal. For all she knew, the feather-light item could be just another cell phone or fancy calculator.

Maude groaned. "What exactly did Dak tell you?"

"A whole lot more than you have," Mackenzie replied. "He said it was all a big mistake."

Maude swallowed with difficulty. "I'm supposed to fix it. And Dak was going to help me do it."

"But now that Dak's gone, you need another authority on ancient Pompeii?" Mackenzie asked.

Rick growled and commandeered the interrogation. "No, she needs my intimate knowledge of Dak and what he was doing before the stasis lock, right?"

"Yes!" she cried, and relaxed her furrowed brow. "So, you'll help?"

"Stasis lock?" Mackenzie echoed.

"Exactly what mistake are you hoping to fix? And how do you propose I help you fix it?" Rick countered.

Maude shook her head. "I've told you too much already."

Rick shrugged. "Then the answer is no. My price is information, and if you can't supply it, I'm not interested."

"I understand," Maude replied. She held out her hand for her device.

Mackenzie was reluctant to give it up. Was it really something from the future, or merely a prop in an elaborate hoax or scam perpetrated at Rick's expense? The possibility of either intrigued her. Maude had used the object as bait for Rick, but had landed her instead.

"What about me?" she suddenly asked. "I'm not privy to Dak's inner thoughts, but he shared a few things and I know quite a bit about Pompeii."

"Outrageous!" Rick roared. "Haven't we been through enough, Mackenzie? Or do you thrive on a crisis per day?"

Well, so much for the night of romance she'd planned. She smiled sweetly in his direction but folded her arms. They were at a standoff. Or were they? Rick was hell-bent on protecting her career. And she was intent on protecting him. But the mystery of Dak was still out there begging to be solved. Dangerous? Yes. But she and Rick had proven during the last week that they thrived on risk almost as much as they thrived on each other.

Maude must have realized she had an ally at last. She inched her chair back and held out her hand to Rick. "Thank you for listening." He shook her hand but didn't comment.

"Can you find your way back in the dark?" Mackenzie asked.

"Don't worry about me, Dr. Cates. I can take care of myself." With one last look in Rick's direction, Maude left.

Rick waited a full minute before he exploded. Mackenzie sipped her wine, enjoyed the view, paid their check, and led him out into the cool of evening before he finally ran out of expletives, ultimatums, and threats.

"That's just silly, Rick. You're not going to send me to

bed without my supper so just hush," she finally said when he struck one of his defiant and utterly manly poses.

He frowned at her. "Did I say that?"

Mackenzie smiled and nodded. "And a few other things that sounded interesting."

He roughly pulled her to him and breathed in the scent of her skin and hair. "You drive me wild, Mackie. You know that?"

"Likewise," she said, and lifted her lips to his.

"Just promise me something," he whispered against her mouth.

"I'll try."

"Don't help Maude without learning more."

Mackenzie laughed. "It goes against my grain, but I'll consider taking your advice—just this once." And she did for the rest of the night. But when Maude and Hargrove both joined them for breakfast the next morning, she realized the subject of Dak was neither dead nor buried.

Chapter Thirty-four

Pompeii: Saturday morning

"Just one more time, Rick. It's the only way," Dak said.

Mackenzie was stunned. It was bizarre watching Hargrove's mouth move and grasp that Dak had taken control of her pompous enemy. However, there was no doubt that it was Dak. His signature smell was present and so was his dark and defiant gaze—adding a luminous quality to Hargrove's otherwise weak and watery eyes.

"I appreciate the fact that you're asking me rather than just borrowing my body again," Rick said. "But why don't you use the one you're in?"

Dak laughed. "This guy? I don't have much link with him." He thumped Hargrove's legs with his hands and shook his head. "No sensation yet. I can't move very well. It's a struggle keeping him upright and I need to give Maude a special guided tour of old Pompeii."

The table in the café felt like it was center stage. However, ghostly possession wasn't obvious to the uninformed; most of the midmorning customers were occupied with their meals and conversation. Gina, on the other hand, shuffling between the tables, had eavesdropped on the conversation and alerted Gillespe. Mackenzie could see him out of the corner of her eye, conferring with her and sputtering with disbelief.

She kept Gillespe at bay, and hopefully safe from Dak, with a shake of her head and concentrated on willing Rick to refuse to accommodate the ghost one more time.

"Maude's going back in time to rescue you. That's what this is all about, isn't it?" Rick asked.

Maude grabbed Dak's arm. "Don't tell him! It's the only rule you haven't broken," she cried.

"It doesn't matter now, Maude. Think about it. 'Never tell the past about the future?' Rick and Mackenzie already *know* about the future."

"But, Charlie said . . ." Maude wailed.

Dak snorted. "Rick and I have shared a body and memories. He already knows about Charlie, Core, and the Rogues. And I know all about him."

Mackenzie squeezed Rick's hand until he yelped and shook her off.

"But I don't know everything," he said. "Core is our future. You and Maude are time-travelers. And . . . that's about it. All the rest is guesswork. There's more to this than saving you. What's the big mistake, Dak? And how are you going to fix it?"

"I caused a time rift, a big one, and it damaged the future. Maude's going to stop me before I trigger the rift, and restore the future. If she can rescue me too, it will be a bonus."

Mackenzie suspended her disbelief—again. Would normal life ever return? First there was a moving statue, then a ghost, and now time-travelers from the future. Heck, if this trend continued, she didn't need to suspend her disbelief; she needed to flush it down the toilet.

"Can you do it?" Mackenzie asked and looked over at Maude.

"That's my mission," Maude replied.

The girl didn't look completely confident. Mackenzie couldn't fathom the necessary effort to accomplish the task, but saving the future had to be a tall order of business for one person.

She sipped her coffee. She needed the jolt of caffeine—it proved she wasn't dreaming.

"I gather this isn't a routine mission," Rick said.

Dak laughed again. "Not exactly. Well, the rescue is routine—that's what Time Rogues do. But reversing a time rift isn't."

Maude pushed a chunk of bread around her plate and flashed a humorless smile. "It's a class-ten rift, Dak. We can't reverse it."

Dak reached over and patted her hand. "It's not impossible. The Rogues hadn't ever consulted with a ghost either, till you were brave enough to tackle the unknown."

Maude growled and snatched her hand away. "Thanks."

Mackenzie and Rick exchanged glances. They were like-minded on this one. Bravery aside, it was a huge responsibility for the girl to carry alone.

Mackenzie considered the facts she'd collected on Maude. The girl's wardrobe choices were bothersome. Was Maude accessing a faulty information database? And if she made mistakes on appropriate attire for a time period, could she flunk on something crucial? Also, evidently time travel wasn't yet a perfect science. The margin of error could be small or huge.

"What happens to the future if you don't reverse or prevent the rift?" Mackenzie asked.

Maude scowled. "I'll prevent it. I have to."

Dak cut in. "She'll do whatever is necessary to succeed. Her orders I'm sure are to use maximum force to stop me from sending the SOS that triggered the rift. I trained her. She can do it."

"Maximum force?" Mackenzie glanced around the table. No one spoke for a moment.

Rick finally broke the silence. "That's why she needs a detailed itinerary. It's the only way she can intercept you well in advance of the 'event.' And you want a real chance at not using 'maximum force.' " He looked at Maude.

She finally grinned. "Exactly."

"Okay, I'm in," Rick said.

"Thanks," Dak replied.

"Hey, wait a minute. What do you mean you're in?" Mackenzie protested. But it was too late. Hargrove slumped forward and Dak was gone.

"Damnation!" she cried and pummeled Rick's chest. "Don't do this to me again!"

"Ouch," he shot back and grabbed her fists. "Don't worry. It won't take long."

"We'll just see about that," Mackenzie groused.

Gillespe strolled over and nodded in Hargrove's direction. "What gives?"

"Dak's back. He just borrowed Hargrove's body and now it's Rick's turn."

"Dak? In Hargrove?" Gillespe howled with laughter. "Sweet revenge! That first possession is a doozie. He'll be out of it for a while. Want to put him in a few compromising positions and take naughty pictures?"

"Gil!"

Gillespe shrugged. "Missing a great opportunity, boss."

They sat around the table and waited. No brimstone. No Dak. Maude's brow furrowed with worry. Rick tapped his fingers on the tabletop.

Gillespe leaned close. "How'd all this happen?" he asked in a hoarse whisper. "I thought we pulled the plug on Dak. Or something."

Mackenzie shushed him. Maude had pulled out her chrome mechanism and was pushing buttons. Something was definitely wrong.

The device beeped and Maude flinched. It was a full body reaction to bad news.

"We've lost the stasis lock. Charlie said it might happen," Maude explained. She glanced at them and sighed heavily. "The rift is expanding again."

"That doesn't sound good," Mackenzie said. Rick still looked normal; so did Hargrove and Gillespe. "Where is Dak?"

"Gone—dead. Lost in time. I can't save him now. No one can." Maude's face was expressionless. She shrugged her shoulders and stood up. "I have to go." She extended her hand to Rick. "Thanks for trying to help."

When it was Mackenzie's turn to shake hands, she held fast. Maude's fingers were trembling in her grasp. She might look calm, cool, and collected on the outside, but Mackenzie knew otherwise. The girl was terrified.

"What does 'maximum force' mean?" Mackenzie asked.

"Termination. I have to kill him before he triggers the rift. And . . ."

"You'll die too," Mackenzie guessed in a whisper. "It's a suicide mission, isn't it?"

Maude was expressionless. "The rift and no-transit zone complicate the mission. I won't get a second chance to fix the past, not now. It's my job to terminate Dak to save Core. My life's expendable. It's the only way," she said.

"No. It's not the only way." Rick growled and pushed himself away from the table. "I know where he is three hours before the eruption. But you'll have to take me. I'll have to show you."

"Oh, Rick—you're willing?" Maude cried.

Relief washed over the girl's features and transformed her into something like an adoring groupie. Rick reciprocated with a damned superhero grin.

Maude started pressing buttons again. And Mackenzie squealed.

"Oh no you don't, cowboy!" she cried, and lunged for Rick. "You're not talking about hopping on a plane."

Rick hugged her tight. "No. And it's probably risky as hell."

Maude's big blue eyes reflected alarm. One finger was poised above the keypad of her apparatus, and Mackenzie didn't doubt that it was hovering above the *send* button. The last thing she wanted was to have her atoms scrambled and shot across time lines like a cellular e-mail. But Mac had promised herself that she wasn't going to let Rick walk out of her life again. And then there was Maude—a poor beautiful kid who was willing to be a martyr.

"What are the risks for us, Maude? Your wigs are lovely but is baldness a permanent side effect?"

Rick turned and shook his head. "Don't you worry about it, Mackenzie. I know what you're thinking and it's too risky. I'm going alone."

"If he goes, I go," Mackenzie told Maude.

"Go where?" Gillespe yowled.

"Back to A.D. 79," Rick replied. "Imagine a *Mission Impossible* movie with time travel and an erupting volcano."

"I was thinking more along the lines of a *Lara Croft* flick," Mackenzie added. "Maude looks the part."

Rick raised a brow and reassessed Maude. "Yep, she's a ten in the body department, all right."

Mackenzie hissed and tightened her hold on his neck. "You could have gone a lifetime without saying that out loud, cowboy."

"Hey!" Maude interrupted their bickering.

It startled Mackenzie for a split second, long enough to allow Maude to slap a tag on her chest and another on Rick's, and then to stab the button on her device.

The noise was sudden and deafening—like an out-of-control freight train. If there was more to Gillespe's reaction than flailing arms and open mouth, Mackenzie didn't hear it. The sound drowned out everything. Soon the sight of Gil, Hargrove, and the café blurred into a mass of spinning color and light. Mac's body bounced against Rick's as they seemed to lift effortlessly, suspended in a transparent bubble, while the world whirled about them and light slowly faded. When the roaring noise became nearly unbearable, her ears popped and she and Rick were suddenly sucked into an inky blackness.

Chapter Thirty-five

Earth's Core: Day 237, 16:24

Mackenzie watched Maude from her prone position. She couldn't move. She felt like jelly and floated somewhere within a lifeless shell of a body. Was this death? Had Maude sucked them through hell and killed them? She could hear Rick but he wasn't in her line of sight.

Maude handed over her chrome apparatus to a wild-haired redhead in a white lab coat. "I had to bring them, Charlie," she said. "Can you help them acclimate?"

"Not much," Charlie replied. "We've had to suspend reacclimations because of the rift. And since they weren't prepped for transit, it's best to let them come around on their own."

Mackenzie sure didn't like the sound of that, except that it confirmed she was alive and the amoeba-like qualities she was experiencing were temporary. The floor wasn't too uncomfortable. But the stark slick whiteness that covered every surface she could see hurt her eyes. She squeezed her eyes shut. Hooray, she could move something!

As she opened them again, Charlie moved between her and a booth that looked like it belonged at the entrance to a toll road or a parking garage. "Every time I try to rush new transits, it causes problems," he said.

Maude glanced down at Mackenzie and smiled. "She's coming around," she cried.

Charlie bent down and tapped Mac's forehead with a tiny rubber mallet. "She might be a natural like you. But give her as much time as she needs—and him, too."

"Why all the caution? I've seen you slap Rogues to pull them out of it," Maude returned, stroking her hair.

Mackenzie closed her eyes again. Her toes were tingling and it sounded like Rick was snoring.

"Those were experienced Rogues with triple-digit transits under their belts. I have to pull them around sometimes. But you can't do that with new transits. You get them too excited, and if they've got any latent hostilities those manifest immediately."

"Drutz!" Maude cried and snatched her hand away. Charlie laughed.

"Touching them is okay, but just don't try to rush them. Remember that!"

"Do we have time for all this?" Maude asked. "They're illegal transits. Don't we need to clear the transit pads before they trigger Core sensors and alert the troops?"

Charlie must have used his rubber mallet on Rick. There were a few grunts that sounded familiar and comforting to Mackenzie. Rick was coming around, too.

"Sensors are down in this sector," Charlie replied. "I've had to take transit stations Delta and Zed offline for repairs. And I've got teams running tests on parallel channels. This transit pad is one of the first I've cleared of errors."

That motivated Mackenzie. Illegal? Troops? She pooled her energy and pushed herself up off the floor. This was all sounding like a clandestine operation, and she wasn't sure she was on the good guys' side.

"Here, lean on me," Maude offered and slipped an arm around her waist.

Mackenzie sagged against the girl and moved her head from side to side. The place was the size of a small hangar, and every surface was still gleaming white—except for a yellow flashing light.

"Don't worry about that," Maude said. "Those are code lights. They signal the status of the transit pad. The amber means a transit is still in process. As soon as we clear the pad, the arrival spots will flick off."

Rick was up and moving without aid. "Remarkable," Charlie said. "He's responding well beyond normal limits, too."

"Mackenzie? You okay?" Rick asked.

She struggled to clear her throat and answer. Maude giggled. "I used to sound like a bullfrog and throw up. Charlie's nutritional supplement never agrees with me."

Rick didn't sound like a bullfrog. He sounded like a pissed-off grizzly bear. "What have you gotten us into, Maude? Sounds like this whole deal is illegal and deadly."

Charlie laughed and tucked a clipboard under his arm. "Of course it is. This is a Time Rogue operation. And there's nothing riskier than a mission to save the future by fixing the past." He slapped Rick on the back and shook his hand. "Welcome aboard."

Chapter Thirty-six

Earth's Core: 23:30

Prepping for a mission seemed complicated from Mackenzie's perspective. Fortunately, most of the prep was directed at Maude. It looked like a pit stop during the Grand Prix. Everyone was racing against an invisible stopwatch.

Mac and Rick lounged on padded lifts and watched Charlie's team of assistants work. In minutes Maude had been redenuded of body hair—not that she had much left to donate, implanted with multiple devices, inoculated, and force-fed nutritional food supplements.

Mac and Rick weren't exempt from that part. They were both trying to gag down the requisite two liters. Charlie wanted them filled from stem to stern with his foul-tasting liquid.

The lab space looked like a reclaimed missile silo. Huge generators hummed. Occasional thunder in some distant corridor was a disquieting reminder that this was a future Mackenzie hadn't imagined. She wondered just what had happened to Earth to drive these inhabitants to travel through time and live underground.

Rick reached over and gave her hand a little squeeze. They talked very little during the brief prepping interlude. But she could guess his thoughts—they probably matched her own. This was thrilling and dangerous. They were historians given the unique opportunity to travel through time and witness history in the making. And the glimpse of the future was phenomenal, too.

"All set," Charlie said and signaled for Maude to join them. The girl looked exhausted but still lovely—damn her. She curled up on one of the padded lifts, while Charlie spread a detailed light chart on the table between them.

"This is the no-transit zone," he said, and circled the ancient urban environs. "You'll land here, outside the zone, and make your way into the city. Locate Dak, return him to the transit coordinates, and await auto-transport."

Mackenzie and Rick studied the map, discussed routes and alternates. They had two points of reference: Dak's memory of his location three hours before the eruption, and his final location behind building six and the House of the Chaste Lovers. And once on-site, hopefully Rick would also recall other memories that would help them track Dak down enroute from one location to the other.

"Ready?" Maude asked. She was glowing with excitement.

"Just one more thing," Mackenzie said. "Why was Dak in ancient Pompeii and in a no-transit zone, and what does Falah have to do with everything?"

"I'll answer that on our way to the transit pad," Charlie said. He jumped on Maude's lift which, as he talked, began to hum and move away from the prep area. The others fell in, one behind the other. As they all entered a side corridor, Charlie's voice echoed.

"Dak did it for love," he continued. "He wanted to save Falah and bring her back to Core."

Mackenzie blanched. That answer was too sad. Love? Love had caused a time rift and threatened the future?

"He's going to try to save her," Rick said. "I know him well enough to know he's not going to leave her behind."

Maude nodded. "I'm prepared for that." She tapped her left forearm and exposed one of her new implants, a pronged tool. "This will disable his implants—including his emergency SOS commands—and neutralize his resistance."

Even in the half-shadowed blue light of the corridor, Mackenzie could see it clearly. The device looked lethal.

Chapter Thirty-seven

Earth's Core: Day 238, 00:14

"Okay." Maude said as she scratched her newly shorn head. "We're ready."

Except for their transit armbands, they were all naked as newborns, apparently a condition for this transit. But Mackenzie was thankful Charlie hadn't insisted on the full transit prep that included mandatory hair removal. Maude didn't look comfortable in the least. She was chewing at her close-clipped fingernails.

Charlie looked up from a glowing monitor. The audience of one was enough to make Mackenzie blush.

And, Maude too. Her cheeks were pink.

Mackenzie stretched her toes. The polished floor warmed beneath her bare feet.

Charlie focused on the monitor again. A few stabbing motions at the keyboard produced an unpleasant squawk. The light above the portal switched from red to yellow.

"Don't worry, I'm routing you through wardrobe—it's automatic, and you'll arrive in full attire in ancient Pompeii."

His fingers danced across the keyboard at an astonishing rate. The light switched to a flashing green. The portal slid open and exposed a vast blackness beyond. Somewhere in that darkness a whooshing sound mounted in decibels.

Cool air fanned Mackenzie's bare skin. She shivered and glanced over at Rick. He looked fearless and magnificent, defiant in the face of possible death.

Charlie punched more keys.

Maude flexed her knees a few times. A high-pitched whine accompanied the deafening but familiar freight-train-like noise.

The green light stopped flashing. "It's a go!"

Maude nodded. She turned her back to the portal and closed her eyes.

Mac had learned that everyone entered transit differently. Out of instinct perhaps, Maude pinched her nose closed with one hand and fell backward into the inky blackness. Mackenzie and Rick followed suit.

Chapter Thirty-eight

Ancient Pompeii: August 24, A.D. 79 10:00 A.M.

Mackenzie rubbed her rump. During the transit she'd landed hard, hard enough to jolt the fillings in her teeth, but it was Maude's precipitous push into the bushes that had caused the bruise on her bottom. Contact with the corner of a stone tomb was the reality check she'd needed. It hurt too much to be a dream.

The rural setting, a small collection of tombs and burial sites just beyond Pompeii, appeared benign. Their transit point had been well chosen. No one had noticed their arrival, and Maude had concealed them behind a screen of shrubbery while they recovered.

There was a odd stillness to the warm morning air. Mackenzie sniffed and scanned the horizon dominated by Vesuvius—a vastly different silhouette from the volcano in 2005. The odor of sulfur was faint and nearly undetectable. And a gray dusting of ash on the volcano's slopes was the only visual evidence remaining from the first event, which had taken place before dawn. They had arrived on time and on target. A second and more significant eruption would take place in three hours and herald the subsequent eruptions that would continue for days, mounting in volume and intensity, involving earth, wind, and fire until Pompeii was decimated.

The pending tragedy didn't quell Mackenzie's enthusiasm. She was awestruck and grateful for the singular opportunity to observe a thriving ancient culture in full flower before it ceased to exist. She trembled with excitement.

"You guys are in great shape," Maude cooed. "I can't believe this is only your second transit."

"Except for the bumps and bruises, I'm feeling pretty good. But I'd feel a whole lot better if I wasn't revealing more flesh than a swimsuit model," Mackenzie answered. Rick was checking her over and brushing dust from her skimpy toga.

"The attire is accurate, Mackie. And you look wonderful in it," he said, planting a kiss on her brow. "You might want to try this look when we get back to Dallas."

"Hey, Rick," Maude cried. She pointed in the direction of an approaching chariot. "Transportation."

"It's Showtime!" he returned, and pulled Mackenzie to her feet.

The chariot was ideal. A few minutes later, after Rick had performed his first criminal act in the ancient world and tucked his now unconscious victim out of sight, they climbed aboard and headed toward town.

Maude surveyed the landscape. "Everything looks different," she cried. "How will we ever find our way back?"

Rick reined in the horse and gave Maude a quick course in triangulation. "Use one of the tombs as a landmark," he said. "Fix it with a point in the bay—that island will do—and use the rim of Vesuvius for your other reference."

Maude used her telescoping implants, marked each with an infrared signal, and correlated the points. "Okay. Got it," she said and grinned. "All we have to do is return to this general vicinity, and the auto-transit commands will lock on."

"Good," Rick replied. He kept his voice low, because a line of tethered slaves led by two men on horseback were passing by.

Mackenzie frowned. The slaves were mere children, some gaunt and bent. The sight tempered her enthusiasm for this trip. At least the slaves were heading away from town and toward the distant orchards. Would any of them survive the eruption? And if they didn't, would it be a blessed end to their short, tortured lives?

Rick glanced over at her. "I know that look, Mackenzie. Remember, we're witnesses to history. No distractions, no side trips, and no crazy heroics. I want your word on it," he demanded.

She forced herself to agree. It was a timely reminder. She was powerless to intervene in human or natural events today—with the exception of Dak—and avert disaster. And with the strict time limit on this visitation to the past, she needed to shift her concentration to the goal of absorbing as much information as possible about the ancient and soon to be extinct society.

"You either, Maude," Rick continued. "We're only going to get one shot at this. Let's focus on finding Dak and getting back here in time to transit."

Maude nodded and rechecked her chronometer. "We're on schedule."

Rick seemed relieved. He cracked the whip and the horse responded instantly, pulling back onto the roadway at a trot.

As they topped the rise, however, they encountered their first obstacle, a herd of sheep. A few minutes later, they suffered another barrier, a plodding train of handcarts all loaded with goods, and their forward progress slowed to a crawl.

"Hell's bells," Rick raged and inched the chariot past a

cart loaded with wine casks. "We need a new plan. I forgot about the festival."

So they ditched the chariot and set off on foot. The Stabian gate was clogged with merchants and celebrants, but once they were through, the flow of foot traffic moved them steadily toward the center of town.

The temperature within the city walls was stifling. Smells of animals mingled with the aroma of baked bread and sweaty humans. And when Rick paused at one intersection to get his bearings, Mackenzie noted an undercurrent of alarm.

A pervasive atmosphere of unease undermined the festivities under way in the arena and marketplace. Some of the citizens were pointing to the ash at Vesuvius's summit. Others were concerned with the failure of the city's water supply, and angrily pushed past the festival crowds carrying empty amphorae and buckets in a futile search for a fountain that had not run dry. Still others were packing up carts with their belongings—perhaps they had survived the dreadful earthquake seventeen years earlier and recognized the pending threat.

"They know something's happening," Mac whispered to Maude. "If they panic, we'll have a hard time negotiating the streets."

Rick nodded as he exercised his limited knowledge of ancient Latin and some blunt contact to deflect attention and discourage a persistent merchant. "Let's get moving, and for God's sake stick close," he hissed. "I've been offered food and coin in trade for both of you."

Maude glanced down at her attire. "They think we're your slaves?" she cried.

"I've been meaning to tell you," Mackenzie said. "There must be something wrong with your wardrobe database."

Maude groaned. "It's got to be the time rift again. Errors are popping up all over."

"Shhh," Rick returned, and signaled for them to follow. He set off toward the Marine gate. "We can use it to our advantage."

Fifteen minutes later, they reached the docks. Rick found a fairly safe and unobtrusive vantage point and nodded toward the thick knot of people disembarking from the morning ferry.

"Dak's supposed to be here, Maude. He's searching every vessel for Falah," Rick said.

"I hope she escapes all this and gets to Misenum. If she's aboard one of the departing ferries, she'll make it," Mackenzie added while Maude scanned the travelers. They had to rely on her for positive identification. Neither she nor Rick could hope to match the features of a plaster body cast with Dak in the flesh.

Rick brushed at the sweat teasing Mac's brow and grinned. "Having fun yet?" he whispered.

She nodded. She hated to admit it—given the impending doom—but she was. She'd gathered enough data in the last hour to equal a lifetime of research.

"Me too," he added. "Maybe we can collaborate on something when we get back to Dallas."

She was about to agree, but something caught her attention. "Is that him?" she asked, and pointed to an enraged male stalking away from one of the overcrowded ferries.

Maude gasped. "It is! How did you know?

"Dak!" she yelled.

He stopped short, whirled around, and bellowed like a wounded bull. "Falah?"

Mackenzie flinched. No way, no how was Dak going to depart peaceably without his woman. Mac inched toward Rick to voice her concern, but noted that he'd already surmised the same. Somewhere en route to the docks, he'd picked up a stout stick. Knocking Dak senseless could work if reasoning failed.

Rick was on the same wavelength. He held her back as Maude finally caught Dak's eye. "Let her do all the talking," he hissed. "If she's smart, she'll stun him and we can hire a litter to haul him back to the transit coordinates."

Dak grabbed Maude by the arm and muscled her into some shadows cast by a stack of off-loaded goods. Their heated debate didn't last long. When it ended, neither looked victorious.

Maude called them over. "Here we go," Rick growled under his breath to Mackenzie. "And remember your promise."

In spite of Dak's murderous expression, Mackenzie couldn't keep the smile off her face. Seeing him alive, she felt like she'd just bumped into an old friend.

"This is an insult," Dak growled. "I don't need to be rescued. I've got everything under control. This is a private mission and none of Charlie's business or the Time Rogues', and I don't need a bunch of misguided novice Rogues compromising it!"

He looked Mac over and Rick too. "Who are you? You aren't Rogues."

"We are now! This is Rick and I'm Mackenzie," she said and gave him a quick hug. It caught Dak off guard and undercut some of his fury.

He sized up Rick and the stick he wielded. "Go home. I'm busy."

"Sorry," Rick said. "No can do."

Dak tried to stare him down, but Rick didn't flinch. "I'm not going back without Falah," Dak hissed.

"I figured as much," Rick returned. "We don't have much time. Where do we start looking?"

Dak was tireless and thorough. They had reentered the town and were now searching the temples and public spaces. Rick didn't hinder or discourage him, even though they all knew the search was futile.

Mackenzie accepted that Rick knew what he was doing.

He wouldn't allow Dak's obsession to trap all of them. But after half an hour, she was getting nervous, and she kept one eye on Vesuvius and the other on Maude's wristband. The chronometer, disguised as jewelry, was counting down the minutes until auto transit.

At the temple of Jupiter, they felt the earth shake. A brief, barely noticeable shiver of current rippled beneath their feet. But it was significant enough to shift masonry. A shower of pebbles bounced to the ground and Rick pulled Mackenzie beneath a main brace until the danger passed. Maude and Dak checked their chronometers, and Maude glanced meaningfully in their direction.

Yes, it was another minor event and prelude to eruption. They had less than two hours until auto transit. And now, with the local unease and alarm shifting into high gear, they might need every second to fight through panicked crowds to reach the safe-transit zone.

"Go back," Dak said. "All of you."

"I can't leave you behind," Maude said.

"You mean, you *won't* leave me behind," he snapped. "I trained you, Maude, and I didn't train a fool. Get out of here while you can. It's my choice to stay."

Maude shook her head. "Not any longer."

Dak looked down at the pronged tool she'd unholstered. In the cool quiet of the temple, it hummed like a cranky bumble bee.

Mackenzie backed away. It might only be on stun settings, but she didn't want to share in any of the displaced energy.

"This isn't just a rescue, is it? Just how badly did I mess up?" Dak asked quietly. He glanced over at Rick, who still carried his big stick.

"Catastrophic time rift. In the first expansion, it will kill thousands of transits and lose the lock on thousands more. In the second, it will unravel the future time line."

"And you'll die here today," Mackenzie added.

Maude nodded. "Your emergency SOS triggers the rift and Charlie can't save you. You have to come with us. You don't have a choice."

Mackenzie recognized the man's expression. It was pure Dak, undiluted by Rick's features. But like Rick he was hardheaded, and he was determined to save Falah at all costs. "There's one last place to check. If she's still in Pompeii, she'll be there."

"Trust me, Dak. She's not there," Rick said.

"For what it's worth, Dak, I don't think Falah dies here today. You must have realized it too in the last moments. Does Claudius Maximus or Misenum tell you anything?" she suddenly asked. "You gave us those clues but I don't know what they mean."

Dak's gaze flicked away from Maude's humming tool and settled on her. "It means everything. If she went with Maximus, she'll be safe," he replied. He scrubbed his face with his hands. "If."

"You're going to come with us, aren't you?" Mackenzie cried.

Dak didn't reply. Maude shook her head.

"I'm not taking any chances," she said. She flicked a button on her device and the red stone on Dak's wristband glowed brightly. "The future of Core is at stake. I'm not unlocking the targeting system until we're clear of the no-transit zone."

He glanced down at the stone. "Termination?"

"It's necessary," Maude replied. "You know I can't deactivate your emergency SOS implant, but Charlie programmed an override command. You'll self-destruct if you attempt to contact Core while in the no-transit zone."

Dak nodded grimly. "Tough assignment, Maude. I'm proud of you."

Maude didn't acknowledge the compliment. "I'd hoped to save your miserable hide, too."

Dak chucked her under the chin. "You did."

* * *

Well within the safe-transit zone, the group collapsed in a pool of shade beneath a tree, exhausted and speechless. The struggle through the hot and glutted streets had been difficult, but once beyond the town walls, with a slight breeze at their backs, they had plodded steadily forward and reached their goal with time to spare.

Mackenzie's sweat-soaked toga weighed down her body and her spirits. The heat was stifling, and her every muscle screamed in agony. And even though they were safe, she couldn't rejoice. No birds chirped in the trees or flew above them in the cloudless sky.

This was the prelude to disaster her exhibit design couldn't mimic. The air, the stillness, the oppressive heat, and the fear were all palpable.

Settled around them were countless others who had fled Pompeii and sought shelter from the hot sun among the tombs and sparse trees. Some of the people were resting, and others were debating the wisdom of abandoning their homes and possessions. But everyone watched Vesuvius and waited.

Mackenzie studied their faces and squeezed Rick's hand. Surely these people would survive.

"Thanks," Dak said when Maude deactivated her targeting system, retracted her stunner, and handed over a temporary transit band.

He turned to Rick and Mackenzie and stared at them long and hard. "And to you too."

He stood up and faced the mountain, rolling the transit band around in his palms. Mackenzie shaded her eyes and watched him, his silhouette dark against the sunlit volcano. And in that moment, she realized again that he wouldn't go back without Falah. Dak wasn't returning to Core.

"No, Dak. Don't do it. It's too dangerous," she cried out in a hoarse whisper.

Maude yelped. "Damn you, Dak. You can't go back

there!" She retrieved her pronged stunner and struggled with the buttons. Dak reached over and stilled her hand.

"Core is safe and I'm alive, Maude. You accomplished your mission."

Mackenzie watched Maude in horror. Her hands were shaking. She flipped the switch and her stunner hummed.

"I give you my word—I won't trigger a rift," Dak promised. "Cross my heart."

"Maude," Mackenzie cried. "I believe him."

Rick stood up and held out his hand. "Good luck, Dak. I hope you find her."

An explosion knocked them off their feet. *Vesuvius!*

Rick crawled toward Mac and held her fast. She lifted her chin from his chest and faced the mountain. She had one glimpse of the plume rising above them before the colors blurred and swirled around their bodies and the winds of time sucked them into the future.

Chapter Thirty-nine

Earth's Core: Day 238, 03:16

The silence was stunning. Mackenzie lifted her head slowly and blinked. *Where . . . ?*

She nodded as her focus cleared. This was Core. White, sweet-smelling, cool, and quiet. She had survived. Rick?

She trembled with relief. He was beside her. Maude, too. But not Dak. His auto-transit bracelet had returned without him, and it lay on the polished white floor.

Awareness slowly crept into her consciousness, along with sounds. A distant hum mounted in pitch until it popped like a giant soap bubble. Then everything descended on her at once, sight, sound, sensation, and relief. She staggered under the weight of it and felt Rick slip his arms around her waist to hold her upright.

All three of them had arrived standing, and Mackenzie realized that it was something rare for new transits. When the roar from the transit tunnel faded, she could hear cheers and applause from the Time Rogues circling the transit pad.

One minute she had been a witness to an apocalypse—the sky filling with ash, the earth bucking beneath her feet, the cries of young and old knotted together in horror—and the next, she was sucked back into a slick white corridor in the future and engulfed in a pink sterilizing fog.

She blinked back tears. They'd done it. They'd fixed the past!

Joyful Rogues slapped Maude on the back and plucked off her singed wig, tossing it into the yawning tunnel behind them. The girl swiped at her eyes and grinned.

"Are you two okay?" she asked Mac and Rick as they vacated the pad and climbed aboard lifts for the journey down to reacclimation.

Mackenzie nodded, then took her time assessing Rick as they floated along an access tunnel. He not only looked okay; he looked better than okay. Filthy with caked ash and sweat, he was the most wonderful thing she'd ever seen. He was alive—they all were—and that was the answer to her prayers. But it tipped the scales on what her emotions could accept. All the stark whiteness, the echoing cheers from the Rogues, the lovely smell of roses, and the absence of Dak overwhelmed her. She closed her eyes and collapsed in Rick's arms in a delicious faint.

Chapter Forty

Earth's Core: Day 249, 03:16

Reacclimation. Mackenzie had a name for her malady. It was a devilishly thorough and necessary process that Maude had warned her about. She'd been scoured stem to stern with a curious blend of body scrubs and herbal mists that would have been pleasant if she'd felt less like a mannequin in a super-duper car wash for people. And the humming lift that moved her near-lifeless shell from place to place would have been pleasant too, if she didn't ache with the need to see Rick's face. When the disorienting process concluded, she was too exhausted to care what happened next. But Maude did, thank goodness.

"No, you can't erase their memories," she was saying. "You didn't prep them for download. They don't have the memory chips or much else either. And the little dab of protection you applied expired on reentry."

Mackenzie lifted her head up off the cushioned platform and watched the debate between Maude and Charlie with mounting interest. Her fate—hers and Rick's—evidently hung in the balance.

"It's not optional. I have to erase their memories," Charlie replied. "We can't send them back otherwise. The rift corrupted multiple time lines before you fixed it."

"Fixed it?" Maude cried. "I stopped it from happening. I changed history. Everything's supposed to be okay now."

Charlie shook his head. "It's not, not entirely. Class-ten rifts defy full containment. Your fix changed some history, but not everything. Rogues are mopping up the residual damage throughout the Continuum. Dallas 2005 contains significant parallel transference."

"Transference?"

"Echoes or shadows of both realities." Charlie nodded in Mac and Rick's direction. "They can't accommodate both realities. Few of the earliest Rogues could. Not even Dak. The resulting psychosis was problematic. But now all Rogues have extractable memory and buffer system implants. Selective downloads circumvent the vulnerability. It'll be messy—I'll have to overlap the timeframe to ensure all Core images and associations are removed."

"How much overlap? An hour on either side?" she asked.

Charlie's features scrunched into a mask of concentration. "Rick's will be tough. It's my fault. I sent you back to his summer dig in Pompeii on your first recon mission."

Maude looked aghast. "Good grief, Charlie. You can't erase that, too." She glanced over at Mackenzie and offered a flat smile. "That's a horrible idea. Besides, they can assimilate the information without jeopardizing the future. They're not a threat."

Mackenzie cleared her throat. She had an opinion on the subject, too: *Stay the heck out of my brain!*

"Charlie, Charlie, Charlie," a voice from somewhere behind her said. Mackenzie knew that voice.

"Dak!" she cried, and spun around on her platform. "You're alive."

He smiled, but the guy next to him didn't. Rick was scowling.

"Stay the hell away from my memories," Rick snarled.

"Ditto," Mackenzie said.

Dak laughed. "You're going overboard as usual, Charlie."

"You're a fine one to talk, Dak. You're the king of overboard. Nothing is ever simple or easy with you, not even falling in love. My entire staff has been working around the clock for weeks to clean up after your mission," Charlie snapped. He crossed over to shake Dak's hand. "Glad you finally made it back, though. How is Falah's reacclimation coming?"

"She's not a natural like these two. She'll need maximum rotations and supplemental boosters because of the baby."

"Everything good with that?"

Dak grinned. "She's still in her first trimester. The baby's fine. But let's get back to your plan to neutralize Rick and Mackenzie's memories."

"It's necessary if I'm going to send them home. You of all people should know that." Charlie circled Mackenzie's platform, and sized her up. "She's not a problem. I can selectively erase her Core experiences. Rick's another matter. You shared more than his body when you possessed him, Dak. You shared all your basic Core knowledge. I scanned his brain while he was processed through reacclimation. It's all there."

"Use your famous intellect, Charlie. Think of another option," Dak insisted.

"Stop talking about us like we're not even in the room. We can hear you, Charlie," Mackenzie said. She stepped forward and poked her finger into his chest. "If you think I'm not a problem now, you just try and zap one single memory in Rick's head and you'll be pushing up daisies."

"You don't want to mess with her, Charlie," Maude added. "She means what she says!"

Charlie leaned on one of the platforms and stroked his jaw. "You could always stay in Core. Historians are valuable. We could use your skills and knowledge. We send Rogues back to your century all the time to collect data. Plus, you're both naturals."

Rick folded his arms in silent protest, but the gesture and his stony expression didn't fool Mackenzie. She knew full well that he was considering it.

Damn, so was she. It was a strangely appealing offer. Joining the Rogues. Rick would certainly fit into the team. And she was intrigued by the time-traveling society. It was a fabulous opportunity for a historian who loved research. The missions weren't all high risk. And the life would certainly offer rewards and challenges.

However, there was one tremendous disadvantage attached to this job offer. Relocation. Core was worse than Pompeii. It wasn't just on the other side of the planet from Dallas and her family; it wasn't even in the same century.

If Rick chose to stay, Mackenzie might take Charlie up on his offer to erase her memory. She could request that he purge Rick Mason from her body and soul.

"It's worth considering, but we'll have to discuss it," Rick said. "And get back to you."

Mackenzie nearly fainted—and not from post-transit shock. She'd been holding her breath. Rick winked. It was his promise that it wasn't going to be a repeat of five years ago when he'd taken the Pompeii job without consulting her. And, apparently, that was a promise she could trust him to keep.

Chapter Forty-one

Dallas: 2005. Monday night

"Don't move a muscle, Rick," Mackenzie whispered. "I think I know where we are."

In the dimly lit space, she had to trust her instincts to lead her to the nearest wall switch. She flipped it and bathed the hallway in pale yellow light. Her instincts were right. They'd bypassed Pompeii in their transit back to 2005 and landed smack dab in the middle of the Dallas museum. To her left were the holding pens, to the right the study cribs for undergrads. And ahead was the stair access to B-4 level and the special exhibits.

"Here? What about Gil and Hargrove, are they still in Pompeii where we left them?" Mackenzie asked.

"Charlie said things would be different," Rick replied. "Are you sorry I cut the deal with him to keep our memories?"

She shook her head emphatically. "Absolutely not. How about you?"

Rick answered with a resounding kiss. "So far so good," he said after a long moment.

Mackenzie agreed. Their chemistry together had changed, too—it was even better.

She wasn't sorry to fast-forward to Texas and her museum. She let the elemental smells of metal and mortar trapped within the labyrinth help her reconnect with the world she'd left behind the moment she thought the body cast moved. The museum anchored her to reality. She'd experienced a lifetime of excitement in the last two weeks, and she was ready to touch base with her roots. That meant a good bit of cat-cuddling, dancing the Texas two-step with her favorite cowboy Rick, and fussing with cousin Bubba while eating a double platter of barbecued ribs.

"I wonder what else is different? I'm all for starting at the top and working our way down. How about you?" she asked.

"The exhibit?"

"Yeah."

"Me too."

"Here goes," she said when they passed through the last portal and stopped at the security booth. She tapped on the glass.

Harry grinned when he saw them. "When did you two get back?" he asked. "Rumor had it you ran off to get hitched."

Mackenzie glanced down at her ring finger. It was bare. That much hadn't changed. Nor that she'd taken off during the exhibit.

Rick grinned. "Nope, not yet. But keep a bag packed, Harry. One day soon I'm going to kidnap her and haul her to Las Vegas for the nuptials. And I'm counting on you to be my best man."

"You got it!"

They waited for Harry to buzz them through and let the door slap shut once they were inside. Her exhibit still worked. She'd seen the actual city in crisis and her plan blended facts with imagination. It might be a mere snapshot of a disaster, but it was accurate.

They didn't speak. What would be in Dak's place? Mackenzie didn't know.

Rick grabbed her hand as they rounded the next curve. Mackenzie stopped short. Dak's body cast was gone, and another was in its place, but this one was prone rather than upright. It was unmistakably one of Rick's body casts. He checked it for telltale signs, the mark between the shoulders where he'd accessed the cavity and poured the plaster. They stood quietly, listening and watching.

"I've got to do it," Mac whispered, and Rick nodded. She leaned over and touched it with her bare hand. Nothing happened—no visions, no sensations other than her flesh making contact with the artifact.

"It's over," Rick said. He pulled her hand to his lips and kissed her palm. "No more ghosts, no more mystery. It's just me inside here," he said. "Still interested?"

She gasped. The dangerous glint in his eyes was there again—but entirely his own. His smell was all-male, a blend of leather and spice that stirred her passion. And his touch, where his lips pressed against her palm, superheated her flesh.

"You better believe it, cowboy!" she whispered.

His smile was slow and sexy. "Take me home and prove it."

The house was quiet except for the cat yowling a greeting. Everything was back to normal. They were just coming home after a short vacation, right? Ha!

She crooked her finger in Rick's direction. "Why don't you feed that cat and then meet me upstairs," she said. She scampered beyond his reach and called over her shoulder, "I'll be waiting."

In her bedroom, she flicked on the lights and turned

down the covers on her big brass bed. Rick, in her home, in her bed. She wanted him here permanently, every night. But it wouldn't happen. Her job—if she still had one after what she'd done—was still in Dallas. And Rick's was still in Italy. Everything was back to normal.

Except, normal could never be normal again after Pompeii, Dak, and the Time Rogues.

Strangely, Mackenzie didn't care. Granny Moon never had, and she'd died happy, surrounded by friends and family. Not a bad example for living a full life.

Trust. That small word packed a wallop. Mackenzie wasn't stepping lightly around it anymore, she was wading in knee-deep and soon she'd be in over her head.

She slipped off her clothes, dropping them one by one to the floor as she walked into the bath and flicked on the shower. Her remaining clothing, little bits of satin and lace, slid from her flesh into a puddle at her feet.

Mackenzie felt Rick approach. Heard his breath catch before she stepped beneath the warm spray. She turned her face into the shower and let it cascade over her skin. Washed clean of Core's sterilizing treatment, Mackenzie felt only the minute aches from their recent adventures. A stiff neck. Tender flesh. An empty belly.

Rick stepped inside the stall. He dipped beneath the spray and shook himself like a dog before he looked at her. They stood apart. Just inches. But it was a gulf between them, widening by the moment.

He scooped up some soap and lathered his hands. "Turn around," he growled.

He worked the knots out of her shoulders. He pressed his thumbs along her spine. Mackenzie tilted back her head and leaned against his chest. Giving over control. Willing him to touch her.

Rick's lathered palms slipped around her waist and crossed beneath her breasts, circling and stirring with gentle strokes. Near but not yet near enough.

He held himself away. Mackenzie felt the tension in his muscled limbs whenever flesh touched flesh. The simple mechanics of washing her body aroused more heat. His breathing deepened. His lips against her ear eased out growls of longing. Gasps of air rushed past her face and feathered her neck and shoulders.

Mackenzie felt her body respond. Far beyond her mind and reason, glands worked overtime. Neurons exploded. Herds of nomadic urges sensitized the planes of her skin, gave her goose flesh, and willed her to surrender. She throbbed in response. Buckled under the sensual onslaught.

"Rick." Her voice sounded far away to her own ears, as if she called from a distant peak.

"I'm here, babe," he whispered against her.

She turned into his chest. The water sluiced between their bodies. And suddenly it was too much. She opened her eyes and her heart to him. She pulled his head toward hers and claimed his lips. He swamped her senses.

Rick curled his palms around her bottom and lifted her against him. Lean hard muscles throbbed against her flesh. A frenzy of need mounted within her. She pulled away from his lips. Her voice was harsh, demanding, a cry for more.

She could see it in his eyes. His own desire matched hers—breath for breath, ache for ache.

"I want you," he said. "Forever." His voice was a hoarse whisper that echoed in the stall and bounced back, again and again, till Mackenzie embraced the knowledge and the man that had opened her eyes to the power of fate.

She nodded against him. Her eyes flooded with tears of joy.

"Forever," she returned.

As she said it, tears spilled down her cheeks. She couldn't foretell the future, but she wasn't going to turn her back on love again.

Chapter Forty-two

Dallas: a week later

Saving Dak and preventing the time rift had changed some events in Mackenzie's Dallas 2005, but seemingly left others intact. Charlie had warned Mac and Rick about the glitches, echoes or shadows where threads of the alternate time lines had crossed and snarled. Total recall without their new buffering implants would be impossible. But as Core's newest "on-call" Time Rogues, they were equipped to accommodate conflicting realities as necessary. And since arriving back in Dallas, Mac's buffer had been working overtime to sort out her fate with the museum.

In both time lines, Mac had taken an unscheduled leave of absence from the museum during the Pompeii exhibit and pissed off Proctor. And a week after her return, she was holding up with her smile intact, but just barely. The first hour, the first day, and the first argument with Proctor had been tough. She was back, but she wasn't back in his good graces.

She didn't know about Rick, but for her, getting back to

normal was a challenge. Thankfully, Gillespe and Hargrove appeared normal, lacking any noticeable effects of possession or the other time line.

"You're on probation, that's all," Rick said as he helped collect the discarded brochures after her last tour. "You were gone less than a week. You apologized. It hasn't totally ruined your job or your chance at promotion."

"I've disappointed Proctor." Mac glanced up at the glass-walled office that overlooked the museum entry, and watched the museum director's shadow pacing to and fro. She groaned and shook her head. "He thinks it's all about romance and women's hormones."

"And Hargrove thinks it's all about the Savaion research." Rick shrugged. "I'd say we lucked out, Mackenzie. By the way," he leaned in and whispered in her ear, "thanks for saving my butt."

"No problem. Anytime." She offered him a weak smile, accepted his chaste kiss to her brow, and headed back to collect the next group assembling for a tour.

A few minutes later, she was standing in front of the new body cast and remembering Dak, the man who for better or worse had rocked her world. She owed him a lot. Her career with the museum was iffy now, but she'd rediscovered love. And although Rick hadn't yet acted on his threat to kidnap and marry her, she didn't doubt that he would. As soon as the exhibit was over.

"Excuse me, miss?"

Oh dear! Her tour group was getting restless. They had questions and she'd left them in the lurch—again.

She fixed a smile on her face and nodded in Rick's direction. He was there, as always, within earshot and tailing the tour group.

"Perhaps Dr. Mason, the archaeologist who unearthed the artifacts we have on display, could answer some of your questions."

Rick stepped forward and dutifully responded. Soon

he'd taken over her tour, delighting the patrons with the mystery, intrigue, and passion that he always conveyed when talking about Pompeii and the day Vesuvius erupted.

Mackenzie fell in with the group and let him work. Rick winked in her direction and moved them on to the next section of the exhibit, and she trailed along grateful for the respite.

The man knew how to lift her spirits with one glance. And he certainly knew the secret to pleasing her heart. What now happened behind closed doors and without Dak's interference was a passion that would last a lifetime; past, present, or future.

So why did she feel uneasy? Was it just the conflict with Proctor, or was it more? Maybe her intuition had been scrambled during transit. Or maybe it was just the letdown after her jaunt to the past. Whatever the cause, Mackenzie couldn't shake the feeling that trouble still lurked on the horizon.

"What do you want me to do with all this research on this woman in ancient Pompeii, boss?" Gillespe asked when she returned to her desk. He tapped the stack of neatly organized materials he'd placed in her inbox. Her notes on Falah.

She groaned and covered her eyes. Another glitch in the time line. "I hate wasting research, but I don't need it now. May as well toss it, Gil," she replied.

"Really? It's a great start on women's social history for the era," he said. Mackenzie peeked at him through her fingers.

"Be my guest. Have at it, if you want."

"Great!" He collected the materials and started to leave. "You know, I owe you."

"Me?"

Gillespe nodded. "You were right. I'm hooked on artifacts. And I think we make a pretty good team. I'm looking forward to our next exhibit."

She had to smile, even though she wanted to dig a hole and crawl into it. A fine mentor she was; she'd exposed the kid to a ghost, subjected him to exorcisms, and a few other, less-than-legal activities. But Gil had survived. And she would too.

"Good. But I've got to warn you, most museum work is boring, tedious, and anything but exciting," she countered. "In a few weeks, we'll pack up the Pompeii exhibit, and we'll get back to our normal humdrum routine."

Gillespe chortled. "Not with you as the new director. And you're not going to scare me off. It's too late. I'm hooked."

She had to admit it, Gil looked happy. He looked hale and hearty. Maybe he had found his passion in ancient studies.

"I am too," Rick said from the doorway. He still looked concerned. He was still hovering. And she'd had just about enough of waiting for the other shoe to drop.

"Don't you have a lecture or something?" she snapped.

"Little hot under the collar, Mackie? Sorry. I shouldn't have taken over the tour group, but you looked like you could use a break."

She waved him off. "No, no. I'm sorry. I did need a break. I still do—a long one. Thanks for taking it."

"She's probably just worried about the directorship," Gillespe said. "They're going to make their decision tomorrow."

Mackenzie pressed her lips together and nodded. Funny, she was a little relieved. It was finally going to be over. If Hargrove got the job, she'd be disappointed but not devastated. She had other things in her life.

Rick came up behind her and pulled her palm to his lips. With one kiss, he soothed her spirit and unsnarled her troubled thoughts.

Yes, she had gained something more precious than a promotion. She had discovered faith and the courage to trust her heart and life to the dark and dangerous cowboy next to her. No, whatever the outcome on the directorship, she would never regret what she did for love.

"Can I help you find something?" Gillespe asked Hargrove. The study crib was small, dark, cluttered, and more than a little off the beaten path for an important patron of the museum.

Hargrove tossed down the folder he'd been perusing and folded up his reading glasses. "You shouldn't be researching this kind of stuff," he said. "You're a bright lad, and Mackenzie's wasting your talent. You need a project with meat on it—something big and flashy that will make everyone take notice. Mark my words; the right thesis will launch you in the right circles."

Gillespe glanced at the folder. Thankfully it was only the research he'd collected from Mackenzie's desk and not the file with the incriminating evidence the university administration had provided on the gray man. Proof that Hargrove had stolen research from countless graduate students, including Mac. He'd handed that over to Proctor earlier that day, completing the director's special assignment in time to eliminate Hargrove as a viable candidate for the directorship.

"What project would you recommend?" he asked.

"The Savaion expedition," Hargrove replied. "I've done a bit of research on it myself, but I'd be willing to share it with you—give you a leg up."

Gillespe nodded. So, this was how Hargrove baited the hook! He offered the old reprobate a flat smile. "Very generous of you."

"Not at all, lad." Hargrove unfolded his body from the chair and shook his hand. "I know you are loyal to

Mackenzie. She's a pleasant girl, of course. But our kind needs to stick together.

"Walk with me," he added. "I'm meeting with the board in a few minutes to discuss the directorship. You might appreciate an opportunity to sit in on the meeting."

"Thank you, Dr. Hargrove. I would."

Gil and Hargrove settled into seats in the hall outside of the boardroom. Not surprisingly to Gil, the closed portion of the meeting to debate and determine the director's replacement was running long. This had been a long time in coming. And Gil was glad for Mackenzie's sake that it would soon be over.

Hargrove checked his watch. If he was concerned, he didn't show it. He looked smug and barely able to contain his arrogance. Proctor's special request, that Hargrove attend, was irregular. Apparently Hargrove assumed he'd won the position.

Hargrove cleared his throat. "I think I can find a place for you on my staff, Gillespe," he said, and flicked a speck of dust from his immaculate gray suit.

Gillespe gritted his teeth. Mackenzie had taught him patience along with everything else, but today it was in short supply.

"Thanks, but I'll pass." He stretched his mouth into a rigid smile.

Hargrove raised one brow. "Are you giving up my previous offer? It would be a mistake to disappoint me, Gil. You don't want me as your adversary. I can ruin a promising career with a few well-placed comments."

It broke the tension for him and he doubled over with laughter. "Jeremy, old buddy, I think you already have."

"And we hope you will accept the position as our new director," the chairman of the museum board said.

"What? You're kidding!" Mackenzie cried. She looked

from face to face, searching for confirmation to the words that she'd just heard.

Proctor's mustache twitched. Biddy held a hankie to her nose. Gillespe gave her a salute from his station by the door and ushered Mrs. Jay into the room.

"Tell them yes, Mackenzie," Proctor roared, "so we can pop the cork on the champagne."

She sputtered and nodded.

"I'll take that as a yes," the board chair said and brought down his gavel. Everyone applauded.

"Happy, dear?" Mrs. Jay asked a few minutes later, after the glasses were passed and the toasts concluded.

"Yes, I'm thrilled," she replied. "And very surprised. I thought Hargrove was the preferred candidate."

Gillespe topped off their glasses of champagne and grinned. "His application was removed from consideration."

Proctor shook his head. "Don't frown, Mackenzie. You won it fair and square."

"Did I?"

"Certainly. Information came to light that cast serious doubt on Jeremy's fitness to serve in the best interests of the museum."

Biddy waved her hankie and sniffed. "He always was a nasty little boy."

Now that didn't surprise Mac, but the about-face of the board *and* Biddy did. Unless? Had someone finally documented Hargrove's penchant for theft of research?

"It took some time, Mackenzie, but thanks to Gil, I finally won the argument," Proctor whispered. "Hold your head up high. You earned this promotion. And I'm proud to hand over the reins to the brightest and most capable lady I know."

It was the second job offer in a week. Mackenzie didn't have to think about which one to take—she could do both. With her on-call status with Core, the compromise Rick had worked out so they could keep their memories, she could do both. So why was her stomach suddenly flopping around like a fish out of water? Rick, that's why!

"Tell me. Do we have a problem? Can we survive this?" he demanded when she got home that night.

She couldn't move beyond the kitchen. Her feet felt anchored to the linoleum.

Rick shook his head. "Are you trying to tell me you're not happy? You just got offered *the* job of your career and the news that Hargrove is going, going, gone, and you're not smiling? We need to give you a refresher course on joy."

He held up a fistful of long-stemmed roses and waved them in front of her face. "I thought flowers would be enough, but I can run out and get you a twenty-dollar box of chocolates."

She pushed aside the flowers. "No, I'm not happy. Not entirely."

He leaned against the wall and contemplated the ceiling for about half a minute. "So I should probably cancel dinner reservations and skip the head to toe massage I'd planned to spring on you afterward."

That did sound nice. Mac's lip twitched. If she wasn't careful, the urge to make merry with her cowboy might sidetrack her.

"I'm serious, Rick. I don't want to lose you just because I'm committed to a job here in Dallas and you're committed to yours in Pompeii.

"Okay." He sauntered over to his laptop, which was plugged into the wall jack by the breakfast bar. He typed something and clicked the mouse. "You've got mail."

Hm. Another good sign.

She picked up one of the roses that he'd dropped on the counter. They weren't the showy red ones that he could have found at any Safeway. These were rare little buds, the soft lavender hue of a prairie at twilight. And their exotic fragrance was like crushed grapes trapped in a honeysuckle bower. It was more proof that Rick never did anything halfway. Not flowers and not relationships—even the long-distance variety.

"I guess you're telling me that you'll stay in touch."

"I'm telling you that and a whole lot more. When I first came back to Dallas, I told you I wanted a second chance. You gave me that and more. I'm telling you that Dak taught me a lot about loving a woman. If death and two thousand years couldn't destroy his passion for Falah, I'm positive a measly ocean won't impair mine for you!"

She grinned. "Really?" She snatched up one of the flowers and breathed in its delightful aroma. She backed away from him, inching toward the back staircase. She stopped when she reached the railing and made a stand—hands on hips, nose in the air.

"I'm not convinced," she said and batted her lashes. "Care to prove it?"

Rick's answering grin could have lit up a ballpark. And his threatening growl sounded like the rumbling magma at Core.

Dark, dangerous, and on a mission, Core's other newest Rogue accepted her challenge. He caught up with her beside her big brass bed. And although it took him several hours to do it, he convinced her in the end.

Epilogue

Dallas: the next day

Using the Sonic drive-in as a rendezvous point worked. It was close and, at ten in the morning, fairly quiet for a fast-food joint. Mackenzie and Rick had managed to slip out of the museum without Gillespe noticing and now sat across from Maude, who was devouring a basket of onion rings.

"I know it was part of our compromise with Charlie so we could keep our memories," Mackenzie said, "but we've barely been back a week. If this on-call status for Time Rogue missions is going to interfere with my museum responsibilities all the time, I'm going to have to back out on the deal."

Maude looked sheepish. "Charlie doesn't know I'm here. Dak sent me. He said he owed you two a favor."

Rick raised a brow and they exchanged glances. He stretched his arms overhead and then looped one around Mackenzie's shoulders. "So, this isn't official. What's up, Maude?"

The girl washed down her last mouthful with a gulp from her tall cherry lemonade. She was stalling, and Mackenzie couldn't figure out why.

"Is it another time rift, or a rescue?" Mack asked.

Maude gulped. "A rescue. And Dak wanted you to know he's handling it personally, and not to worry."

"Oh my gosh, Maude, who is it?" Mackenzie gripped Rick's hand.

"It's your daughter."

Rick's features flattened into a controlled mask, devoid of emotion. "We don't have a daughter," he said carefully. He looked over at Mackenzie. "Yet."

"Mackenzie, you look great!" Bubba crowed and swung her around the dance floor of the Rib Joint a few hours later. "Where have you and Rick been hiding?"

Mackenzie put on a brave face that passed the test for the moment. She allowed her cousin to twirl and two-step her right into his favorite booth without protest.

"He's *with* you, right?" Bubba looked over her shoulder toward the doorway.

"He's meeting us here," she managed between her clenched teeth. The truth was, she was scared to death that he would show up and deliver bad news.

Bubba pulled at her left hand and eyed it with disdain. "I thought when you hauled his sorry ass back to Dallas from Pompeii, you were going to have a ring on that finger."

"Oh, that." She had to laugh. Yesterday, that had been on her top ten list of priorities, too. But after Maude's visit, everything had changed. "Maybe after the exhibit closes. That's two weeks away, but there's no rush."

That wasn't entirely true. Soon—Maude hadn't been specific about when—she was going to be a mother, and it would be nice to be married before she gave birth.

"No rush? Bull hockey!"

"We'll tie the knot, Bubba. Don't worry." Mac's smile

flagged. She couldn't keep up the good humor, even for Bubba's sake. She was flat-out miserable. She was terrified for the child she had yet to hold in her arms, and the father that had rushed to her aid without even knowing her name.

Rick chose that moment to swing her into his arms for one of his wonderful toe-curling kisses. "Hi, babe. Sorry I'm late."

For a split second Mackenzie found her balance in his smile and touch. Her heart skipped a beat. So much had passed between them; it was difficult to imagine the future without him.

"Everything okay?" she asked.

"Lara sends her love," he said, and chucked her under the chin.

"Lara. My mother's name," she whispered.

"Hey you two, what's going on? Who's Lara?"

"Never mind that, Bub. Hand it over," Rick said and held out his hand.

Bubba shrugged his shoulders, pulled out a ring box and tossed it into Rick's outstretched hand. "You going to get down on one knee? I think she'd like that."

"Thanks, but I'll take it from here," Rick replied. He shouted to the barkeeper, "Hey, Marv. Hit it!"

Mackenzie watched all of the proceedings in stunned silence—that is, until he popped the lid and flashed a diamond ring in front of her.

"You're asking me to marry you?" she cried in a hoarse whisper.

All the lights in the Rib Joint dimmed. Blue spotlights flicked on and searched the room until they zeroed in on their table and the sight of Rick on bended knee.

"You bet I am." He winked and slipped the ring onto her finger, and the crowd cheered. "And we better get to Vegas fast."

Mackenzie looked at the beautiful ring and laughed with joy. "Fast? Any special reason?"

"All I'm going to tell you is that we're going to be up to our eyeballs in diapers real soon. And that you better learn how to cook in large quantities."

"Not just Lara?" she cried.

He smiled and shook his head. "Nope. Not another word on the subject."

"But what about us? Your job is in Pompeii. Mine is here in Dallas. How are we going to work it all out?"

He swung her into his arms and kissed her. "You'll have to trust me. We will!"

STILL LIFE

MELANIE JACKSON

Snippets of a forgotten past are returning to Nyssa Laszlo, along with the power to project her mind. Each projection thrusts her into a glowing still life of color and time, and her every step leads deeper into undiscovered country. Things are changing, and dangerously so. She is learning who she is—whether she wants to or not. She is also learning dark things are on the rise. From the Unseelie faerie court to Abrial, the dauntless dreamwalker who pursues her, the curtain is going up on a stage Nyssa has never seen and a cast she can't imagine—and it's the final act of a play for her heart and soul.